The Kingdom

of

Winter

By

Sir Windham the North Wind

Transcribed by

Dorothy Papadakos

"The Kingdoms of the Seasons" Series

Book I: "The Kingdom of Winter"

Text © 2016 Dorothy Papadakos

Paperback: ISBN-10: 0692830839
ISBN-13: 978-0692830833

Second Edition

For

Tracy, who believes in me
and the world of infinite possibilities!

And

Robin & Karen,
dream builders who know what it takes
to pursue a passion with
perseverance!

AUTHOR'S NOTE

I was there. I've always been there, here, for everything, everywhere! It's true, we battled the fearsome Fire Witch. But nothing could prepare anything in nature for what came after ... when fear reinvented itself.

My superstar colleague Orion pressed me to pen my memoirs to immortalize the extraordinary heroic events that restored Earth's Seasons. Winter, Spring, Summer and Autumn relied on me, Sir Windham the North Wind, to keep them on schedule ... until one Winter Solstice when it all went terribly wrong. You see, there appeared a fifth season created by Man. We called it the Season of Fear.

About the languages: yes, the girl knew Wind from birth. The boy was predisposed to learning it, for he was a student of the stars and planets. The ancient Faerie dialects spoken by the Seasons, particularly The Kingdom of Winter—whose lineage pre-dates Earth's five Ice Ages and who's heyday was the Cryogenian, or Snowball Earth Period—have been translated here to avoid misinterpretation.

I am often asked where is the Great City? It is your city, of course. And if you live in the countryside, well, you already know about building on a Faerie highway: DON'T.

About the Fire Witch: yes, she is real and ever plotting her return. That candle on your dinner table? Do keep an eye on it. It may appear calm and content, but thinks one thing only: "I want more."

About my transcriber: I am indebted to Dorothy Papadakos for her painstaking attention to detail. Wind is the world's first and oldest language, easily misunderstood by the untrained ear. To her I say, >WHüa'ih-Háaîoh\/ < (Thank You!)

About me: well, you'll have to read my story!

Sir Windham the North Wind

v

TRANSCRIBER'S NOTE

*I love weather! Hot, cold, wet, dry, stormy, sunny – I
love each day's new look and feel. As a child I always wondered,
'Who's behind the weather? What exactly are the Seasons?' And
then I met Sir Windham the North Wind up at Lake Tahoe in a
blizzard ... and again in Manhattan during a Nor'easter! Soon
after, I met several of his Wind Family relatives one Winter in
Russia, one Spring in Japan, one Summer in the Galapagos
Islands, one Autumn in England. They taught me this: 'No matter
the hemisphere or continent or Man's kingdoms, religions or
inventions, the Four Seasons rule all life on Earth.'*

*Being a musician, I always perceived the sounds of the
Wind as a beautiful ancient language. Then one Winter Solstice
Eve, quite unexpectedly, Sir Windham whispered his tale to me.
By lantern in my cottage I scribed day and night, windows and
chimney wide open so he could freely dictate Winter's epic tale.
Working with the Wind is, quite literally, mind blowing. He is an
ever forward moving energy, and a tremendous flirt, as anyone
with fur, feathers or hair knows!*

*Hoping to avert a repeat of Earth's near cataclysm, the Four
Seasons have granted Sir Windham rare permission to reveal
what has been kept hidden from humankind until now: an intimate
knowledge of their realms, the Kingdoms of the Seasons.*

*The Wind changed what Man thought possible. The next time
a breeze tickles your ear, messes up your hair or flips the pages of
your book, stop, look and listen ... Sir Windham has something he
wants to tell you!*

Dorothy Papadakos
Transcriber to Sir Windham

CONTENTS

My
heartfelt
gratitude & hugs
to Mom, Dad, Athena,
Maxfield, my family, Al, Meher,
Helen, Clay, Elaine, Jonathan, Dao, Tess,
Samia, Robert, Jerry, Amy, Louis, Nicholas,
Joy, Martin, Elizabeth, Haley, Sondra, Yellowstone
National Park, the biologists & scientists on my many treks,
expeditions & eco-tours around the world from bat caves to coral
reefs to glaciers! A special shout out to Finland reindeer, Japanese
wisteria & Ireland's Cliffs of Moher and wild *winderful* howls to
Paul Winter whose
St. Francis Day and Summer & Winter Solstice concerts
heal the Earth and to my stellar editor Milda Devoe, illustrator
Laura Diehl & graphic designer Lorraine Gelard for your genius.
To Orion and his dogs, *The Great 88* and Pine Trees everywhere,
especially Jeffrey Pines at Lake Tahoe,
Central Park's Pinetum,
Loblolly Pines in
North Carolina &
Rocky Mountain
Blue Spruce!
>WHüa'ih-Háaîoh∨<
(Thank you! in Wind)

Special acknowledgement for their tremendous help to:

Richard Giard, Weather Observer & Education Specialist
and all the Meteorologists at
Mount Washington Observatory,
White Mountains, New Hampshire

❄

Dr. Philip Jones, Assoc. Curator and Keeper of Collections,
The Babylonian Section, University of Pennsylvania
Museum of Archaeology and Anthropology

❄

Serafín M. Coronel-Molina, Ph.D., Assoc. Professor
Dept. of Literacy, Culture and Language Education,
School of Education, Indiana University Bloomington

❄

Alex Bangyin Zhang, Visiting Lecturer in Chinese
Dept. of World Languages and Cultures,
University of North Carolina Wilmington

There is Friendly Fire
*   and Unfriendly Fire;*
Visible Fire
*   and Invisible Fire.*
One we desire ...
*   Two will conspire;*
Three we admire ...
*   Four is a liar.*

Viggo Vespa, Northern Swedish Flyer

PROLOGUE

W *h'woüh'eh°° Uwh háhoo//<* Welcome, my friend!
<Hua'poh whåe hyhy'jhoò wH'ua° < I always look forward to seeing you.

<W°hua> wH'ua° hyø'huú, haho Whoo'Sh∨ Oh? You don't read Wind?

Ah, you don't speak Wind. We can easily fix that! Pucker your lips – yes, just like a kiss … then breathe in, whispering: *>Who'he-håh hüh'hsi°* … then breathe out: *<Whøø'sh Haåh∨*

Even louder! Try it again and aim it out your window … Aha! Hallooo to you, too! Well done!

You've just greeted, that is breezed, me in Wind, the world's oldest language. When greeting children, animals, plants, bodies of water or Fire, this greeting translates to "Want to play?" but when greeting human adults and all Soil Families, it translates as "Forget your cares, come with me!" Wind is a complicated language.

Now, before I grant you entry into the Kingdoms of the Seasons, two things: first, I know you wonder if we Winds get scared? The answer is no. Contagious as Fear is, we've never caught it. That's the trouble with Fear: no one can catch it, yet everyone's caught it! Except us, the World's Winds. But we do get surprised.

Two: as you read our story, don't hesitate to ask the Season outside what it knows. One hint on royal protocol: the Kingdoms of the Seasons are passionate realms where everything is art. We have one forbidden word and you must find your way around it: *monotony*. Around the world, 'round the clock, two Seasons at once, each the other's Polar opposite, work in tireless sync in perfect balance: Winter/Summer and Spring/Autumn. No two days or nights on Earth have ever been alike. Do not take this *Pas de Deux (Dance for Two)* for granted – your life depends upon it. Other than this, the Kingdoms of the Seasons are known for their impeccable manners and on-time arrival – until, that is, things went terribly wrong … in the Kingdom of Winter.

"O ROAR, AURORA BOREALIS!"

I felt it before I saw it: the whisper. From silhouetted frosty lips, it clung to the air, floating imperceptibly, then *WHOOOSH!* It streaked to the heart of the lavender-rose Arctic sunset illuminating the Arctic ice shelf. That one historic puff fluttered me, tingled me … me, the one who flutters and tingles everyone else! Funny how loud a whisper can be in frigid night air. It thundered, *Regnum Autumnus, summovendum Lux Brumalis! Beatus Solstitium! (Kingdom of Autumn, make way for Winter! Happy Solstice!)*

In seconds, a glistening reply streaked back: *Regnum Hiems, Castrum de Tempore quod tuum est! Beatus Solstitium! (Kingdom of Winter, the Castle of the Seasons is yours! Happy Solstice!)*

The official Season Salute (left and right hands to the brow at once) and His Majesty's deep bow were met with the traditional Changing of Color. In the distance, Autumn's orange-gold-red-copper crystalized into Winter's white-silver-lavender. It was done. Who could have known the venerable *Changing of the Guard Protocol Between Kings* would never be the same after this night?

Why Latin, you ask? Each Solstice and Equinox the Old Season is handed off in a different language. Each New Season gets to choose. That year it happened to be human Latin, a favorite of the Winter King. The Four Seasons speak all 8.7 million languages of Earth's species. You should hear *The Protocol* in Orchid or Koala or Octopus! But back to Winter Solstice …

My best friend and sovereign, the Winter King, cut a gallant figure. His ice blue eyes twinkled like starlight, his feathery ice-hair glistened. I remember he seemed particularly robust and daring this night. By now I knew his every subtle move, and as his breath quickened, alerting me our Solstice ritual was seconds away, eons of tradition kicked in. I ruffled and billowed his ice-woven cloak, dusting everyone he passed in fine powdery snow.

Astride his Arctic white stallion with deep blue-violet eyes, His Majesty wore a luminous ice-jeweled Constellation Crown which still to this day receives and translates starlight messages. *"HAPPY WINTER TO EARTH!"* rang billions of celestial messages from our distant stellar friends that night.

As if on cue, we, the Royal Retinue, held our breath – something I, as the Wind, don't easily do – eagerly awaiting this year's wondrous moment, precise to the millisecond, when Earth's North Pole would tilt furthest from the Sun.

"A 23.5 degree tilt, to be exact…" calculated the Winter King, trusting his inclinometer's precision. Winter Solstice was about to plunge the Winter Palace into 182 days of Polar Night.

"Sir Windham! Five, four, three, two, inhaaaale, annnd – *NOW!!*" boomed His Majesty in joyous echoes across the North Pole.

The air pressure plummeted as I roared to life, in fits and bursts then in great howling gales:

ʜʜHUUFFFFFFF! PPUᴜᴜFFFFFF! HHHOWWWWWLLL! FFFFFFFFFFᴜᴜLLLLLLL SPEEEEED AHHHEAD!!!!!

His Majesty loosened his stallion's crystal reins, leaning in hard. Faster and faster they galloped, surging to near flight, snow billowing in a spectacular wake from thundering hooves. We roared ahead of the 1,000 mile-long Winter Caravan for the four-billion-five-hundred-and-ninety-nine-millionth year in a row.

At 70 mph, I aerodynamically piloted His Majesty's gleaming ice-scepter into precise alignment with Polaris, the North Star, a binary-Cepheid (a senior star with junior companion stars), who is one of the brightest lights in the sky. Its triple dose of starlight flashed as it hit the scepter's tip and like lightning shot into the King's blue stellar-ice gloves designed especially to translate pulsating Cepheid greetings: *RRighttt onnn tttimmme!* it chimed.

"HAPPP-YYY WINNN-TER SOLLL-STICE!!" His Majesty cheered exultantly, thrusting his scepter to the sky and thrusting the Northern Hemisphere into Winter.

Aurora Borealis, the King's flashy kaleidoscope of a cousin, and Old Magnus, the quirky keeper of Earth's magnetic field, ignited the First Night of Winter. Their supersonic dance partners, the sunsational Solar Winds, streamed showers of the Sun's plasma into Earth's magnetosphere. How can I describe the Northern Lights, Aurora's shimmering curtains of color, what they look like – and feel like? Have you ever felt silk? Or chinchilla or a butterfly's wing or powdered sugar? Then you know. I especially loved seeing Aurora's reflection in everyone's eyes … how the Winter Caravan's crystal costumes, carriages and banners absorbed her colors like prisms of captured rainbow.

"SHAZINGA-ZASSS!!" we all roared in reply to our Yellow Dwarf Star's shimmering gift … all, that is, except for Frescobaldi.

Field Marshal Frescobaldi, the King's bald bold First Officer, watched. And shivered. He always shivered. He wasn't a true Winter Faerie, but a Spring-Summer, a *Mixed Seasoning*. How did he come to be with us? Ice ages ago, the Kingdoms of the Seasons took a Solemn Oath of Security to defend each other against all enemies. The biggest enemy they'd ever encountered hit 66 million years ago: the asteroid that killed the dinosaurs – and rocked Earth's climate. After that, the Royal Courts agreed to share their top strategists. This ambassadorial appointment grew into four distinguished and highly coveted positions: the Season Sages. To keep out dead wood and ensure fresh ideas, the Season Sages are appointed every 2500 years when the comet Hale-Bopp passes by Earth. At the time of our story, Winter's venerable counselor, Lord Brumal, was sent to the Kingdom of Autumn and Dame Tropica was leaving us to return home to the Kingdom of Summer. Frescobaldi was already here, having come years earlier from the Kingdom of Spring. As Season Sage, he had so impressed our King that he was invited to stay and serve as Winter's Field

Marshal. His cunning strategic thinking and training of the Northern Knights earned him the King's trust. But I admit my nagging doubts about him gave me no rest. As Chief Emissary between all Four Seasons, however, I had to abide by the Oath and put up with him … which meant I kept an eye on Frescobaldi.

In time, we grew accustomed to his shivering and noisy chattering teeth, for though he was never in command of the cold, he was quite in command of Winter's legions. His portly gait was more walrus than penguin, but tonight he moved as if trying to impress someone.

"Attennnn-tion! Northern Knights, forward march!" Frescobaldi boomed.

The titanic squadron of Northern Knights, Winter's bravest and finest in Winter Dress Ices, proudly hoisted their ceremonial ice shields and swords, lurching the procession into motion. At the same time, the rising moon's silver-blue light glistened across millions of ice-shields bearing snowflake family crests from the great Northern Knights Families. They've guarded The Kingdom of Winter ever since I was a baby breeze!

"On your mark! Snow Delivery Corps, ready... aim... *snNNOWWW!*" boomed the second order.

The sky was remarkable. A sharp line of voluminous snow clouds stretched as far as the eye could see. The new moon made it all the more dramatic: a heaven-sized wall of white encroaching on the clear, starry midnight-blue sky. Heaving a gargantuan wind chilling gust, my Great Uncle Squamish blew, propelling the Snow Delivery Corps into action, quickly hiding the moon and stars.

Before all the stars disappeared, Frescobaldi's chubby hands clasped the carved hilt of *Hibernal*, the Kingdom of Winter's legendary blue-ice sword. As if thrusting his own soul to heaven, he thrust *Hibernal* to the sky, east southeast, 72° above the horizon. With airtight accuracy, he sliced ten sharp cuts in the air – ten whistling slashes that tickled me to no end! – outlining overhead our superstar guardian, everyone's favorite Winter Constellation, Orion the Hunter.

Orion's twenty brightest stars laughed, twinkling dazzling colors back at us. *Hibernal*, designed to capture high intensity starlight, reflected ruby from Red Super Giant Betelgeuse and pulsated sapphire from Blue Super Giant Rigel like I'd never seen! It was magnificent yet eerie … Rigel, my intuition hinted, had something urgent to tell us. How many times have I recalled that moment and regretted not urging His Majesty to check his Constellation Crown?

Arms high in the sky, Frescobaldi turned 45˚ left, slicing another six cuts outlining *Canis Major* (Major Dog), keeper of the brightest star in the sky: Sirius. A blazing team of two stars, a Blue Giant and White Dwarf, Sirius flickered rainbow colors that would be seen long into the next day. Between Aurora Borealis and the Constellations, this was Winter's version of Opening Night fireworks.

Sloosh! One last slash of *Hibernal* and *Canis Minor* (Minor Dog) twinkled to life like a big happy puppy. Orion and his beloved dogs, Major and Minor, joined Winter's party which would last for three merry months. Thus was Winter officially launched and we began our Royal Progress down the Northern Hemisphere.

But that was just half of what was going on.

At the very same moment at the South Pole, the Kingdom of

Summer was noisily launching its own Royal March. Aurora's magnetic twin sister, Aurora Australis, outdid herself. Orion reported the view from space, ringing loudly: *"Herr Fesstivval of Phhotonns, herr ssullltry Southerrrn Liiights, wrrrrapped the connntinnnent in nnneonnn grrreen, gilllding Eassst annnd Wessst Aunnt Arrrcticaa lllike shimmmerrrinng Prinncesses at a ballll!"*

Aunt Arctica's daredevil Winds, my mighty cousins the Acrobatic Katabatics, did our family proud. No one celebrates like the Wind! No one makes a bigger mess, and no one cleans up faster. We just blow it all away, as did my cousins celebrating Summer. In fact, their aerobatic gusts and gales broke all World Wind records. This is a championship sport for us Winds and for Aunt Arctica (though humans never see it that way). We call it the Whirled Wind Cup, our Olympic Games.

Back in our hemisphere, if I thought a whisper or Northern Lights felt amazing, there was yet one more sensation to come, one beyond words. The chill … the shiver … ooh I'd know it anywhere! Dainty, elegant, high up above me … the thing I love most, and you may, too … the first snowflakes of Winter! Down, down they floated, zillions of geometric crystals, each hand crafted, one of a kind, drifting from fountains of clouds. Highly social in nature, they took on the shapes of everything they touched, adorning the beards of grazing goats and the eyelashes of the last bear peering from his cave before hibernating, as if to say, *sweet dreams.*

Icicle carvers adorned rivers' edges, porch swings and covered bridges with lavish ice sculptures. I did my part in creating hard rime, or wind swept ice – literally freezing fog! Trees, flags, clothes on the line, all frozen in motion. Ice-floes

silenced rivers, streams and ponds, while some lakes and I made ice waves that jingled like glass chandelier prisms clinking.
A whipped-cream stillness blanketed Earth in the rhythms of Winter's ancient chant, the *Solstice Carol.* Louder and louder the chant grew as we marched, sung by Faerie Folk whose bonfires greeted our caravan as Winter arrived in their lands:

Light your lanterns! Here we come!
We Kingdoms of the Seasons drum
What's that hint of us in the air?
'Tis a tease of gifts we bear!
All hail the Seasons! Hail our King!
We're not Summer, we're not Spring;
No brighter star the sky has seen
Than Winter's Queen Crystalline.

Whose Solstice Kiss each snowflake brings!
Blow, Sir Windham, our good tidings
To all the Earth now merry make
With Solstice cider and frosty cake!
All Faeries, women, men and beast
We're all one in the cosmic feast
Of stardust thrust through time
Hark, Orion, chime our rhyme:

O roar, Aurora Borealis!
Light our path unto the Palace!
Friends and loves who warm our hearts,
Raise a frosty chalice
To love for love is always in season,
Always the reason,
Let the Season start!

Will ye dance the Solstice Dance mi' lady?
Good Sir, let's dance away fear and malice;
Don your shoes, you're invited to
The Snow Ball at the Palace!

 Shazinga-zasss zoon-zoon!
Shazinga-zasss ring! Sing!
Ye Yellow Dwarf, Blue Giant stars
Red Super-Giants and Pulsars,
Our Solstice chant merry and bright
Light our longest darkest night!

O roar, Aurora Borealis!
Light our path unto the Palace!
Friends and loves who warm our hearts,
Raise a frosty chalice
To love for love is always in season,
Always the reason,
Let the Season start!

AN ACT OF WINTER WAR

I t was Queen Crystalline's *Solstice Kiss* which always triggered the first snowflakes – yet this year they had fallen without her presence. "How very strange," His Majesty and I wondered amongst ourselves (a bit nervously, I confess). Unnoticed in all the excitement, his Majesty slipped back to the Winter Palace. There, on the ornately carved ice steps, he ordered a courtier to find Queen Crystalline and the infant Prince Cerulean, both of whom had been strangely absent from the ceremony.

We Winds hear and know every single sound on Earth, large and small. But what I heard next you never want to hear. I can't forget it: BLOARRRRGRRRGGRRRARGH! There's no scream like a she-Polar Bear's ear splitting shriek. It crackled, it shattered my merry mood – it HURT!

I whipped around to His Majesty's side and witnessed the unthinkable: the Prince's Polar Bear Nanny hurtled and heaved toward the King, panic stricken and clutching in her massive furry paws the wildly screaming infant. Her sharp fangs, never shown to the Royal Family, flashed violently as she reared onto her hind legs.

With a spine-chilling roar she yelled, "Your sister has killed Queen Crystalline! Her Majesty vanished into thin air right before my eyes! Then your sister tried to steal His Highness Prince Cerulean!"

The King reeled in horror, for he knew of his sister's burning jealousy and hot desire to rule the Kingdom of Winter. But this? To act against his wife and son? It was an act of Winter War! Murder belonged to the realm of Men, not nature, let alone the Four Seasons' royal families.

The King took his son in his arms but his own trembling terror worsened the child's cries. Then His Majesty bolted for the Queen's chamber. "There, there little one, we'll find her, your dear mother! I'm sure she's not far –" he gasped through freezing tears. The Polar Bear Nanny sprinted past them at explosive speed ready to pounce if she saw trouble. I soared ahead into the chamber and couldn't believe the sight: Queen Crystalline's chamber looked like a blizzard had blitzed it to smithereens.

"Her Majesty was here, at her vanity, brushing her hair," the Polar Bear Nanny recalled. "She was singing a lullaby to the Prince in his cradle and rocking him gently. That's when your sister, Princess Frostine, entered, unannounced. Without a word she started smashing everything in sight. I tried to stop her, even showed my fangs! But she lunged at the Queen and shattered the vanity. The Queen dodged her, trying to protect the Prince. When the vanity shattered, the Queen's beloved mirror of Saturnalian Ice fell to the floor. Frostine grabbed the mirror and cornered the Queen here, in the turret – then a strange thing happened. Frostine held the mirror up to the Queen and ordered her to look into it. The Queen quickly suspected dark magic and tried to dodge Frostine who kept shoving the mirror's face to the Queen's face. Forcing the Queen against the wall, Frostine shrieked "Look into your mirror!" As the Queen tried to turn away, she caught her eyes in the mirror and *SLUSH!!* A sickening crush of dried-ice crystals fell to the floor! Her Majesty, she – she just – vanished!" the Nanny sobbed. "But then Frostine turned her hungry glittering eyes and the mirror's face on the cradle. 'You'll have to kill me first,' I growled. Then I grabbed the Prince and ran till I found you!"

The King lay a calming hand on the traumatized Nanny, her white furry shoulders heaving in despair. His Majesty stepped into what used to be the Queen's magnificent turret of tall, carved ice mirrors, now a shattered ice heap.

"You broke Winter's heart, Frostine, now see how bitter cold I can be!" he vengefully resolved. Grief stricken, holding his son and brandishing his scepter, he let the words fly to the sky that would change Earth forever:

"I banish you, Princess Frostine, my sister, from the Kingdom of Winter FORRREVVVERRR! I brand you *Burnadine*! I condemn you to eternal heat outside the Four Seasons!" he thundered. His icy wrath pummeled me, for anger's vibrations attack all who hear their launch. I knew that ice can blister and burn as painfully as fire and these words seared the frost off his sister, Frostine.

The Kingdoms of Spring, Summer and Autumn upheld the Winter King's decree in a unilateral show of force. Any adversary evil and cunning enough to kill Winter's Queen deserved the ultimate punishment: exile outside the Seasons, trapped in eternal *monotony*. And so Princess Frostine melted into Burnadine and came to be known as the terrifying, unstoppable Fire Witch. Worse, her Torches became her *ears* in *fears*: she learned what scared each and every being and used it to take control of the world.

Many thousand Seasons passed. Our Winter ceremonies lost much of their luster, traditions lost their details, some even faded away. Humans didn't even notice the change. All seemingly went on without event. Little did they know.

The Winter Solstice that Prince Cerulean, now a good nine years old (times ten thousand in Ice Age), joined the King and me in leading the Winter Caravan was no small event. The moment marked the Prince's Coming of Ice Age, the time when every young Winter Faerie develops new ice in his or her veins. Months of preparation preceded the great *Week of Wonders* culminating in the ancient but thrilling *Winter Rites of Passage.* These Rites not only bound together Winter Faeries young and old, male and female, but they were the envy of the other three Seasons whose Rites didn't have quite the same mystique. You see, Winter's Rites were, and still are, all about one thing: Winter Water, the most prized water on Earth.

For the First Rite, Cerulean swam the traditional polar swim with Beluga Whales who escorted him from the Aquatine Iceberg to Sapphire Seal Cove. From there he mushed a team of snow-loving sled-pulling Malamutes. All along the route Winter beings cheered him on and tossed the customary snowballs, some filled with permafrost candies and others exploding in midair (thanks to me batting them!) and creating mini-blizzards. When Cerulean arrived at the Winter Palace, he was officially presented at Court and invited to read from the primordial *Cryo Codex*. This ancient volume is so massive (millions of ice sheets) that my job is to blow it open and flip sheets until the reader shouts, *"Freeze!"* And I did. So did the Codex. Curiously, the pages that freeze open always seem to have an uncanny way of matching the reader. Cerulean's reading, to our dismay, was about how our mothers are always with us, near or far, present or passed. He read it slowly, spellbound by its intimacy, as if every word was from his mother to him.

Field Marshal Frescobaldi broke the spell by offering the Prince the Rite everyone loved most: the Snowing Birch Branch. Cerulean raised the branch, snow pluming out in sparkling flakes. I blew him a musical pitch, sweeping the snow up in swirls. In his crystal boy soprano voice (Winter is renowned for its children's choirs) he started to chant the haunting *Ballad of the Brumal Brume (Winter Mist)* which everyone joined in Olde Glaciatic dialect. Their chanting enveloped him like a musical hug as he ice skated down the grand ice aisle, smiling and waving the Snowing Birch Branch, streams of glittering snow billowing behind him. I can still hear them singing with him and to him:

 Go forth, young soul of Winter, go!
Know what's above and what's below
Is known to those alone who know
The wisdom, bliss and kiss of Snow!

Cerulean besnowed blessings on them all and ice skated back up to his father's throne. There his father closed the ceremony by giving him what every Winter Faerie cherishes their entire life: their very own Saturnalian Ice flagon of Winter Water.

Right on cue, a howling chorus of white Arctic Wolves heralded Winter Solstice and signaled all to move outside. There Cerulean lit his first Aurora Borealis and soon found himself leading the Winter Caravan with the King and me. No sooner had we crossed the Arctic Circle than we intercepted a Pigeon Post: a strangely out-of-season communiqué from the King of Autumn. I felt the poor creature struggling in my currents, frost-bitten yet determined, losing altitude. I scooped him up and landed him right on His Majesty's arm, startling them both.

The King read the pigeon's mini-scroll. "Ah, another false sighting," he said dismissively, trying to fake what he really felt. Oh how His Majesty had aged. He was weak and tired from having his hopes dashed time after time over thousands of Seasons. In spite of the Queen's death, without fail, some Spring, Summer or Autumn rumor would surface that Queen Crystalline was still alive. It wasn't malicious, it's just that no one wanted to believe she was gone. Eventually though over time, all but me, had given up hope of ever finding her. We Winds are optimistic and only move forward. We know no other direction. Oh we may suddenly make a sharp turn, it's rare, but there's always a good reason …

On this fateful night, as Winter arrived in the Eastern Forest, our route was blocked. The Four Seasons travel twelve Great Faerie Highways, meridians, crisscrossing Earth. These ancient

well worn routes had never in history been blocked, but tonight
Winter was stopped cold. Prince Cerulean called on his best
friend, Sir Jack Frost, also nine years old on his first Solstice
Caravan, to inspect the blockage: a lifeless bundle lying in our
path.

"Sire, he's an old human man! He's barely alive!" Jack
shouted.

The King himself approached, with Field Marshal Frescobaldi
anxiously shuffling behind. His Majesty cautiously knelt beside
the snow-crusted figure and lurched in disbelief.

"Zhu Zhu?? Can it be you? Old friend, what's happened?" the
King urgently asked. But the old man made no answer. "Quickly!
Take him to my carriage! Get the rime rum!" he ordered.

Attendants carried the mysterious old man into the King's
crystal bed chamber. Soft lacy sheets of finely woven ice were
laid on him to absorb the cold away from his body.

"He lies near death, your Majesty. This man has been beaten,
he's nearly frozen," said the royal Rabbit Shaman, whose long
ears listened intently to Zhu Zhu's heart and head crackling with
noise. "He's been told terrible things, seen terrible things. His
great old heart is breaking."

"Who is he?" Prince Cerulean asked.

"Behold the most famous person in the Eastern Forest,
half-human and half-Faerie. He has upheld our Faerie highways
and traditions for centuries," whispered a Solstice Sentinel in
deep reverence.

The Winter King spoke gently. "Zhu Zhu, it is I, Winter. We
love you well and are here to help you. What evil misfortune has

befallen you this night?"

Zhu Zhu, barely able to speak, searched the King's eyes. "Y-Your Majesty? Ah … old friend. She – she's in terrible danger! H-Help her!" Zhu Zhu cried out desperately.

"Who?" asked the King. "Who's in danger?"

"My granddaughter! In the cabin beyond the clearing. Lily, my little *Lilykinlichen*. She has The Gift, Sire! She's one of us, a Daughter of Autumn. But her father was seduced by the Fire Witch –"

"NO!!" Frescobaldi blurted out. "I-I mean no … good … she's up to no good –"

The King was puzzled by Frescobaldi's strange outburst and stark, pale demeanor. To me, Frescobaldi's shifting eyes thinly veiled a deeper disturbance. Why would this news of the Fire Witch's latest seduction upset him?

Zhu Zhu clutched the King. "The Fire Witch has blackened my son-in-law's heart! She made him one of her own – a Torch! Now she wants my Lily!" he gasped.

Searing fear shot from Zhu Zhu's eyes. It burned and steeled the King's resolve. "The Fire Witch killed my beloved Queen, the Heart of Winter, but she will not – I swear by Winter's Oath – she will not get your granddaughter!"

Here it was. The moment the King dreaded, the confrontation he had imagined over and over thousands of times. Would he even recognize her, his deadly sister, Fire? Or her Torches? He scanned his loyal inner circle. We waited, anticipating our orders. At first he faltered. We could all read the thoughts behind his eyes: when Fire and Ice meet it generally doesn't end well for Ice. Yes water is stronger than Fire. But in the Kingdom of Winter, water is frozen. Sir Yukon, General of the Northern Knights, shifted his weight, tilting the carriage, jolting the King from his thoughts. Me, I was eavesdropping, anxiously whipping up, down, all around the carriage listening and looking through every window at once.

At last His Majesty spoke. "Cerulean and Jack, arm yourselves and come with me. Sir Yukon, form a party of Northern Knights to lead and flank. Frescobaldi, stay here, guard the caravan."

Through a window he summoned me. "Sir Windham, scout ahead! If you encounter the Fire Witch, gust a report at once. Arm yourself with snow aplenty!"

"Your Majesty, I shall blow her out!" I howled, slamming the window shut and whooshing away in gales of excitement. I love dramatic events and showing off my prowess. Well it's not really showing off. I am the Seasons' most loyal emissary – and spy. They trust my reports, for the Wind knows everything about everybody everywhere all the time – or so I thought.

"Give our guest anything he requests," the King told the shaman. "Zhu Zhu, you are legend among us. Drink this and you shall become one of us, a Son of Winter," he added.

"But Lily, she's all alone! She – she –!" Zhu Zhu coughed painfully.

"Calm yourself, my friend. You will see her soon," the King assured Zhu Zhu, who weakly sipped the rime rum. No ordinary drink, its healing effects went straight to his head and heart and spread Winter's cooling calm through Zhu Zhu's veins. For the first time in thousands of Seasons, Zhu Zhu slept well.

LILYKINLICHEN

By the time the Northern Knights reached the lone cabin, I had whipped up one of my finest blizzards. Snow blustered so thick it was impossible to see, unless you were a Winter Faerie.

"There doesn't seem to be anyone here, Sire!" Jack Frost yelled, his voice muffled by my howls. Young and inexperienced, he only looked for and understood Winter beings.

But a Solstice Sentinel, a proud snowy owl, cocked his ears. "Your majesty, I think I hear something in this wall, by the chimney! It sounds like crying."

The King heard it, too. "We must be quick. I feel enormous heat from this human house – indeed now an abode of the Fire Witch. We won't last long in there. And depending on the strength of the child's Gift, she may not even see us," he cautioned, stepping towards the door, his scepter tilted to sense heat levels. "She is only human, after all."

Jack Frost boldly cut in front of him. "Your Majesty, permit me to enter first!"

The King's taut face relaxed into tender warmth. "Tonight Zhu Zhu's loyalty is repaid at the highest level. I do this for my friend. I admire your courage, Jack, but you'd be easy prey for my sister's cunning. I command you to guard the Prince. I'm counting on you."

"With my life, your Majesty!" beamed Jack, proud at the honor and confident in an easy task.

I swooped in closer and broke away from my blizzard. "Majesty, tread with care! The vibrations are of a Torch. It's very dark energy," I warned. They all hesitated, knowing the accuracy of my senses – and that Winds never exaggerate.

"Windham," he commanded with a strategy in mind, "cool this abode as best you can without knocking it down! We'll be quick. Howl if she comes, and remember, Fire strengthens with you, so resist her temptations no matter what!"

A hot sting of shame shot through me, yet I knew the King's warning was valid. "Sire, that's all in the past," I humbly assured him. Truth be told, I was trying to reassure myself.

Part of me hovered on alert outside the frosty cabin windows as the rest of me blew open the front door. I swept in and pushed the cabin's warm smoky air out into the night. The rescue party entered the cabin. The King walked to a locked coal cupboard beside the chimney. With the touch of his hand the lock froze and shattered into sparkling crystals on the floor.

The coal cupboard's door slowly creaked open and there, crouched on a pile of coal, crying and disheveled, was a little girl with golden hair. Her face was streaked from crying, smudged black by coal dust. Her clothes, tight and too small, were in the Eastern Forest style of beech wood fiber and spun llama fleece. She clung tightly to an old soft leather vest, which was much too large for her. I wondered if it was a token from someone she loved. The girl looked grimy compared to the glistening silver-white faces and attire of our rescue party. The bright light of the room blinded her, and she shielded her eyes.

"Are you Lily, Mistress of this Wood? Your grandpapa Zhu Zhu has sent us," the King said.

"Is someone there? I hear a voice – I can't see you … where –?" asked Lily. She seemed utterly disoriented, but strangely not frightened.

Inexplicably drawn to her, Cerulean stooped down and took her hand. He saw her faint smile in response, in wonder at her hand's coolness. "I am Prince Cerulean of the Kingdom of Winter," he said warmly. His unusual speech soothed her.

"I am Lily. You speak an ancient language – how is it that I understand you?" she asked.

"Zhu Zhu is right – you have The Gift," said the King, smiling, as he gently brushed her tangled locks away from her face.

"You saw grandfather? Is he OK? Show yourself to me! I can't see you!" Lily cried.

The King nodded and Cerulean raised his glistening ice flagon of Winter Water to Lily's lips. "Drink just one sip," Cerulean gently urged, utterly mesmerized by her.

"Mmm, it's so sweet and cool … *huh??*" gasped Lily, astounded. I knew that hazy twinkles of silver, crystal and white were coming into exquisite focus before her eyes. Cerulean, in dazzling costume, helped her stand. She looked at him as if he were a marble statue come to life, for his skin was white as snow. The two children stared at one another, transfixed, hand in hand.

"I've never met a forest girl before," said Cerulean, taking in her every lovely feature.

"I've never met a Faerie Prince before," replied Lily, memorizing his ice-blue eyes and unusual voice. I could tell each thought the other to be the most extraordinary being they had ever beheld.

"The Fire Witch will come soon, Sire! Out this way!!" urged Jack Frost.

Clinging to Cerulean's hand, Lily grabbed her pouch of herbs and seeds from the cupboard floor and hastily tucked it under her belt. She trembled – I suspected it wasn't from cold, it was terror. Or maybe it was relief … and the excitement of freedom with wondrous beings – beings like her who'd understand her special way with plants. Lily was learning *Chroma*, an ancient Earth language understood by all of nature. It has to do with light and its colors and has lovely dialects especially among plants, lizards, birds, fish and stars. Much of nature sees colors humans can't even imagine – just ask any Mantis Shrimp! As the forest plants taught Lily their medicinal properties, she learned how to use them to heal people and their animals. In her pouch was that day's special recipe of herbs, flowers, roots and bark to make grandpa Zhu Zhu's herbal tea before he went missing. He never mocked her tinctures as *mud mix*, the nasty name Lily's sister Kir gave them, even though they worked like magic on Kir's colds and allergies.

Cerulean, Lily and the King made for the door just as Lily's father walked in … accompanied by Kir, his eldest daughter.

He was a man known to all as Papa, built like a lumberjack, but he trudged in wearily. His face, square and rugged, would have been handsome were it not trapped between desperate boredom and desperate dreams. Already it had begun its slow distortion into permanent disappointment.

Kir was a younger angrier version of that disappointment who believed her pretty face was her only hope of escape. *Maybe a handsome young man, if I ever meet one, will whisk me away from this hateful forest?* It was a chronic yearning thought. She hungrily stepped up to a small cracked wall-mirror into which she stared obsessively, hourly, like an addict controlled by a drug, looking to see who she wanted to be instead of who she was – and making sure she hadn't yet changed, terrified as she was of the Fire Witch's threats to burn her face if she didn't follow orders. The only control Kir had was over her body, her lithe teen figure, which, like her face, still masked the unhappy soul trapped within.

It was clear that these humans couldn't see any of us Winter Faeries. Neither Papa nor Kir exchanged a word or a glance. Their brooding resentment stifled the air in a cloud of mutual denial: not only were they blind to our sparkling splendor, they didn't seem to care much for each other. And from their expressions it was very clear that both of them loathed Lily.

"It's my father and sister," Lily whispered to Cerulean.

Papa surveyed the scene. "Lily, what'd ya' do to that door, huh? How'd ya' get out? Who are ya' talkin' your gobbledygook to?" he demanded angrily.

"No one you'd know!" Lily shot back, cut off by my raised alarm.

Historic records vary on what happened next. Winter Faeries who survived claim they saw her first. All I know is when I felt that unmistakable wall of heat, and got a whiff of her burnt-wood scent, I instinctively howled my alarm down the chimney, *"GET OUT!!"* The fact is that no matter who saw or felt her first, we were all too late.

The cabin shook with a jolt. For a moment nothing happened, then the fireplace angrily back drafted, hissed wildly, sucked the cabin air up and out the chimney in a choking, whirling-dervish vacuum. WHAM! It slammed back down and thrust a wall of searing heat, a spewing fiery wraith, the Fire Witch, into our midst. Even the hot stunned silence seemed to hold its breath in terror.

Papa and Kir stood motionless, numb. Yet their surprised faces revealed frayed threads of dying hope, *Maybe there's still a way out for me?*

The King, too, stood motionless, astonished by the sight: he could barely recognize his sister. Her former Winter white complexion had darkened dramatically in an unexpected way. Fire's relentless hungry burn had turned her into an eerie, and staggering, ethereal beauty. Later he told me he had been surprised to catch himself admiring the transformation, then jolted back, remembering her volatile temper. *Strange how mesmerizing fire can be,* he had thought to himself upon noticing the first tiny drips of his own melting self. What I thought to myself was far more panicked: *Here's my sovereign, frozen in contemplation of his transformed sister, and he should be fighting her!*

The Northern Knights drew their swords of Saturnalian Ice, the hardest ice on Earth. Neither Papa nor Kir could see or sense them. To the rescue party's astonishment, and relief, it seemed as if the Fire Witch had lost her ability to see Faerie folk, perhaps when her heart of ice melted into fire.

The Northern Knights spread themselves strategically to protect the King and Prince as the Fire Witch approached the fireplace. The fire sparked and hissed something in tongues of fire only she understood. She smiled, nodded and knowingly surveyed the room for magical beings.

In a sickly sweet voice she asked, "Tell me, Lily, have you been playing with your imaginary friends again? Where are they? I'd like to meet them."

Trembling with fear, Lily inadvertently looked at the King who slightly shook his head in a gentle no. The Fire Witch followed Lily's glance and, quick as lightning, hurled a fireball at His Majesty. In a flash of sparks, swords of ice repelled the fireball in a sizzle, ricocheting it back to the Fire Witch. It hit her hard and left a steaming hole where it passed through.

"Whoever you are, you're no match for me!" she shrieked.

She lit a torch from the fireplace and slowly moved along

the walls. Water started running as the Northern Knights began to melt. "Aha! My fortunes are changing! Has my family come to pay me a visit?" she laughed in vengeful glee, for she knew which Season's Faeries can't bear Fire.

"What the –? Water? My walls are a' leakin'?" asked Papa in disbelief.

"Let us leave peacefully and these innocents won't get hurt," the King warned his sister.

"Innocents?? Ha! This man called Papa had me torch his enemy's business so he could prosper. I burned it to the ground, I did! Even brought his enemy within an inch of his life! I'm very thorough. Now he *owes* me! That girl is *mine*. She's payment! I grant *you* exit, brother, but *she* stays," she spat spitefully, eyeing Lily like a ravenous animal.

"What? Who are ya' talkin' to?" Papa asked the Fire Witch.

"Cerulean, don't let go of me," Lily begged the Prince, who held her even tighter.

I watched Lily's response to his embrace. She seemed at once warmed and tingled by his coolness, and it surprised her. They both seemed completely aware of each other's unusual power for their age.

"Papa, she's doing it again! That weird talk of hers," Kir cut in, glad to see Lily in trouble, yet jealous she was getting all the attention.

But the Fire Witch recognized bits of that weird talk, her native tongue. "*Cerulean??* You're here, too?" she scoured the room with her maleficent coal-black eyes.

Cerulean stood frozen silent like a deer before a hunter's gun.

He squeezed Lily's hand over and over as if their lives depended on it.

The Fire Witch sauntered, marveling at this incredible turn of events. "These are my woods now and Winter has no power here!" she scowled.

"Winter Solstice is already three hours old. I've laid the northern climes fast asleep under a blanket of white. Step aside, else my snow will snuff you out! My Northern Knights have you surrounded. Cerulean and Jack, remove the girl," ordered the King.

"What the hell's goin' on here? Tell me who yer talkin' to!" Papa demanded of the Fire Witch.

"Will you shut up and let me handle this?" she snapped, sparks flying at him.

The Fire Witch waved her fiery hands. Right where each Knight stood, fire broke out. The heat was intolerable. The Knights' mighty ice shields started melting. "Can't take the heat? Ha ha ha!!" she cackled.

"My house! You're burnin' down my house! Stop it! Are ya' crazy?" screamed Papa.

She turned on him. "There are bigger issues here than your crummy little house! I've waited thousands of Seasons for my revenge! When I destroy Winter for good, Earth will know eternal Summer! Searing scorching summer! And it will all be mine! I'll be the envy of the Witch Head Nebula!" gloated the Fire Witch.

"D-Destroy winter? What's a neb-neboola?" asked Papa, utterly bewildered.

The Fire Witch rolled her eyes at his ignorance of the sky.

"You never could control your temper or your greed, sister. It will be your downfall!" the King threatened her. His icy words stung, for he was hardly melting at all and she was losing steam to his coolness.

But Fire is unpredictable. In a flash she lunged at the Prince. The King easily blocked her, sizzling her heat with his icy frame. She was thrust back as the Knights cleared a path for Cerulean's and Lily's exit.

Cerulean urgently whispered to Lily, "If we get separated, come to the Faerie Crossroads. That's where our caravan is. Here, take this!" Cerulean reached in his vest and carefully handed her a pulsing, glowing light as he kissed her on each cheek. His cool kisses crystallized on her warm skin, leaving small droplets like tears.

Kir, staring at Lily in unbridled hate, saw the beads of sweat appear on Lily's cheeks and something glowing flash in her hand.

"If you ever get lost, ask Orion the Hunter of the night sky for help. He's my Guardian Constellation and will never fail you," Cerulean confided to Lily.

"Please, please don't leave me here!" Lily begged him in a desperate whisper, clutching his arm. In that instant, the King nodded to Knightmare, Winter's fiercest Northern Knight, who grabbed Cerulean just as Papa lunged for Lily, wrenching the two violently apart.

"Lily! No –!!" yelled Cerulean, reaching for her wildly, kicking Knightmare. "Jack! Forget me – help Lily! That's an order!" Cerulean commanded. But Jack knew where his duty lay.

"Knighthawk! Help her!" the King commanded one of his

personal guards.

Knighthawk savagely iced Papa, whose massive muscled arms enclosed Lily, crushing her like a bird till she could barely breathe. Shards of ice tore Papa's clothes and burned his skin, but strangely didn't touch Lily.

In her impossible struggle to break free, let alone breathe, Lily's little pouch fell to the floor. She clutched Cerulean's chrysalis with all her life. She thought of nothing else but him, keeping her eyes locked on him. With what little breath she had left, she let out a heartbreaking scream. No one but me saw her sister slyly pick up and hide Lily's pouch of herbs and seeds.

WIND VERSUS FIRE

I heard that scream. The whole forest heard it. The worst scream of all: when a child is in trouble.

Circling the cabin, I felt the rising heat. Impatience rattled and spiraled me – I knew my friends couldn't survive the heat but a few more moments. I had vowed to never, ever tangle with the Fire Witch again. It always ended badly. But without warning it kicked in, my inner wrestling match: do the right thing or the easy thing? Good behavior or chaos? Then I saw him, my beloved Prince, precious water dripping from his ornately slippered feet. It triggered every gust in me, for I loved that boy like my own son.

Oh no ... No ... NOO! I thought, slipping into the violent surge and spin I dread. Yes – I lost control. With a power I rarely unleash, I *BLEW!* and *BLASTED* down the door! I *SWOOPED* down the chimney! I *THROBBED* every creaking crack and crevice in those rotten wooden walls! Snow billowed blindingly into the cabin as I howled my insane fury, trying to blow her out.

But, to my horror, the Fire Witch flared even hotter.

"Ooh yes! YES!! Windham! Give it to me! More! More!!" The Fire Witch surged in ecstasy, blazing bigger and brighter. It all went horribly wrong. Again.

"Winndhammm! Retreeeat!! Retreeeat!!!" I barely heard the King command, begging me to end my squalling savagery.

He sounded so distant, so alone, and at once the soldier in me recovered my senses and obeyed. I ferociously sucked the air out of that cabin in a giant vacuum-inhale. The fireplace and the Fire Witch choked and smoked for oxygen. I inhaled even harder, deeper, enjoying watching them suffocate. It was working after all!

Lily pleaded, "Cerulean!! Take me with you!"

Papa slapped his hand over her mouth. "Stop babblin' like a lunatic!" He turned to the Fire Witch. "See what I mean? The girl's gone mad! A freakin' loony!"

"Father, we can't leave Lily!" Prince Cerulean begged as Jack and Knightmare rushed him to the open door.

"Cerulean, get out! NOW!" the King yelled. Then turning to Lily, "Daughter, trust what you have seen! Learn the night sky and know us by the Northern Lights. We *will* return for you!"

Kicking wildly, Cerulean grasped the doorway, wincing in pain as he twisted sharply and broke free from Knightmare's iron-hard grip. He wrenched his body with such power he knocked Jack to the floor, flinging Jack's sword into the fireplace where it sizzled and sparked, fighting for its life. Just as Jack lunged for his friend again, a colossal icy heat rose up inside the young Prince: a force he'd never felt before.

He yelled to Lily in a new voice, staggering Jack, the King and all the Winter Faeries: "I AM WINTER!! I will seek you out every Solstice until I find you again!"

With that the Fire Witch seized her prize. She cut down Knightmare in a fiery move so deft that it has since been added to Winter Faerie self-defense manuals.

She shrilled, "You pompous little upstart! I strip you of your Princely pride!"

In a stormy swirl of ice shards, steam, and sparks, the Fire Witch and Cerulean viciously fought and tumbled in a spectacular crash, abruptly vanishing into thin air.

"Cerulean? CERULEAN!!" we all screamed in disbelief. The King lunged desperately at the place where his son had been. The boy's cool vapor barely clung in the air.

"She's taken the Prince!" the King yowled in horror. "NOOOO!" he thundered, his voice vibrating the cabin violently, completely terrifying Papa and Kir who could only see their walls expanding strangely outward.

Jack Frost felt sick, disoriented. He had not only failed to save the Prince's life, he didn't even die trying. Dishonor and shame burned down the back of his throat into his stomach. His heart lurched. He had never known self-hatred, but in that moment when he let everyone down, most of all his best friend and himself, he believed a new thought, despising himself: *I'm not enough.* Never mind the King's warning that he was no match for the Fire Witch, his only way of facing the situation was to beat himself up like no one else could.

Jack wailed in shock, running out the door wild eyed in panic, "NO! Take me! I should have died! Not him! Not my Prince! AHH!!"

Outside, I desperately tried to pick up the slightest air trail signature of their direction. But there was no scent. No heat. No sound. No wake. No vibration. Nothing! Absolutely vanished into thin air, just like Queen Crystalline.

WHAT KIR ALMOST DID

Terrified the cabin's creaking walls would crush her, Kir panicked and rushed for the door where the King stood. Neither good like Lily, nor evil like the Fire Witch, Kir had no image of herself. She was the missing piece in her own puzzle – isolated, undefined, hidden in a room in a cabin in a forest where no one would ever say about her, *Wow! Look what I found!*

She reached the door just as the Northern Knights grabbed the distraught King and Jack. In a biting gust of sleet, the rescue party fled. In their wake, ice crystals flew everywhere, prickling Kir and Papa, but strangely not Lily, still in Papa's crushing grip.

Wincing in prickling pain, Kir noticed a growing pool of water at the fireplace. "Papa? Something evil is here! I feel it!

Spirits! Ghosts!" Kir yelled, pointing at Jack's sword, melted in fatal surrender.

She ran to the mirror, hysterical over her stinging red pockmarked face. Horror stricken, she wondered if ice crystals scar? At first, she had relished seeing Lily in trouble again, calculating how she could use it against her later. She'd always felt left out of Lily's and grandpa Zhu Zhu's imaginary world, so she quit trying to see it or hear it, so it never appeared to her. But now Kir's heart blackened.

Her thoughts erupted hotly, *I HATE you, Fire Witch! I HATE you, nature! This crappy cabin, Lily, her imaginary friends, all of it I HATE IT! All I want is to be beautiful and popular in The Great City and BE THERE NOW!* She closed her eyes, fiercely willing her small trapped life to somehow magically transform. She opened her eyes.

Upon the Winter party's exit, the cabin instantly returned to normal. No scorch marks, no heat, no ice, no wind, only curious water puddles on the floor.

"What was THAT? *Who* was that?" Papa shakily demanded of Lily, uncovering her mouth. He was genuinely terrified – and suddenly aware his daughter couldn't breathe. "Who ARE your imaginary friends? Devils, I say!" he cursed, shaking her violently.

Lily gasped for air, gasped for Cerulean, shell shocked by his demise at the Fire Witch's hands.

The fireplace hissed and flared as the Fire Witch returned, swooping down the chimney and startling them. She was perversely calm … and spoke to Papa in the soft, alluring voice he loved and loathed. Kir knew her father couldn't resist it.

"You want an end to your troubles? There's a clearing just beyond your cabin, a crossroads. Build a mighty iron works there and –" lured the Fire Witch enticingly.

"No, Papa!" Lily interrupted. "You can't! Not there! You can't block a Faerie highway!"

"– and give me that girl!" continued the Fire Witch, circling Lily and Papa like a vulture.

Kir saw her chance. "Do it, daddy! DO IT! Get rid of Lily! She's ruining our life! She hates me and my beauty 'cause I was your favorite! And 'cause Mama –" Kir was cut off.

"You did something to Mama! I just know it!" Lily shot back furiously.

Kir may have hit a nerve, but Lily hit a bigger one: Mama's death. Kir lunged at Lily but the Fire Witch flared between, happy to stoke each girl's fire.

"Shut up, Lily! You killed Mama by being born!" Kir yelled. "Go back to where you came from, you freak! You're not wanted here! You're not one of us!"

"The truth won't die with me, Kir! The trees whisper it, the Wind howls it – you are BAD! You're hideously ugly, inside and out!" Lily blitzed her, knowing which bombs to drop.

Kir reeled. "Ugly?? She called me ugly! Papa, am I ugly?" Kir cried.

"No honey, you're the prettiest girl in the whole world," he answered, trying to appease her.

"How would you know? You've never left the forest!" the Fire Witch snapped. "… But, are you sure you're giving me the right girl…?"

The Fire Witch's eerie focus on Kir made Papa's blood run cold. Kir's melodrama awakened his paternal sympathy and he reached for her. The instant he loosened his stranglehold, Lily seized her chance and bolted out the door into the snowy night. Kir shoved her father's outstretched arms aside and ran to her mirror. But she saw the open front door flailing in my deliberate blizzard wind: an invitation just for her.

For an instant, something in Kir understood, tempting her to bolt for the door in a thrilling mad surge for freedom and escape. *"Here's your chance! Do it! RUN!"* I wished for her. I knew exactly what she was thinking. It was etched on her face, in her eyes: *"Lily escaped. Maybe I can, too? Would her imaginary friends help me?"*

Kir could barely breathe as indecision and fear fought her visions of the Great City. I saw her energy surge powerfully, like a race horse at the starting gate. There she stood on the brink of her life's dreams – but then I saw that oh so subtle shift. A numb paralysis crept over her. It was as if her legs and soul were screaming "GET OUT!" But, like a lone candle in the wind, her one shining moment of possibility was snuffed out by her fear of the unknown.

The Fire Witch barred Papa from following Lily. "She's mine now! She won't get far. My Torches will track her heat in the snow and catch her before she even reaches the old covered bridge. Any creature who aids her will be singed to the core!" she hissed, relishing her supreme power. "That includes you."

Papa put his arm around Kir as if she were a precious, fragile doll. "Good riddance to Lily!" Papa said huskily, bleeding from his icy slashes.

"I never say no to a free child. But I'll ask one last time: you are certain you gave me the right one?" hissed the Fire Witch. Like an artist, she framed Kir's face with her molten hot hands and locked eyes with her. It seemed to Papa they exchanged an enmity so deep that its dark energy shuddered him to his gut. What no one knew was the Fire Witch's secret hold on Kir. Humans have always lived under the misconception that nature is blind to their bad deeds, or at least silent about it. For the most part we were, and still are, except of course for Parrots who have an embarrassing habit of spilling secrets. Fire, however, traded in secrets. A consummate opportunist, Fire seized a person's weakest moment to use and control them. Be they a world leader or Kir in a crummy cabin, each was held hostage to the Fire Witch's worst torture: *Invisible Fire.*

"There will be no getting her back. Ever. Handing a child with The Gift over to me is a far darker deed than giving me one already in decay," she added. She brusquely released Kir from her mind controlling gaze. Again Kir pushed her father aside and ran to her mirror, her eyes stinging with tears.

Papa's voice anchored Kir in place. "Lily's birth brought death into my house. I was never sure she was even mine! My dead wife Gala and I were happy … until her crazy father Zhu Zhu came to live with us! Huh! He brainwashed her, took her to weird starlight rituals with animals and Faerie banquets and other crazy humans who think the wind and stars talk. They tried to get me to go, too! Ha! I'm no idiot. I don't believe in that stuff!"

The Fire Witch studied him. "You don't, eh? Lucky for me you believe fire can talk. I'll tell you what you want to hear: there are no Faeries! No Faerie highways! It's all Faerie tales!" she spat, steam spluttering where her sparks hit the water puddles reflecting her every brazen flaming gesture.

She turned on him, her hot breath raising beads of sweat on his anxious face. "You want power? Wanna be Top Torch? Bend them all to your will? I need a human to build an iron works at the crossroads."

She then fanned out beautiful, iridescent flames like an angel of peace.

"God, she's beautiful when she does that," Kir helplessly whispered, reeled in like a fish who keeps forgetting what's on the other end of the hook.

But I rattled the front door and it rattled Kir. "And if we say no?" She heard the words slip from her lips, astonished by the reckless danger of it. "Aren't we doomed either way? With no escape –"

Papa went pale as a ghost. Even the fire in the fireplace seemed to hold its breath. The Fire Witch, a master manipulator, knew exactly how to bring Kir back from the edge of this cliff, the cliff of losing fear to fatalism. The Fire Witch needed Kir to stay hopeful and scared. She knew the girl hated her. But she also knew which dangling carrot would keep Kir from giving up. Much as she hated doing it, a trick she learned from humans, she turned on her charm.

"You and I, Kir, can't we start over? We all want the same thing. You want beauty and popularity in the Great City. I want an ironworks. Your father wants prosperity and power. You help me, I'll help you. I'll teach you all my secrets," she enticed. "I'll scorch the Earth barren for your father to mine and drill all he wants! And you'll see, all the young men will flock to you! Here! You'll be and have all they want and need. Tonight dawns a new age! A fifth Season! The Time of the Torch is at hand! Break the Underground, Earth's last stronghold, and you'll see who – I mean what rewards await you! We'll not leave one tree standing! Not ONE!! I'll silence their chatter forever! And all the Earth, the Seasons, the Wind, they will ALL bow down to me, their Queen!" she proclaimed triumphantly.

In a defiant shower of sparks she slammed her arms together above her head and combusted, leaving Kir and Papa to nurse their wounds … and leaving me to wonder why they of all people were her chosen ones to build an iron works? Who was waiting for them underground? Or was that just a slip of her fiery tongue? What did the Fire Witch know that we didn't? Her seduction, perfectly aimed at their thirsty hungry dreams, had worked, oh yes. But something told me it was the raw primal fear of being burned alive that catapulted Kir and Papa to seek out other Torches, fellow humans driven by *Invisible Fire*, to build the ironworks exactly how and where she told them to.

A MOTHER TREE

"Silence our chatter? Well she's just about done it, hasn't she?" declared Coco, the lovely Oak Dryad. In her large craggy oak tree roots, she cradled Lily, now a beautiful fifteen-year old girl dreamily playing the spider silk-harp that Darwina, their bark spider friend, had made for her. Six years had passed since that night of horrors and it had become a tradition between them, this re-telling of Lily's story, every year as Winter Solstice, long since banned worldwide, drew near.

They sat beside a small quiet lagoon where a twilight mist floated and lilted above them as if it were being serenaded by the ethereal music accompanying the tale of Lily's escape and the terrible blows suffered by the Kingdom of Winter.

"I always wondered why the Fire Witch didn't chase me? Why did she let me run from the cabin?" Lily asked.

"She never thought you'd get away. Child, you're the only one who's ever escaped her clutches! And she has hunted you relentlessly ever since. Remember all those drills we practiced? They weren't drills – those were alarms from other trees that a Torch search party was closing in. Don't think for a moment the Fire Witch has forgotten you. The Underground is your home now, your safe-house," Coco reminded her. "Your *medicine chest*, as you like to call it!"

Lily's life with Coco was so happy it almost made her miserable former life with Papa and Kir seem unreal. They had resented Lily's happy rapport with the forest and its beings. And her being half-Faerie/half-human didn't help – it scared them. Instead of trying to understand her, they surrendered their thinking to the lowest frequencies of envy and fear. On the rare occasions when Kir or Papa needed Lily's *mud mix* for themselves or a friend, they mustered a smidgen of warmth, but it was cold comfort.

To Lily, her forest was the finest *medicine chest* anywhere and Coco was delighted to cultivate the girl's knowledge of which plants cured diseases and cancers while others cured a bad mood or a broken heart.

With the whole world turned upside down by the Fire Witch, not only were most humans displaced persons, but so too were animals and Faeries. On many occasions, Coco invited famous traveling Faerie shamans to stay for weeks at a time as they passed through on their journeys. These brilliant Faerie botanists and herbalists from around the world found Lily to be a thirsty sponge for their vast plant knowledge and healing practices. She learned about Ayurvedic medicine in India, Chinese herbs, the thousands of Rainforest plants used for Man's medical compounds, African and Native American healing arts … she couldn't get enough. The shamans told her how humans everywhere relied on traditional medicine, but with Earth's herbs and plants dying to drought and floods, Man not only was starving but his remedies and cures were disappearing for even the basics like headaches and burns.

Soon the "clever little girl in the leafy frock" and her pretty spider silk pouch of herbs and seeds were in demand throughout the Eastern Forest. She healed sick children, pets, parents, even lone spinsters and woodsmen with no one to care for them.

What broke Lily's heart, though, was that she couldn't heal the plants themselves, who were suffering terribly from the Fire Witch's intolerable heat. Some of her most therapeutic plants finally simply gave up, exhausted. So happy to give, yet they needed to receive something simple in return, like a drink of water. For Lily it was like losing her best friends one by one; for the forest, it was like losing its memory and self-worth.

Lily pondered that fateful night when she fled, lightly strumming her hummingbird feathers across the spider silk-harp strings. "I remember after the Fire Witch killed Cerulean, and the King and his Knights fled, Papa was about to hand me over to the Fire Witch. The second he loosened his grip, a strangely powerful force erupted inside me – I felt like a shooting star and burst out that door! I sprinted in the snow, amazed at myself, how I ran like a deer, like I'd never run before. That is until the clouds blocked the moonlight and I ended up in total darkness surrounded by trees," Lily recounted.

"Faithful stalwarts, those trees! Now long since gone, burned to death by the Fire Witch for helping you flee," Coco shuddered.

Her hand on her heart, Lily felt Cerulean's chrysalis which she had secretly sewn into her leafy frock. Only Coco knew about the chrysalis, not one other soul. She and Lily never spoke of it, lest fear's ears were about. Its warmth on her chest reminded her how tightly she had clutched it that night in her hand under her vest, running in the snow.

In her panic, Lily had gotten lost in the dark. The more scared she grew, the more she felt Cerulean's chrysalis pulsating. She soon realized it was glowing with light. She slowly shone the chrysalis around her, risking being seen by the Fire Witch's Torches, but she had no choice. It was dark and she had to keep running – the question was which way?

The chrysalis illuminated the forest in new fallen snow in wondrous ways she'd never seen before. Snowflakes sparkled like little rainbows. Every tree looked new and different, strangely alive yet dormant. But at the same time her familiar forest became confusing; there were a million different ways to run and no time to decide. So she asked the pulsing chrysalis which way to go. Small iridescent beams shot out like shooting stars. She followed each turn and dip, running for her life, overjoyed Cerulean was still somehow with her and guiding her.

It led her here, to Coco, after she had run what felt like an eternity. Lily stopped to catch her breath, and her feet fell out from under her as Coco opened her broad craggy root arms and swallowed Lily underground before the poor girl even knew what was happening. Being a Mother Tree, Coco's root network ran deep. As each deeper and deeper layer of roots opened to swallow Lily down, the upper roots quickly and efficiently covered her, and themselves, in dirt and snow to hide Lily's tracks and heat. Similarly, Coco's friends' and relatives' roots had been erasing Lily's tracks the entire time she ran. If the Fire Witch had been counting on snowy melted tracks, there wasn't a hint or trace to be seen.

"I still don't know how you found me, child," Coco pretended, careful not to reveal a thing out loud. "But I'm so glad you did. We've kept your story to ourselves, for no one but Oak trees can be trusted to keep secrets anymore," hushed Coco.

Lily played along. "It was your children, brave young trees who led me to you, Coco. But tell me, no one's heard from Prince Cerulean or Queen Crystalline ever again?" asked Lily.

"You know they haven't," sighed Coco, "though occasionally Sir Windham will circulate rumors that both are alive, optimist that he is. We trees once told the Wind everything, but even he, in all his winsome loyalty, got caught off guard by the Fire Witch one too many times. She seduced and tricked him into fanning her flames, devouring what was left of the forests in Siberia, Brazil, Indonesia, Canada … we've never trusted him since."

Lily silenced her silk-harp. This was quite an accusation, for Lily and I had become best friends. "I think we may not know the whole story … and not all of Windham's relatives are good Winds. Some can be very cruel … they find forest fires to be highly entertaining. That's what Windham says. And a forest doesn't need Wind to burn! Just fire!" Lily's youthful defense of me was endearing. Someday she would learn my whole story – and I hoped she wouldn't hate me. It was very special being her friend.

"Coco, I wouldn't be alive if you hadn't rescued me …" Lily reminisced. Coco hugged her warmly, wrapping more craggy roots around her.

"And I wouldn't be alive if *you* hadn't rescued *me*!" chirped Darwina, hard at work on her latest giant orb creation, a web that spanned the misty lagoon. No other spider on Earth dared spin, let alone span, over water and Darwina made sure everyone knew she was one of the last heroic bark spiders on earth.

Tingsparlkingdingz! sang the miniature rainbow-fan of weightless hummingbird feathers strumming Lily's silk-harp. Audible to all but humans, no sound is more soothing in nature, especially when there's a crisis. Everyone knows spiders are masters of vibration, but with so few left alive, their worldwide web of silk-harp music was all but silenced. Oh to strum Fiery-Throated Hummingbird feathers (the most musical of bird feathers) across a bark spider's silk-thread panels (the strongest fiber on Earth) anchored in an oak-twig hoop (courtesy of Coco) … it was more than music – it was survival. It kept all of us hoping.

Ping-ting-jing-a-ding! Darwina plucked her web, each twang rippling her gossamer net, undulating in waves of cluster tones. It tickled the Mist, whose laughter flung dew drops on Darwina and her web. I mention this because laughter had gone pretty much extinct. Its occasional occurrence between friends was, well, like hearing a silk-harp – survival. Lily rotated her silk-harp and strummed another panel, this time from the center outward, sending shivers up Coco's oak spine. As the feathers strummed outward, the silk-harp threads grew longer and chimed reassuring tones, like your favorite song when you're sad.

A *Thank-you-for-saving-my-life!* gift from Darwina, Lily's spider-silk-harp was unlike any other: most silk-harps were sixteen to eighteen web panels (musical keys) with fifteen to twenty spiral threads (notes) connected by radial threads. But Darwina outdid herself: Lily's silk-harp started out with fourteen radiating panels and fourteen spiral threads. Then Darwina doubled both to twenty-eight. You could play both sides and using a Nightingale feather double your options to fifty-six keys! Humans make music in twelve major keys and twelve minor keys – not nearly enough! In nature, our musical keys are on a sliding scale based on temperature. We have cool keys and hot keys, and everything in between. Millions of years ago, spider webs, which catch all vibrations, were the first satellite-dishes and musical tuning forks. Do you sing better in hot or cold, humid or dry, above ground or underground? Spider webs near you know! Darwina loved Lily's music and if a harp string broke, she fixed it on the spot.

Searching the twilight sky, Lily saw it first. "Look, Coco! The first star! Orion will soon rise above the trees!" she exclaimed, as breathless as if it were the first time.

Coco sighed, reluctantly letting the nightly ritual begin.

"Child, every night you speak to Orion and he pays you no mind. I'm afraid the Seasons and our Faerie world are gone forever. Fear has trained us, big and small, to look out for our own kind. Orion has no care for you or the Earth. The stars have forgotten us."

Lily frowned thinking about this. "But what happens to your neighbor, happens to you," she replied. "You taught me that."

"Yes, and there was a time when no one feared their neighbor's differences or the adventure of meeting a stranger. Only the silly Wind keeps us all loosely connected," Coco mused.

"Orion's all I've got left of Cerulean … and Cerulean promised Orion would guide me," Lily murmured dreamily, staring into the sky. "I still see his piercing blue eyes … feel his strong, cool arms. Winter Solstice is just a few days away and I mean to be at the Faerie Crossroads, in spite of Papa's horrid iron works. Winter will come this year! You wait and see!" she said, as if willing it to be.

"Maybe it will, dear, maybe it will," Coco sighed, knowing full well it wouldn't.

Lily stood up, enveloped in the thick evening mist, and hurried off to her secret place, her silk-harp attached to her belt.

SKYLAR'S ANGEL

Skylar sat alone under the stars. Very alone. Even the darkness seemed afraid to come near his solitary lanky figure. I wouldn't dare breeze against him. The one time I had tried speaking to him – ever so gently flapping his coat tails, mind you – the boy hurled such brutish insults that even my mischievous nature felt polluted. So I blew his hat off! That made things even worse.

He was unusual, almost spooky, yet impossibly intriguing. I couldn't stay away. He was different in an attractive, dangerous way.

His odd black clothing said he came from the Great City, a good 370 Land Marks away (how Wind measures distance, roughly 500 human miles.) I could tell he was a bright young man with two passions ruling his imagination: astronomy and horses. I could smell the horses on his boots, but it was the way he gazed into the night sky that intrigued me. One minute his eyes darted, as if he were reading a stellar map; the next he would focus longingly on a single spot, as if looking at someone he loved.

In the dirt he drew a line. He then poked it with holes to note the moon's position and easy to see Venus, Jupiter and Saturn, his favorite planet. But even more important, here on the ecliptic, the line of the Sun's annual path across the sky, lived the Zodiac Twelve. With meticulous care, Skylar sketched each Constellation along the line as if he'd known them forever … Virgo, Aquarius, Leo, Taurus, Scorpio … the *Dazzling Dozen* he called them. From there, he configured the Constellation 'neighborhood' floating above him at that moment. He drew outlines of Ursa Major, Ursa Minor, Draco, Cassiopeia, Hydra, Monoceros … but to his favorites, Orion the Hunter and his dogs Major and Minor, he gave great artistic and heroic detail. He then put a smile on Orion's face. That made him smile – which made me smile! He wrote WINTER SOLSTICE and underlined each word in wonder, realizing he had deduced by stellar calendar that Autumn's end and Winter's beginning were nigh. He sat back and pondered his drawing.

I gently breezed over it in amazement, careful not to mess it up. His advanced grasp of the night sky astonished me – and the Sky. But what warmed our hearts was the Changing of the Seasons not only mattered to him, it brought him happiness.

Skylar observed the Moon waxing towards full, yet it seemed not as bright as in former years. *The moon is fading,* he thought, *like me.*

The boy is fading, thought the Moon, *like me.* It knew there wouldn't be any Northern Lights or Winter this year. The emptiness was contagious, and the Moon couldn't be its best self. *Why get my hopes up?* With Earth's atmosphere so muddy, Sunlight, Moonlight and Starlight simply couldn't get through. *Ah, to be a Winter Moon on snow*, the Moon mourned its lost best self nostalgically.

It was true, the lights were going out: with no Aurora Borealis or Aurora Australis to produce, what fun was there in being Old Magnus or a Solar Wind? Earth was so out of sync that its magnetic field shifted from positive to downright negative.

When the Kingdom of Winter had lost Prince Cerulean, all joy had left the Earth and Sky. Winter beings carried out only the barest minimum of their Winter responsibilities. Some places were lucky if they saw frost, for Jack no longer found pleasure in the mischief of hinting Winter's arrival without his best friend whom he was supposed to have protected. And in the unusual warmth, frost would have melted instantly anyway.

The other Seasons would have complained about Winter's lax performance, but they each had troubles of their own.

The Kingdom of Summer, once a master of control, couldn't stop overdoing it. In many places its heat cooked man and beast, caused drought, lightning struck without rain and, for the first time ever, Summer couldn't tolerate its own temperatures! It frankly didn't like the Fire Witch's plan for eternal Summer – it was exhausting. No Season should have to work that hard. And besides, what she was creating wasn't Summer at all! It was a scorching oven of planetary death.

To Summer's Royal Family, the Fire Witch seemed oblivious to the obvious: when all the fuel to burn was gone, what would happen to her? In creating Earth's demise she was creating her own. And those who helped her, her Torches, erroneously believed they could rocket to Mars and be spared.

No one was spared.

The Kingdom of Autumn, once a favorite Season, was now redundant. Unnecessary surplus. The ultimate blow. Summer's heat burnished leaves crispy brown to the ground. No matter how fast trees, bushes and vines over-produced leaves just to breathe, Summer wilted and shriveled them even faster. Autumn's ego was badly bruised, which made Winter's job harder, for Autumn refused to leave no leaf unturned, wanting more time to paint red, orange and yellow anywhere it could.

So Winter grew shorter and shorter, which secretly pleased the Winter King. So bereft and lonely was he that he wasn't sure he remembered how to even make snow anymore!

But of all the Seasons, Spring was the most fragile in self-confidence and artistic sensibility. Birth is serious business. From the smallest Edelweiss to Honey Bee to Giraffe to Blue Whale, Spring Queen Terra saw to it that each being regenerated to perfection. Some beings she even evolved to higher states. It was all about the show: a global spectacle in loving microscopic detail. But for Spring's audience to lose appreciation for its special effects, well, every artist takes rejection quite personally. Rather than a jubilant welcome after a good harsh Winter, Spring was now greeted with utter dread: everyone knew what would follow … another blazing Summer.

The Spring Princesses Flora and Fauna actually threatened to boycott if attitudes didn't improve. And their brother Prince Rainier, the moody Master of Monsoons? He gave *Tropical Depression* a whole new meaning. First everyone complained there was too much rain, then not enough – he couldn't get it right. The oceans and skies were too warm for him to form clouds that stuck together. He needed cool air. (Imagine how I felt as the North Wind, unable to find any for him!) Without clouds, the Sky became a vast empty desert of bored hot air.

Worst of all, rainforest tribes stopped their rain dances to Prince Rainier. They vanished. No rain, no forest; no home, no tribe. Thus were sown the seeds of the Water Wars. Once humans knew rain was less and less scientifically possible, they realized they themselves were less and less scientifically possible. War took their minds off a doomed future … which was *precisely* what the Fire Witch wanted.

You may be wondering why I don't mention the King of Spring? It's because – well there once was a great Spring King you see, that is until he – he … he's still hard to talk about, the darkest of the Dark Natures in all of nature. Virile virulence. Savvy savagery. His tale I've saved for the telling through those who survived in the Kingdoms of Spring and Autumn in Volumes II and IV.

But back to Winter's story, speaking of clouds … above Skylar a few clouds quietly crept along, unsure of their duties, too proud to mutiny, afraid to go it alone. They revealed a panoply of stars. Skylar wondered what it would be like to be a Constellation,

seemingly in eternal peace, while Earth was in ruinous chaos.

Skylar, too, was in ruinous chaos. He couldn't believe his predicament. He bounced his legs with unconscious wired energy. He grabbed them, and held them firmly, realizing his mind and body had been in a perpetual state of alert or panic ever since he ran away from the Great City. He furtively whispered inside his breast pocket.

"I hope you're happy! I'm in the middle of nowhere lost, hungry, tired, paranoid – all because of *you*, starball!" He paused, as if expecting it to answer, which it never did. He didn't know what else to call it but a starball, because that's exactly what it looked like: multi-dimensional and spinning like a mini-galaxy. One minute it glowed like gaslight in a lantern and the next it shone in colorful fluorescence like bioluminescent phytoplankton he'd seen snorkeling at night at the beach. Skylar didn't hold back.

"So what are you, anyway?" he asked the starball. "And by the way, you weird little sparkly electromagnetic whatever … I didn't steal you! More like you stole me! Yeah, that's what I'm saying. Hijacked! You know if she finds us we're dead. Like DEAD. Like everyone I know – knew. Ugh!"

Skylar was freaked out, all the time, ever since the entire world was hit by the Great Catastrophe. In his short fifteen-year lifetime, human civilization which had taken millennia to evolve fell apart when fragile Earth lost its balance. Nations and politicians blamed each other until their voices vanished into silence and borders disappeared under flood waters or were rewritten by earthquakes.

The Great City fell. Like all the other cities, it had no food, no water, no electricity, no phones or internet. Each city was cut off from the rest of the world. And then his school burned down, the starball found him, his home burned down and now he was being hunted like an animal – it was more than any fifteen-year old could take! He never took the starball out of his vest pocket. Sometimes he even forgot it was there … until he'd meet another person and suddenly all this crazy weird anger would just spew out of his mouth! Not even connected to his thoughts! He was pretty sure he was losing it – and the starball had something to do with that.

Skylar jumped when he heard the noise and pulled out a dagger he fashioned from metal he had stolen from a nearby iron works. He nimbly scooted behind a large rock and hid. I heard him gasp imperceptibly to himself, "Huh…? Is she –? Is that an … angel? A glorious golden haired angel!" I couldn't resist fluttering Lily's hair and leafy frock for added angelic effect.

"How strange …" Skylar continued, "the Wind is blowing her face and hair, like it's asking her a question. And – and she's answering?"

The more Lily spoke to me, the more Skylar couldn't believe his ears.

"Whoa … she talks – sounds just like Wind. Well that's normal, I guess," he surmised. "Angels would speak Wind, everyone knows that. Why, it's how angels fly and get travel directions."

I surmised this must be one very scared or lonely boy to imagine he was looking at an angel. Skylar's imagination went into overdrive. "This is irresistible … a mystery I have to solve. If she's an angel, where are her wings? She plays a harp, ok, but why can't I hear a single note? And her frock, it looks like leaves, not poufy white angel-wear."

But this was nothing compared to what he saw next: Lily began speaking to the stars, addressing, in particular, Orion the Hunter. I could tell Skylar couldn't make out what she said, but he knew it was heartfelt, because he saw her shed tears.

"I better stop giving the Wind such a hard time," Skylar said to himself. Then it struck him. "What a strange thing to say, as if the Wind were –? Pff! Impossible."

He was so spellbound that his dagger slipped from his hand, clanging loudly on the rock. It startled Lily and me. She leapt off the hill and vanished into the trees. Skylar rubbed his eyes, certain he'd seen a hallucination. He emerged from behind the rock and stood on the place where his angel had stood. Taking several breaths, he blew to see if the Wind would answer him.

"Will you answer me, Wind?" he asked softly, half mocking, half serious.

I didn't dare answer.

He lifted his eyes to Orion the Hunter and … "What was that?" he asked huskily. He could have sworn he saw the great Constellation turn his head to … "Are *you* looking at *me*?" Skylar asked.

His intuition knew the answer was yes and it freaked him out. The starball started pulsating hotly against his chest and the one person who came to Skylar's mind, as she always did when things got weird or rough, was …*"Coral,"* he whispered. Coral, the pretty Asian girl he had had a crush on ever since she came to the Great School. Coral, the oceanography whiz who spoke three languages. Coral who spent lunch everyday with him and their friend Rocky, a geology whiz, on their Constellation apps quizzing each other on who among the *Great 88* was floating above in broad daylight invisible to everyone but them. Coral who finally said yes to going out on a date – on the day of the fire. Coral, the first girl he ever loved and whom he couldn't bear imagining dying, let alone in a fire.

He had had enough of death. Losing his mother the year before when the Great City's hospital couldn't save her was the worst experience of his life. "No Medicine! No Doctors!" was the sign posted on the shuttered emergency room doors. It had all been so surreal that her funeral still felt like a bad dream … someone else's bad dream; their mom, not his. And being placed in a foster home with other orphaned kids only deepened his disconnect.

His only solace was sneaking up to his foster family's roof and stargazing night after night – nights when the smog would clear out enough to see the stars, that is. When his mom died, people didn't hesitate to tell him where she had gone: some said to heaven to be with the angels. Others said she reincarnated into her favorite animal. Still others said she became a new star in the sky. This last one captured his imagination most, and on those nights when he saw stars, he wondered which one might be her, and if he could see her, could she see him?

Being an astronomer, Skylar categorized things by color. To him, his foster parents were grey energy. Not hot, not cold, not mean, not fun, just grey. They weren't into science, let alone stargazing. The only times they showed any color, angry red, were the many times they were convinced Skylar was out partying when he was in fact above their heads lying on his back hanging out with his Constellation friends.

The astronomy lab was the last place he saw Coral. Just an hour before seeing her for the last time, he had been unceremoniously escorted off the Great School's grounds by the headmaster who took umbrage at Skylar's one man Dickensian *Hamlet.* Skylar thought he was being innovative by changing *"Something's rotten in Denmark"* to *"Something's rotten in the world."* He changed the names of Hamlet's enemies to the names of powerful people whom everyone knew were behind the Water Wars, which he dubbed Man's *Waterloo*. But the plot thickened: these powerful people were not only the headmaster's best friends, they were the school's biggest donors. Being expelled was humiliating. The headmaster made sure a lot of people saw Skylar get the boot. Along with Dickensian Hamlet, out went Skylar's not-so-secret *Banned Book Brigade* and *Atmosfears Club*, both of which had kept students secretly up to date on the world's demise outside their school bubble.

Outside the gates, the thought of never seeing Coral or Rocky again sent Skylar sneaking round the back where he climbed over the brick wall and slipped in a side door. So what if a few people saw him sneak back in? He didn't care, he had nothing to lose. He had to tell his friends what had happened and, if he was being expelled, he sure wasn't going to leave his astronomy notebook behind – not with all his ideas, dreams, sketches and Coral's note in her pretty handwriting saying *Yes!* in it.

But no sooner was Skylar in the lab and caught sight of Rocky and Coral, did he hear his professor say to another student, "Watch it, Daniel, these are stellar gases! One wrong

measurement and –" KABOOM! Skylar was blown out the
window. All he remembered was a force field knocking the wind
out of him, then the hard ground knocking it back into him as he
landed outside, narrowly missing the brick wall's iron spikes. He
couldn't believe what he was looking at: his school was a giant
ball of flames. A second explosion blew out a wall and caused
the roof to cave in, slinging a swirling starball to his feet. He
intuitively grabbed the small, strange gassy sphere of light, and
since it wasn't hot, he mindlessly pocketed it, all the while desperately trying to find a way to help his friends. He shouted for
them at the top of his lungs, "Coral! Rocky! Professor!" The heat
became an impenetrable wall as the smoke started to choke and
blind him, as if it were after him. Then he saw the headmaster
staring at him accusingly and knew he was really in for it. In
terror he ran home, utterly grief stricken about Coral and Rocky
– not to mention his irreplaceable notebook. But more was yet to
come.

His foster mother was preparing dinner when Skylar ran
into the house and breathlessly told her what had happened. He
lived there with seven other foster children, all of whom had also
lost their parents to the medicine shortage. Out of nowhere, the
kitchen stove suddenly caught fire, a fire which seemed eerily to
have a personality – an evil one at that. Skylar's foster mother
tried to put it out with towels but the fire hungrily hitched a ride
on them to leap to the curtains over the sink. She ran for the fire
extinguisher as the fire sprinted onto cabinets, the ceiling, the
table, then took command of the floor and marched toward Skylar.

"Give me back what you stole!" he thought he heard the fire

scream. The fire lunged at Skylar repeatedly, each time getting hotter and closer, flames swiping and lurching as if grabbing for him.

Skylar's foster mother did what any mother would do: she jumped to the boy's safety putting herself between him and the fire, spraying the extinguisher. The Fire Witch did what any fire would do: whipped around behind her and attacked her clothes and hair. Skylar panicked, screaming "Fire! Fire!" looking for some way to help. Another foster kid ran in with a blanket and helped Skylar snuff out the burning flames on their foster mother.

"Run, boys! Get out! Go that way!" she yelled as they all ran for the door. The entire house was ablaze. The three barely got out with their lives. As Skylar leapt off the front porch he again heard behind him, "Give me back what you stole!" He turned and could have sworn he saw a wraith of fire pursuing him off the porch. Skylar ran for his life into the night.

He fought with every fiber not to cry. He knew he could never go back to the Great City, that it looked bad, like somehow he was responsible for both fires: *'crazed expelled teen goes on pyro rampage in angry revenge.'* All he had wanted to do was say goodbye and get his notebook. All he got was a starball in his pocket that somehow inexplicably seemed to have made him an enemy of fire. Skylar took off running back to the cave where he had been hiding. There, he stopped fighting. Finally he wept like the wounded boy he was.

I quietly accompanied him, breezing behind, liking him more and more.

ꞚO SWIMMIꞚG!

M ost mornings Lily picked herbs along the lagoon's edge
for her tea. Playing her silk-harp, she sang ancient tree
songs Coco had taught her. This morning another voice joined
her, a beautiful voice. It was light, feminine and ghostly, oth-
er-worldly. Lily stopped singing to hear the voice better. The
voice stopped. Lily resumed and the voice resumed. Then Lily
halted and the voice halted. This happened several times until
Lily knelt down at the water's edge. Though it was a misty
morning, it was sticky hot.

"I'd love to go for a swim," she sighed. She'd never swum
in this lagoon before. Come to think of it, she'd ever seen any
other creature swim in the lagoon, either. She lifted her frock to
dip her toe in the water.

"Stop! I wouldn't do that if I were you!" the voice warned. Lily jumped back on shore, looking all around her and in the water. There was no reflection. Her heart pounded.

"It's very misty here so I can't see you – who are you? Where are you? Show yourself!" Lily commanded in the ancient tree language she'd been singing in.

"I can't show you more than you already see," answered the voice.

Lily was confused, but not to be trifled with. "If I can hear you and supposedly see you," she said, "touch me so I can feel you."

"I am touching you," whispered the voice.

Lily scanned her body. "I don't feel a thing," she replied, slightly irritated.

"Close your eyes," soothed the voice. "You want to cool off?" the voice asked.

"Oh yes, please – I'm sooo hot," Lily swooned, as if she might faint.

A cool, refreshing wet sensation brushed across Lily's face and body.

"Mmmm*mmist?*" Lily murmured. She opened her eyes to find herself enshrouded in a thick vapor. "*You're* who's been singing with me?" Lily asked in disbelief.

"I am," replied the Mist.

"Why can't I go swimming?" asked Lily.

"You didn't ask permission," said the Mist.

"Is it your lagoon?" asked Lily.

"It is my Soul," the Mist answered wistfully. "Swimming

in these waters will change you. And I like you the way you are. Even just a few moments underwater and you'd be transformed into anything you wish. It's rather dangerous," warned the Mist.

But Lily saw it another way. "It sounds ideal. A new me, a chance to find *him*."

"Would you let go of everything and everyone you love? Because if you change, everything else changes."

"I do have something and someone I love," Lily answered. She thought of the glowing chrysalis in its secret place, sewn into her garment over her heart. "I love Coco and Sir Windham. But there must be an upside to the lagoon's magic? What if I just stayed a few moments and –?" Lily mused. Her big toe tickled ripples in the cool dark water.

The Mist could tell this girl had pluck. "A few moments are never enough. If you drink the lagoon water, you forget your old self forever and permanently transform. For a few, this is a good thing. For most, it ends in disaster. Especially those who want only riches, fame or power. They suddenly change into a mighty ruler or a rock star, but since they never earned it or learned it they can't play the part. One thing about wishing you were someone else: the greater a person, the greater the tests. Unless you can stomach the tests to become great, please remove your toe from my soul," the Mist warned her. Lily brazenly dunked her whole foot! She held her breath wondering what would happen next.

The two regarded each other silently until the Mist spoke again, "I've watched you grow beside my waters in Coco's care. I know your legend by heart."

Lily was jolted. "Legend? Isn't it true?" she asked.

"Everyone has a legend they are writing, one deed at a time. And all are called to great deeds, but most give up when it gets hard, just when their best self is about to emerge and make their journey adventurous and rich," said the Mist.

Lily thought of Cerulean's bravery. "Is this why I understood Cerulean's language?" she asked. "I was called?"

At last! Maybe she's the one! thought the Mist.

"I've listened to your exchanges of plant wisdom with the great shamans who have passed through these woods. You understand that all essences have senses. Take me, I used to be a Faerie in human form, like you" the Mist said. "Now I can't go anywhere in this misty state, for the lagoon is my soul and I can drift only so far. Without a human body to carry me, I will never leave here. It will take someone who willingly wants to get to know me, then be me, to set me free."

"You would take over someone's body? For how long?"

"I don't know. I've never done it. I've never met anyone I trust enough until now … until you."

"And if someone does become you? Say hypothetically I do it, not that I will …" Lily dug deeper.

"Remember your 'imaginary friends' and their 'Castle of the Seasons' in the Great Forest?" the Mist inquired enticingly.

"Yes, I still dream of them," answered Lily.

The Mist ventured, "I've heard stories that some have seen a Mistress of the Castle. Some say she is Queen Crystalline imprisoned; others believe her to be your mother, a Daughter of Autumn with The Gift, like you, half-Faerie; and others say the

Mistress is the Soul of the Castle wandering her empty halls, melancholic, since the Seasons no longer take turns holding court every three months."

The words seized Lily's mind and heart. Her throat swallowed her voice.

"My *mother??*… My mother is, *alive??* She didn't die? She was half-Faerie? *I'm* half-Faerie? Is that why I can talk to you and the Wind? Can I go see her, my mother?" Lily asked huskily. Her knees gave way, and she plunked down on a rock in a jittery jumble of feelings. "Papa and Kir never ever spoke of Mama. Not a word, except to remind me that my being born killed her. Though I'm pretty sure I must be a lot like her, because every time Papa caught me speaking what he called gobbledygook, I mean Faerie, he'd stare right through me saying mama's name like he'd seen a ghost, *'Gala'* … then he'd snap out of it, get furious and tell me to stop it!"

The Mist was still, careful not to betray its feelings.

Lily asked again, urgently, "Please, tell me, can I see her? Does she know I'm alive? Can I go live with her? What's she look like –?"

Lily was cut off by my furious intrusion out of nowhere. I'd been listening and had had enough! I blasted the Mist.

HOWWWWWW DARRRRRRRE YOUUUUU??
FORRRRR SHAAAAAAAAAMMMMMMME!

I howled and blew that Mist to bits. It tumbled, toppled, curled, rolled, and spun and still, it continued to speak to Lily!

"Whoa! The heat isn't good for me! I say foolish things when

I – I – whoa! I shouldn't have raised your hopes on rumors! Winddd-ham, stop! Lily, come back tonight and – ahhh! Ohhh! Windham, enough! Down boy! Ouch! That hurt! Do – Not – Go – Swimmm-mmmming …!" the Mist admonished Lily, fading as it scattered in every direction.

Oh but I squalled even harder! Darwina clung to her web for dear life. Her silk, the toughest biological material known to Man, was built for maximum wind load. The cluster of sounds it made was quite extraordinary! I don't know who lost more leaves, Coco or Lily's dress, but I gusted till that Mist was gone Gone GONE … or at least invisible.

"Mists are fickle airheads who should keep their spray to themselves!" Coco shouted. "No manners, no morals!"

The Mist's words were infuriating, yes, but also frightening. I made sure Lily understood the dangers around her. "The Castle of the Seasons is top secret! Its location is known only to the Seasons, the Blue Spruce Guard and to me! The Mist knows better than to talk about it in the open! The Fire Witch's spies are everywhere: no candle or lantern is to be trusted. You have a gift everyone wishes they had for themselves and which she would love more than anything to destroy: the power to heal others. Never take your powers for granted, for they will be required of you when the world most needs it. As for your mother, dear child, even I wouldn't start a rumor like that. It's heartless!" I scowled. I loved Lily like my own little breezling and wanted to protect her.

"Why is the Castle's location so secret?" Lily asked, not sure I'd answer. But the answer was common knowledge.

"Because it's an H.C.S.," I whispered. "An Harmonic

Convergence Site, one of the few places where Constellations visit on Earth."

"Even Orion?" she bubbled spontaneously.

"Especially Orion," I said.

"Windham, where do you go when you're not here? To the Castle of the Seasons?" Lily asked, spontaneously.

"No. I go … *there*," I evaded her.

"No, not tonight. No riddles," she groaned. "Where do you go? I miss you when you're gone."

This tugged at my heart. Lily was my close friend and confidant, but I couldn't tell her. No one could know but those who already knew. And she would soon find out anyway.

"I blow around with other winds!" I retorted, hoping to quench her curiosity.

But she pressed on, "Coco says you carry the Tree Spirits of the world. That you pick them up and drop them off as they birth and die, ever choosing new places to grow. Coco wants to be a Baobab Tree in South Africa next time around, or a Red Wood in California."

"Ha! Everyone wants to be a Baobab and live over a thousand years or be a Red Wood and stand 300' tall – they have the best views," I laughed. "There's more to it, but Coco's basically got it. We Winds know every spirit of every being that has ever been on Earth. And the more spirits traveling, the mightier we blow! It changes constantly, especially now with all the forest fires, floods and storms. Human, Animal and Tree Spirits are being released in the billions. And Faerie souls that are stripped of their chrysalis or entrapped, they revert to a natural essence."

Lily took in the awesomeness of this, feeling the warmth of Cerulean's chrysalis over her heart. She wondered what natural essence he might be and where? We waited by the lagoon for the Mist to waft in, which it didn't. The Mist knew it had pushed a boundary and though it was hiding, I felt it listening to us. Lily and I watched Darwina dine on the one lone fly ensnared in her web. Who would've ever imagined flies could go extinct, too?

Lily stared at the stars, daydreaming of her mother, the Castle of the Seasons and the legendary balls every three months at the *Changing of the Seasons* ceremony. I loved telling her my stories of The Golden Age and cooled Lily as best I could, but it was such a hot sticky December night that moving the air seemed to only make it hotter.

Overhead, Orion began his journey across the night sky. At last Lily gave up waiting for the Mist, and I accompanied her silently to her secret place. She didn't have to say it, I could feel it, how the Mist had changed something deep inside Lily. I felt like someone had been stolen from me. Lily felt like someone had been given to her.

FACES IN THE MOONLIGHT

Skylar was prepared tonight. If he saw his angel, he would find the courage to communicate with her. But how? Ever since that life changing moment at the fire at his school, the words that flew out of his mouth were cruel, bitter and never connected to his thoughts. He was pretty sure it had something do with the starball, the weird souvenir from his burning school … or did it? He didn't know why he picked the starball up. But the minute he did his every instinct screamed *RUN!* And ever since, it was like he had lost control of his mouth, so he simply stopped talking – not that there was anyone to talk to out here, except himself … and his starball.

His mother always told him he was a good natured boy. He thought it was because he loved nature more than anyone, being a city boy where the only natural things around were the sky and the carriage horses he helped care for in the Great City Park which long ago had lost its trees. Yet now, nature itself seemed to trigger embarrassing reactions not of his own devising.

"Maybe my souvenir is something more than a shiny trinket? Would you care to answer?" he asked his vest. No answer. "Maybe there's an alien inside me?" he wryly mused to himself. He'd been through so much, especially the gruesome fiery deaths of his friends and his professor. "Maybe my mind has snapped? They say when you go insane you don't know it," he mused again, scared it might be true. He wiped the sweat from his brow. I could tell it unnerved him to realize that even I, the Wind, was hesitant to touch him in the way-too-hot December air. Much as he wanted to befriend me, not even the feistiest badger, wasp or vulture would come near him, for beasts are inherently kind and instantly sense confusing energy. And how his energy confused me! To his credit, Skylar understood the beasts and plants were going through the same ordeal he was: since the Great Catastrophe, all beings, plant and animal, were losing their homes, their friends and families, they had little food or water, and each relied on the kindness of those different from themselves for survival.

The boy seemed plagued by his thoughts as he waited. At long last his patience was rewarded: his angel appeared. Exactly as the night before … "She's playing her silent harp-thingamajig … speaking to Orion … and crying," Skylar quietly observed in every minute detail. He saw me breezing around Lily, billowing her thick hair and leafy dress in soft pillows of faint moonlight.

"The Wind loves her," Skylar whispered enviously. "And she loves him." He saw Lily blow me a kiss as I swirled in a delighted funnel.

I knew Skylar wished he could catch that kiss for himself. "I wonder if this magical being, my angel, can rescue me from this nightmare? But if she could, what can I offer her? Vicious words that sabotage everything? Great. Oh who cares? I have to try! I'm all alone, I'll never see Coral or Rocky again, and this angel may be my last chance."

Skylar stealthily snuck toward Lily and me. I confess I grew in agitation the closer he crept, gusting in Lily's face so violently that she yelled and stomped, "What has gotten into you??"

In a flash of silver-blue moonlight on two young faces, Skylar and Lily faced each other, each giving the other a solid fright. Lily was transfixed, for the face staring at her was dirty, marred, almost beastly, but underneath wore a penetrating, handsome intensity. His clothes were tattered, black and cut oddly – they were from a time and place she didn't recognize. He even wore a funny black top hat, which I quickly blew off his head!

"No manners!" I twittered.

I had assumed he was one of those humans who lost everything when the ice shelves melted and flooded the lowlands. Lily, Coco and I often spoke about the Great Catastrophe and how billions of humans died and those who migrated to higher ground were killed by those who wouldn't share their food or water.

Water … the foundation of all life. Each Season once played its part in bringing fresh water to Earth's beings. It was fun, it was rewarding. In many parts of the world, the Wet Season was a time of celebration and rejuvenation. Be it monsoons or April showers, the Seasons' rains, and especially Winter's snows, were gifts most humans appreciated. Yes, there were those who called rainy days "awful, depressing, ugly, a pain" and even "it's a bad day outside" … until heat-induced rain shortages led to Man's terrifying Water Wars. Then everyone wanted rainy days back. The Water Wars triggered floods of displaced persons on every continent and each continent's lakes, streams, rivers, waterfalls, geysers and glaciers were cannibalized.

As much as humans desperately missed these, the Sky, Sun, Moon and Clouds missed seeing their reflections, especially in the world's mighty lakes: the Caspian Sea, Baikal, Tanganyika, Tahoe, Victoria, Titicaca, the five Great Lakes, Malawi – each once a very proud healthy being. We Winds used to gauge our wind speed by ripple and wave size and we missed our old lake friends terribly. The Kingdoms of the Seasons had seen it coming: when the world's lakes fell, the Great Catastrophe was inevitable.

But humans had help in their self-sabotage and their rescue, though they didn't know it. They long believed in dark forces against them, usually found in each other, and good forces helping them, often assigned to spirits and gods. But curiously they weren't aware of the Kingdoms of the Seasons living right beside them! Faeries were the stuff of fairy tales and Earth's problems were consigned to scientific explanation, which thrilled the Fire Witch and the dark lord who – no, No! Not here! Not another word about him, that monster! But I will say, for these dark beings the fun in being evil was getting away with it right under Man's nose … with Man's help.

Without water the world starved, just as the Fire Witch planned. Weeds grew where trees and crops once stood, but the land was now so damaged that even indestructible 'irritating' weeds – that's what humans call them, we Seasons know nature's soldiers better – even poor ole' weeds couldn't hold on long enough to keep soil in place.

The few trees that were left had huddled for safety in small clumps, like Coco and her friends. Mother Trees, one of nature's best kept secrets, were stunted by drought which ironically hid them from the Fire Witch's trained eye. For the very first time in Earth's history, we Winds could count how many trees remained. It was like a man going bald counting his last hairs. Man now valued shade and topsoil more than gold; fruit and vegetable seeds replaced money. Why several famous bank robberies were at seed banks!

Lily greeted Skylar in Wind, unable to remember well enough the language of Men.

Much to my surprise, and his, he understood her. "I'm hot and hate it here!" he yelled bitterly.

Lily was taken aback. This boy spoke a broken ancient Faerie dialect, yet was very rude. "You don't have to be nasty!" she shot back.

I urged Lily to leave at once, for now I picked up a very odd vibration from the boy. I couldn't place it, but I no longer trusted him and I let him know it: I gusted him a few good ones! To my surprise it tickled him! He laughed like you laugh when you're playing with a friend – but not for long.

"How dare you! Don't you know who I am?" he exploded in rage. He slapped his hand over his mouth.

"I think you work too hard to make friends. Let's try it again," Lily said calmly.

I was surprised, but Skylar was stunned. *She really is an angel,* he thought. He started to tremble, which Lily noticed.

"I am Lily. And this is my best friend, Sir Windham the North Wind," she said.

I breezed Skylar a Wind hello. It unnerved him. He sweat in panic. Instead of speaking, he took a stick and drew in the moonlit dirt: S K Y L A R

"Well how do you do, Skylar? Nice to meet –" she was cut off.

"That is NOT who I am!" he shouted, his mouth momentarily uncovered.

"OK, Skylar – or whoever you are …" Lily cautiously replied.

"Yes! No! Don't listen! This is who I am not!" Skylar fought for control of his mouth.

Lily was utterly confounded by this bizarre boy. "Where are your parents?" she asked.

MA DEAD – NO PA He wrote in the dirt, covering his mouth with his left hand. He quickly etched more.

SORRY!! I'M NOT MYSELF.

I calmed, listened keenly, and whispered to her, "See if he'll tell you where he's from – and what's with the strange clothes?"

"I've never seen clothes like yours. Where –?" Lily asked.

YOU WEAR LEAVES He etched, cracking a small smile.

Lily smiled back. "Yes, I'm a forest girl."

CITY BOY. LEAD IN SCHOOL PLAY He wrote. Then he tipped his top hat to her and bowed as a Dickensian gentleman would to a lady.

Lily barely suppressed a giggle. She may be a forest girl, but she knew what flirting was. And she didn't mind this city boy's style. "How did you end up here, so far from –?" she asked.

SCHOOL FIRE … He cautiously looked around, then slowly wrote the next bit: SOMEONE IS AFTER ME

"After you? Who?" Lily wanted to know.

Skylar nervously swiped the last words out with his foot. A dust cloud rose which I puffed away as he wrote more:

ARE YOU AN ANGEL? ORION HEARS YOU

Tears welled up in Lily's eyes. Orion never gave any sign that he listened. How could this boy know such a thing? In the distance a commotion arose followed by the telltale smoky orange glow of the Fire Witch's handiwork. Lily heard the trees send up the alarm to the beasts.

"Skylar, hide! If the Fire Witch's spies –" Lily cried out. As if Skylar's pallor could get any ghostlier, the blood drained from his face in sheer terror as his eyes caught the distant orange glow. It chilled Lily to the bone.

He instantly shushed her lips with his finger. He felt it: they'd been seen and heard. Not even I dared rustle a hair on their heads. Skylar slowly pulled out his dagger, for they were exposed in the wide open. Coco taught Lily how to survive as a tree, especially in danger. But she was only part Faerie and would have given anything to hide this boy like Coco could with her roots.

"We must go!" I puffed in Lily's face.

"I live by the lagoon in –" Lily hushed to Skylar, but before she could finish I drowned her out and whisked her away. She ran as my urgent howl cleared a path for her back to the safety of Coco's underground sanctuary.

His angel gone, Skylar was more alone than ever. Discouraged, he looked up to Orion and his breath caught. "You're whose gaze I felt?" he realized in awe. Staring, he wondered how Lily hadn't noticed it: Orion the Hunter was brandishing his bow exactly as Skylar held his dagger.

THE MIST'S IDEA

S itting alone at the lagoon's edge, Lily watched dawn break as she sipped her tea. Her toes delicately rippled the still water and she felt refreshingly cool all over. "I know you're here," she whispered to the Mist. As if on cue, early sunlit rays glistened in golden shafts of floating vapor all around her. Darwina's web sparkled like a twinkling golden orb as the little spider set upon a tasty bug breakfast. "I got up early, hoping we could talk –" Lily was interrupted.

"I heard about your new friend …" the Mist ventured, also eager to pick up where they had left off. "… but you should be more careful venturing out alone."

"You should be more careful with secrets and rumors!" Lily jabbed.

"My dearest dear, I'm so sorry! I apologized to Sir Windham and to Coco. I behaved like a smog to you!" confessed the Mist. Tears starting dripping from the Mist into the lagoon.

"Oh, don't cry! I forgive you – we all do. None of us are quite ourselves," Lily reassured her. "We're all trying our best."

"I haven't been myself for some time," the Mist sighed.

"If your lagoon changes people, maybe it's changing you? Just sitting here dipping my toes changed me. I'll never be who I was before yesterday … you gave me new things to think about and I can't forget them," Lily said.

"When the tree alarm went out and you weren't home, Coco was out of her mind – have you ever seen a panicked Oak pace in place? What a mess – now my lagoon is all clogged in acorns and leaves!" The Mist continued in a whisper, "Those fires last night were dangerously close to the Castle of the Seasons."

"I saw the orange glow. He saw it, too – it terrified him. His name is Skylar. I think he talks to Orion –"

"Oldest spy trick in the book!" snapped the Mist. "Men worship Fire. Don't forget, *She* still seeks you – what a prize you'd be for a greedy boy in the Fire Witch's service."

A twig snapped and fell into Lily's lap. "You're listening too hard," Lily mused to Coco, looking up. An astute listener, like all trees, Coco was a Royal Messenger, an honor given only to the Wind and Trees to announce the Changing of the Seasons. This is why you feel a Season coming on the Wind and can read it in the Trees. This is also why Winds and Trees make such good spies.

Lily felt a sensation in her chest. *Is that my heart pounding or his light pulsing?* she wondered, feeling a bit light headed and confused.

The Mist, too, was light headed – but not confused. What no one knew is just how long it had been waiting for the right person. The moment and the girl were here, at last, now.

"Lily, how would you like to celebrate Winter Solstice this year?" the Mist asked enticingly. "Let's ring it in like the old days! Why not throw the biggest party of the year on the longest night of the year? Why, it may even summon the Winter King … I could ask Sir Windham to invite him!"

Her words had the desired effect: a desert stunned by a flash flood.

Lily's mind raced. "But what about the iron works blocking the Faerie Highway?" she asked.

"I think Winter can find a way around that. And if my idea works, you may even find … your Prince," the Mist beguiled.

"Stop it! Her head's foggy enough with him!" reproached Coco.

"Cerulean??" asked Lily eagerly. "When?" Her spirit soared in wonder and hope. "How?"

"A Solstice Costume Ball!" the Mist cajoled. "Not a Faerie or human alive would miss the chance to dust off his or her Solstice dance slippers. I see you as the belle of our ball, my dear!" the Mist glistened. "And I have the perfect costume for you."

"A Solstice Costume Ball??" exclaimed Coco like she'd just been told the Earth is square. "Will you invite the Fire Witch personally? Or should we just let her crash the party?"

"*Secret* Solstice Costume Balls! Worldwide! Winter Solstice above and Summer Solstice below the Equator," insisted the

Mist. "PNN, the Pine News Nexus, they can broadcast through the last-standing-trees. Pine Code: *Top Secret*. Fire still can't crack the language of trees."

Coco was so unusually still, so silent, that Lily dared not move. She held her breath in suspense and saw how even the Mist seemed to hang in suspended motion.

"… What is this perfect costume, Mist?" Coco asked.

"We must speak privately. No one else must hear a word," hushed the Mist.

"Very well, come inside, both of you." Coco opened her roots for Lily, who nimbly climbed in. Then she opened a knot for the Mist, who eagerly sailed inside. Coco quickly closed her roots and the knot so the three could speak privately.

Inside the mighty oak, sound had a gentle cavernous echo, and the Mist's unearthly voice took on an enchanting, even loving, quality.

"All right, Mist, we're waiting," Coco pressed. "If this costume means a dangerous transformation for Lily, I won't let her do it!"

"Calm yourself, my friend. Coco, Lily … allow me to introduce myself. I am the heart and soul of Winter's vanished, but alive, Queen Crystalline," whispered the Mist.

There is no sound so silent as a tree taken by surprise. Lily was so thunderstruck she didn't realize she, too, had stopped breathing. Then Coco, as if seeing dawn break for the first time, swayed, creaking her massive trunk. If the Mist were telling the truth, this was an historic turning point for Earth: a chance to defeat the Fire Witch with Winter's return! Breaking one of the

Fire Witch's oldest and cruelest spells just might be the coup de grace needed to throw her off balance.

"Y-Your Majesty," Coco stammered, "you've been here ever since I was a wee acorn hundreds of years ago. All this time you've been – ?"

"– and long before then, Coco. The only one who knows who I am is Sir Windham, and he only found out recently."

"You mean, all those rumors – they were true?" Coco gasped. "We nicknamed Windham 'the boy who cried wolf' … the 'wind who cried queen'! False sightings everywhere, in all four Kingdoms, by different members of his family. It was too cruel for Winter's King and the Old Ones who remembered you."

"I'm to blame, I'm afraid. For an eternity I sat here as a lagoon … immobile, bored, hot, lonely. And being enchanted meant no beast, Faerie or human could even swim in me. Not even your roots, Coco, drink from me."

"I've always wondered about that …" Coco slowly realized.

"Frostine's curse banished me so far outside of the Kingdom of Winter she knew no one would think to look for me out here. I landed so hard when I appeared that I melted into this lagoon, running deep into the Earth."

"Over generations, I pondered how to escape. One day a cloud inspired me, so I tried and tried by sheer willpower until I figured out how to do it, how to produce mist. I knew it would be the only way to send for help. I had a few encounters with other vapors, an occasional low cloud, a Summer fog, an Autumn Zephyr – each time I'd evaporate bits of myself into the air hoping they'd bring help. But each time they caught my essence, it either didn't convince them or they couldn't convince others. That is until Sir Windham figured it out, with the help of Darwina and her musical web. I taught her a secret musical message of Winter songs. Windham reacted exactly as I knew he would: doubtful, saying no one would believe him after so many false sightings – then Darwina played him my favorite song, *The First Waltz of Winter*. That's when Windham knew.

"Lily, Daughter of Autumn, I am Cerulean's mother. And your devoted love for my son has meant more to me than you will ever know," Queen Crystalline concluded.

"So the perfect Solstice Ball costume, your Majesty, is – *you?*" Coco said.

"Yes. And top secret, of course. Windham and I thought of it. We have spoken many long hours and believe Winter's return is now or never. You, Lily, are my only chance and Winter's best hope. You are a healer. Winter, Earth, my son, my husband and I are broken. We all need healing, desperately … if you are willing, of course," said the Queen.

Lily released a big airy *Whoa!* up into Coco's trunk in amazement at the Queen's astounding words. An intuitive rush of joy and a sense of destiny flooded Lily. She felt like she might levitate and grasped Coco's roots as hard as she could. Coco hugged her back, which set her canopy far above fluttering.

"Your Majesty, Queen Crystalline, it would be my greatest honor to help restore you to your throne and Winter to Earth," Lily said. She felt the chrysalis over her heart. "… And to see Cerulean again? Why it would – I mean, if there's a chance, I – it's so exciting I can barely take it in …" she whispered, her mind racing.

Coco felt a warm wonderful feeling rise up inside her: a spontaneous surge in her phloem and xylem, like a forgotten memory. The Queen felt it, too, as it ascended up Coco's trunk in tingling spirals, waking each branch and its leaves into high-tuned focus. It descended down into her roots and mycorrhizal network and gave Lily wonderful refreshing chills.

"Coco, what are you doing?" Lily giggled.

"Mother Tree Talk! That's how we'll do this! What better way to find out who's still alive? All mothers need support from other mothers and, as far as I know, in my region I'm the last Mother Tree standing. Maybe there's another lone Mother Tree – a Pine, a Maple, a Sycamore, an Elm, a Birch, any Mother Tree somewhere out there, eager to celebrate Winter Solstice? I know those ladies will be among the first to reply to a worldwide PNN news flash!"

"TOP SECRET: Solstice Balls to Woo Winter! Plan Yours Now! Code: Fire Proof," the Queen misted. "Coco, if you please!"

Coco opened her roots and the knot in her trunk. Like a comet, the Mist arched itself backwards over the lagoon and split into two diaphanous figures in a ballroom dance dip: a regal Prince dipping his Princess.

Lily merrily applauded, imagining Cerulean waltzing her at Winter's Snow Ball.

Without delay Coco transmitted the Top Secret announcement to the Pine News Nexus in an ancient tree trill I hadn't heard in ages, a sound only the Wind and other trees can interpret. It's impossible to replicate it in writing, for human letters can't describe any of the sounds of Tree Talk.

"Now, how do we get Sir Windham to invite the Winter King –?" Coco was abruptly cut off.

I whooshed in and did what every Mist dreams of in a dance partner: dips and flips in wispy abandon! I'd been expecting this conversation to happen and as Lily and the Queen emerged from Coco I knew it had gone very well indeed! Winter Solstice Balls! Incredible! At last! In Tree Talk, the word for *Wind* and *Party* are the same … and the world sorely needed both.

"Windham, can we trust you not to blow it? Into the wrong ears, that is?" Coco taunted. "You're so easily tempted by Fire and her sweet smell of smoke," she jabbed.

Coco's words jangled my nerves. My addiction to Fire was a well-known vice and every time I slipped, I felt dirty and used. Here was my chance to prove myself and make things right.

I rippled a message across the lagoon water: *From guilt I long to be set free, the Prince long lost will be found by ME!* Again I blew, even harder, spraying droplets of wet words across Darwina's giant spider web: *What are you up to, Mist?*

HHHHHHHHHHHHHHUFFF! I guffawed across the lagoon and blew the Mist to bits, snapping Coco's twigs.

"Well now, this feels like the good old days!" Coco cheered. "When all I feared was nests fallin' out of my branches!"

Winter Solstice was ON. Ask any tree in that forest, I took off at top Peregrine Falcon speed to announce to my family, Winds large and small around the world, the merry tidings.

But Lily noticed none of it. Unconsciously she moved her

hand over her heart. *Could he really be alive?* she wondered excitedly. Hope made her tummy flutter. For the very first time, she really believed *YES.*

The Queen guessed her thoughts. "Leave it all to me, my dear. All you have to do is step into your destiny – and learn a few Winter Waltzes!"

Lily's eyes filled with tears of joy. "Windham! Can you believe it? Winter Solstice!" she rejoiced. "…Windham?"

"Child, that daft draft is so excited he took off in every direction at once!" Coco mused.

"To tell his family?" Lily bubbled.

"You know he loves nothing more than to gust good tidings! Let's just hope he whispers instead of howls," Coco added wryly. "It all now hangs on Windham and the PNN getting it right."

Without thinking, Lily jumped on a boulder, strummed her silk-harp and started singing. Her voice caught my ear no matter where I was. It rose like perfumed healing balm and all the forest went still. Singing was forbidden by the Fire Witch, especially the song Lily was singing. What was she thinking?? She knew that around the world, singing was punishable by blistering death, yet no one knew why. What did Fire have against singing?

"O roar, Aurora Borealis! Light our –" Lily choked and gagged. The Queen's mist swirled wildly around her, rushed up her nose, down her throat, in her ears.

"STOP! What are you doing??" the Queen sprayed in panic, soaking Lily to her skin.

"What are *you* doing?" Lily gasped. She coughed like she was drowning.

In her cloudy vapor, the Queen rushed Lily back to Coco. "If the Fire Witch hears even one note, if she finds you, she'll – well you know what she did to songbirds! And crickets! Wolves! I know you're happy, we all are. The time for singing will come. But for now, do it in your head," the Mist implored. "Coco and I will join you."

Lily nestled safely back in Coco's roots, quite rattled by the Queen's panic. She started to think she was in something far bigger than she'd imagined. But her joy wasn't diminished. In fact, she had never felt more alive, more loved and protected. She plucked the first four notes of the chant on her silk-harp. And there, in an isolated wood at a lone lagoon, a forest girl, an oak dryad and a misty queen wooed Winter silently, singing in their heads …

"O roar, Aurora Borealis! Light our path unto the Palace! Friends and loves who warm our hearts, raise a frosty chalice to love! For love is always in season, always the reason –"

Thoughts have powerful vibrations. Ask any Wind accompanying you on a walk when you're deep in thought. From far off I sent a small breeze back to them, *"LET THE SEASON START!!"*

THE QUAKING ASPEN

I was a Wind with a mission. With uncommon precision and caution I spread the news of Solstice Balls across the Earth. All the Winds were eager to announce the tidings, from the Polar Easterlies to the Prevailing Westerlies. Even the great Coho, Chinook and Jet Stream Winds altered their patterns to get the word out. The mighty Mistral and Sirocco teamed up with the Levanter and within a few hours all of nature from the North Pole to the South Pole planned their secret festivals to welcome Winter in the North and Summer in the South.

A worldwide Wind relay was easy compared to what came next.

I blew my way toward the Arctic Winter Palace. It was lonely going, for many old tree friends had been torched, cut down or felled by disease. The eerie silence actually became frightening. I flew the deserted Faerie highways which once teamed with commerce. At the first sign of Smoke or Fire I would veer off, undetected.

Of all my downfalls, *She* was the trickiest, my fiery temptress. Much as I lit her Fire, she lit mine. Few beings made me feel so alive! What is it about Fire that we all love so much? For me, I confess, it's our tug-of-war. She's my equal in strength, in cunning, and her unpredictability is downright sexy. I felt desire just thinking about it, then fought it down: *no No NO! Bigger and better things await me! I won't settle for less!* I told myself as thoughts of Machu Picchu saved me again.

As I flew, I noticed the land, once so familiar, had more water in some places and less in others, carving a new map which confused me. More than once I blew the wrong way, getting lost and having to ask for directions. That's embarrassing when you're the Wind. And not all trees were to be trusted, as evidenced by the charred remains of those who had not sworn allegiance to the Fire Witch. And allegiance meant only one thing: you'd die later than sooner.

About one Zoom (roughly two hours in Wind speed) from the Arctic Circle, one such tree, an old Quaking Aspen named Pando shouted boldly, "Windham? Is that you? Haven't felt you in these parts for years! What gossip?"

I hesitated, knowing the Aspen stood in a place that once held a vast forest of Black Spruce, evidently burned to the ground by the Fire Witch. *These Aspen were quick to move in,* I thought. On closer inspection I noticed Spruce saplings by the thousands huddling in discreet groups. I felt relief at the sight and cautiously addressed the Quaking Aspen Chieftain.

"Greetings, Pando. No news, I'm afraid. Being the Wind is a boring business these days. A storm here and there, but no trees or birds to share it with. How 'bout you, any gossip?" I inquired.

The Quaking Aspen, a master maneuverer above and underground, knew me to be too savvy to get bored.

"I don't believe you. You don't blow across the Arctic just to say hello. Everyone knows which Season you're loyal to. If you don't tell me *why* you're here, I'll tell her *that* you're here!" threatened the old Chieftain.

I regarded this tree, whose tired yellow leaves were nearly all gone. I generally loved Aspen, for they danced beautifully in my breezes. But this Chieftain was notoriously the worst sort of tree. He looked out only for trees that looked like him. He was clearly aligned with the Fire Witch.

"I see the sap in your veins has hardened with age! And muffled your hearing!" I chortled. "I'm stunned you haven't heard!"

"Heard what?" demanded Pando. "There's nothing wrong with my hearing! I'm the sharpest tuning fork there is – ask any breeze around!" he bellowed.

In a snap, all the Aspen in the grove prickled with excitement. Many of the young saplings felt for the first time the thrill of the chill of my North Windy self. Even more thrilling, no one had ever challenged their Chieftain so brazenly.

"*She* sent *me* to warn *you*," I said slyly.

Pando froze in disbelief. He felt his roots fleetingly go weak and his sap thin.

"Warn me? About what?" he casually inquired. But I sensed the old tree's deep-rooted terror.

"She doesn't like her colonels betraying her," I guessed. I admit, it was bold of me, but what can I say? I can be fierce!

The Chieftain shuddered so violently that every last leaf fell off his frame. The younger Aspen swayed in such disbelief that their giant common root broke ground.

"Not that you'd care, you wandering nomad, but I did it for my family! And I'd do it again!" Chieftain Pando roared at me. The old tree thrashed and whipped around, breaking several of his oldest branches, striking out at my invisible self.

I swirled, stalling for time, not knowing how to respond to this unexpected turn of events. A prolific risk taker, I didn't understand anyone fearing risk. *How else can one forge ahead and get somewhere new?* I wondered. I felt sympathy for the Aspen Chieftain. He'd taken a risk and I had revealed his secret. I wondered if I could show him I was an ally.

But Pando exploded in rage, "That wicked old hag! And, YOU! You know what's worse than starting a fire? Withholding a fire! Yes, the Fire Witch burned down the Spruce forest here as punishment for their loyalty to Winter – and promised me their land in exchange for my betrayal of them. What she didn't say is that she'd abandon us on this bleak godforsaken plain! No evergreens, no wind, no fire, no snow! The birds fled by the millions. My grove quickly grew sick from disease and loneliness. We need fire to cleanse us above so to sprout below!"

I saw the Fire Witch's double-cross.

"So now at your feet the Spruce rise again. Fire did for them as it would for you," I surmised.

"Yes," lamented the Chieftain. "So I did it! I sent the request. I thought she'd be too busy down south to notice. I'd given up hope till I felt you blow in my branches, though how you intercepted my message, I can't guess!"

I suddenly recalled something odd my Cousin Coho of Greenland said when we'd met earlier that day: *"Ach, Vindham! Some ole' stick up north called on me to fly up a spark – a spark! To your ole' neck o' zi woods. Gone soft, poor old fool. Like he don't know vat a spark'll do? Ach, I blew 'im off."*

Now it all made sense. So cracks were appearing in the Fire Witch's legions. But trust a sick old Aspen who betrayed Spruce? I decided to test him.

"The Fire Witch thinks you're loyal to Winter!" I hissed, trying my best to imitate a Torch.

"Pfaw! What's there to be loyal to?" Pando snorted. "When she killed the Prince, she pretty much did in the King. I hear parts of the Winter Palace have completely melted."

"And how do you know Prince Cerulean is dead?" I pressed on.

"No spell lasts that long. How could she sustain it?"

"Fear. Your *fear* empowers her!" I snapped.

Pando was thrown by this. *What Torch would say a thing like that?* he wondered.

"Give me the names of your Wind collaborators and I might be lenient with you!" I threw down the gauntlet. "Perhaps I may even accidentally toss a spark your way," I tantalized.

But the old Chieftain, bitterly regretting the betrayals that ensnared him, decided. "No more! Off with you! I will not give up any more names for any price! Let us die in peace," he roared in stentorian tree tone.

I tingled at the nobility of the Chieftain's sacrifice and I gusted it down the valley. There was a massive rustle of leaves as the Chieftain's words transmitted tree to tree.

Out of nowhere, an old Nordic Faerie rode up to the Aspen stand, his miniature cart drawn by a snowy white Arctic Hare. His craggy, pointed elf ears heard the Chieftain's decree, hardly believing it. "What's this? What's this?!" he cried in dismay. "Is the Old Stick starting to break?" he taunted. "Ha ha ha!"

Impressed by this pint-sized creature's feisty demeanor, I suddenly realized I'd neither seen nor heard any Faerie folk for thousands of land marks flying up here.

"You there! Sir, Windham, is it?" asked the Faerie. "I've heard a rumor some say you started."

"Spreading rumors is my business!" I proudly exclaimed.

"Not this kind of rumor, no sir," said the Faerie.

"…What is it you've heard?" Pando asked nervously.

"Not trusting faking-Quaking-Aspen is my business!" retorted the Faerie. "Follow me, Sir Windham. I've something to show you."

The Faerie turned his cart from the Aspen grove and began to ride north, with me following close behind.

"Wait! Wait! You must help us! Don't leave, I beg you!" Pando cried.

At once there arose a chorus of Quaking Aspen, one of

nature's most yattering sounds, demanding the Chieftain *"TELL HER SECRET!"*

The Faerie and I stopped: *"Her Secret"* was legend, rarely mentioned. The Fire Witch had charmed the very word, *Secret*, and any Seek-ret Seeker (even spelling it was dangerous) would be hunted down and burned alive.

"WHAT? Throw away our last bargaining chip?" Pando exclaimed.

But they clamored all the more, hurling leaves everywhere. *"The Great 88! The Great 88!"* they chanted.

"Shh!! Her spies will hear you!" Pando barked in naked alarm.

I wondered if this was really happening: could it be I had stumbled on the greatest secret in nature, *Fire's Secret?*

I lashed impatiently at the Chieftain, taunting him. "This bargaining chip can't be worth much – or she wouldn't abandon you into betraying her," I inferred slyly. It worked.

Before Pando could answer, a tall old female Aspen lunged forward and savagely snapped off the Chieftain's brittle wooden crown with a whack.

"I've been wanting to do that for years!" she hollered, to the clacking applause of the entire grove. *"She* doesn't know we know!" she yelled. "Sir Windham, I run the USA: Underground Spying Aspen. We've worked together in Seasons past."

I felt a fond recognition arise. I knew her voice from somewhere in my old memory.

The she-tree continued. "When I was just a sprout, peeping through the snow undercover, the Fire Witch's heat unfroze some ice around me and I overheard her speaking to the night sky. It was a clear night. The *Great 88 Constellations* were rising and setting as usual. Her fiery wraith cast jerky dancing shadows on the snow as sprays of sparks steamed around her. In her hand she held a glowing swirl of energy. I knew it had to be some powerful Faerie's soul, for when she held it to the sky the Constellations burned more brightly, especially Orion," she said.

"Prince Cerulean??" I whispered in dismay.

At this moment the old Nordic Faerie solemnly approached the she-tree, bowed and began to climb her. The tree helped him ascend, offering him sturdy stepping twigs until he reached her main fork. "I must insist, good Aspen, that we – you, the Wind and I – confer amongst ourselves, for these tidings bear the gravest consequences."

The she-tree agreed and creaked, slowly folding her hundreds of branches into a tightly wound full-length nest as I slowly encircled her. A haunting whistle arose as I increased my funnel speed. The Faerie carved the ancient Anglo-Saxon rune *Ansuz* into the bark of the fork, to bless a revealing message, then lay in the sticky sap that sprang from the cuts. He was quickly encased, only his mouth and ears visible, for otherwise my force would have blown him off. When my mini-hurricane's "eye" calmed in the center and we could not be heard outside the funnel, the she-tree resumed.

"All of nature knows *The Great 88*. But humans have long since forgotten their *Guardian Constellations*, except for the *Zodiac Twelve*, who are underused and utterly misunderstood. Bats by the billions had always tuned-in, for as you know Constellations sing, ring and crackle which sonar can interpret.

Whales and dolphins, before they went extinct, would surface at night in the middle of the seas in their massive family pods and share stories with the stars. Afloat and star gazing, they listened to the adventures of their celestial ancestors.

"The Great 88 Constellations, the loftiest mathematicians in the Universe, circle the Earth night and day on an unfailing schedule that is the Heart of Time. Orion was uniquely positioned at a precise moment in time and space the instant of Cerulean's birth. It was he who was born in Cerulean's form."

"Cerulean holds Orion's essence," I breathed. There weren't many secrets I didn't already know. The fact that Orion's starlight traveled light years to be born in Cerulean's form made perfect sense and I felt foolish for not having thought of it before.

Constellations are great adventurers and will travel far to experience any amusement in the Universe. And life on Earth by far is the most entertaining of all, especially to celestial bodies.

"Orion and Cerulean are stellar soul mates – and the Fire Witch knows this for she attended the Prince's birth," the she-tree said, feeling relief in releasing the secret's grip on her.

The Faerie spoke up. "There's something important to add. It's about Rigel, the Blue Super Giant in Orion's foot. It lights the Witch Head Nebula. Rigel dimmed the moment Cerulean disappeared, cooling the Nebula, decreasing births in its stellar nursery – a side effect the Fire Witch didn't anticipate. She's desperately been trying to win back the Nebula's respect ever since."

I grew agitated. "What kind of cosmic spell has she cast?"

"Settle down, Windham!" cried the she-tree. "Every problem

contains its solution. The Fire Witch offered Cerulean's starlight to the Nebula, but they refused it because his energy is incomplete – it seems the Prince either lost or gave away his chrysalis, the missing essence *She* needs, the heart of every being. Without reuniting him with his chrysalis, *She* can neither destroy Winter nor restore the Witch Head Nebula. THE PRINCE LIVES, my friends! Incomplete and fractured, but CERULEAN LIVES! You must recover his chrysalis and rescue his starlight from the Fire Witch and reunite them! I suggest you also enlist a reliable bat, one with solid sonar, one who's not hibernating," the she-tree concluded huskily, exhausted but unburdened at last.

"That shouldn't be hard, given the warm Winter. Earth's sleep patterns are all off kilter," said the Faerie.

"By Jove! I know just the bat: a great Northern Swedish Flyer with crystal clear sonar like that human Mozart!" I exclaimed. "Viggo Vespa! The only bat alive to fly the Arctic Circle!"

The she-tree's branches began to break in my wind, for she was brittle and much weakened by our impromptu reunion.

"Good Aspen, you have served as those of old served: for the common good of all. It will be my honor to bestow a reward upon your tribe," I graciously offered.

"Wait! The rumor!" cried the Faerie, "Is it true? A worldwide *Secret* Solstice celebration?"

"Yeeeeeeessss!" I cheered, calming my hurricane gale to a lazy lull.

The Faerie, now solidly cemented in sap, let out a whistle. The she-tree gave a great shrug of her forked shoulders, cracked open the sap-sac and unlocked her entwined branches in a giant crackle of relief. The Faerie gingerly climbed down, bowed deeply to the she-tree and remounted his cart.

The entire grove leaned in dead silence, earnestly listening, for they had not made out a single word of the private interview.

"Chieftain, if one hint of my visit here leaks out –" I warned.

"No, no! I swear, not a breath! Don't forget us, please," begged Pando, who without his crown was much humbler. "You're just two Zooms from the Winter Palace."

His words kindled an ancient feeling in me I thought I'd never feel again, real happiness. The Faerie, Arctic Hare and I set off for the Arctic Circle, the Aspen tree line fading behind us in the last lavender-rose sunset we'd see for a very, very long time.

CHAPTER TWELVE

QUEEN CRYSTALLINE'S MIRROR

The Faerie and I were silent most of our journey. When we reached the Arctic Hare's nest we bid our furry friend farewell. The Faerie thanked him for pulling the cart-turned-sleigh and wished his large Hare family a very Happy Solstice. From there on, I blew the Faerie's sleigh across the thin sheet of ice. A few land marks later, I at last broke my silence.

"What's your name, my friend?" I asked.

"Frost. Jack Frost," replied the Faerie.

This knocked the wind out of me! "FROST?" I gasped. "My old friend, Sir Jack Frost?"

Breathless, I did what I never do, except in extreme confusion – I stopped! Staring at the old Faerie, I wondered how this Winter legend had aged so much as to be unrecognizable? Everyone knew that Winter Faeries took tens of thousands of years to age because of the ice in their veins.

"I knew you right away, old friend," said Jack. "You've not changed one bit!"

I looked closer, taking note of Jack's clothes. His sparkling white royal livery was barely visible under the tattered patchwork of grey woolens, scarf and cap.

The Faerie felt my penetrating gaze. "When the Fire Witch took the Prince, an odd thing happened. Winter Faeries, for the first time ever, began to feel cold. Our festive costumes lost their protective luster. When the iron works was built on the crossroads, Winter was the first to suffer. The intense heat made ice, frost, sleet and snow impossible," said Jack, painfully reliving the memory. "I'm afraid by now most of us have forgotten who we are and what we do."

"Nonsense!" I bellowed nervously, a feeling I did not like one bit. "Why," I stammered, "Winter Fairies never forget how to make snow. It's…it's in your veins!"

Jack reached into the back of his cart and unwrapped a parcel. "Do you recognize this?" he asked, carefully handling the object.

I knew it right away. "It's Queen Crystalline's mirror of Saturnalian Ice! It sees the beauty in everyone," I said fondly. "One day I breezed by the Queen looking in her mirror and happened to glance … *Huh? Who's THAT?* I spun around and glanced again. I froze in midair. The Queen lifted her mirror to me and I – I saw … well I didn't know who I saw, until I realized it had to be, well, me … and I looked … *handsome.* I had never seen myself before. I didn't know I looked like anything at all! All Winds grow up thinking we're just invisible moving air and if we want to be seen we pick up some pollen, dust, leaves or rain. But this mirror, it showed me, me."

Jack turned the ornately carved blue-ice mirror over, revealing its face covered by black silk.

"Mirrors have memories. Each face who gazes in, a mirror recalls it forever. Every glance, every thought behind the eyes, remembered by every mirror everywhere. Of course mirrors don't tell anyone this. They are the repository of one's love or hatred of his or her reflection," said Jack. "You're in here, I'm in here."

"Princess Frostine bewitched the mirror with an evil curse the night she attacked Queen Crystalline. This mirror, whose vast memory knew only beauty, saw fear and ugliness for the first time. First, it was used as the infamous weapon to kill our beloved Queen, then Frostine, immune to her own spell, laughed into the mirror's face with hideous glee and triumph. Her twisted image, a face distorted by jealousy and greed, repulsed the mirror who repulsed her! She slammed the mirror to the floor. But Saturnalian Ice doesn't break. It didn't so much as scratch, let alone release the horrible scenes it had absorbed. When investigating the Queen's death, some unfortunate Northern Knights discovered the spell had a diabolical second layer: one look was all it took to lose one's youth. Ever since that night, instead of reflecting beauty, the mirror ages the face of any who gaze into it.

"Over time, the mirror was lost and forgotten. One day, sometime after Cerulean vanished, I came upon it among the belongings of a Northern Knight friend melted in battle against the Fire Witch. Not knowing its curse, I saw the name Crystalline on the mirror's back and smiled into its face. My smile turned to horror as I watched my young face age in seconds into the craggy old Faerie before you," Jack said. "I covered its face with this black cloth to protect others. Its care is a heavy responsibility, Windham, sometimes a burden beyond compare. But it's all our Kingdom has left of the Queen."

I lightly puffed across the mirror's face, rippling the black silk. No reaction.

"We've all tried. It refuses to speak," Jack said.

I became aware of how uncomfortable I was, having held myself in stock-still rapt attention to Jack. So I stretched, and felt cool Arctic air greet me. Cool, not cold – but much better than hot.

"Has the mirror never spoken since that night?" I asked.

"It did once, to me. It said only the Queen's face could relieve its torment," answered Jack. "An impossibility. So I wrapped it and keep it hidden and safe, so no one accidentally suffers the fate I did. Angry mirrors are cruel, yet I don't have the heart to tell it that Her Majesty, uh –" he silently mouthed the words, carefully packing the mirror away, *The Queen is dead*."

I kept my knowledge of the Queen's 'mist-ified' state to myself. It became clear to me that Her Majesty's mirror held far more power than Jack knew. It's perfect memory of the past would guarantee the future.

Like two worn, old snowshoes, we resumed our journey with a familiar peace between us.

VIGGO VESPA

I was the first to spot the towers glistening in the early moonrise, casting long pointy shadows across the ice. There were even snow drifts, albeit small ones. From this distance, the Winter Palace looked the same as it had for millennia. Jack seemed invigorated by the mild cold yet his teeth chattered noisily, not what you expect from a Winter Faerie.

I quickly glided to the palace gates, puffing Jack's sleigh in front of me. The palace's massive carved-ice portals stood half open, unguarded. Their hinges were dripping and Winter's heroic coat of arms was blurred from melting, freezing, melting. The legendary phalanx of Northern Knights was nowhere to be seen. Jack and I stopped just inside the gates as our unease grew.

"Jack, it's not right – something's very wrong," I ruffled

suspiciously.

"It's the silence, Windham, it's what we're *not* hearing. No singing, no howling wolves, no Solstice Tree ornaments chiming, no banners flapping their ribbons …"

"No last minute Northern Lights igniters frantically shouting color cues," I recalled wistfully.

Then, out of nowhere like a precision arrow, a flutter and ping shot between us from behind. Jack and I jumped! Moments later, it happened again, this time shearing in from the left. Jack had to duck to keep his cap. I quickly recognized the aerodynamic pattern.

"I know that tail trail signature! No one fools the Wind, no matter how fast you fly! Ha ha!! Viggo Vespa!! The Northern Swedish Flyer!!" I howled boisterously.

But the furry little black bat ignored my greeting. He had waited toooo long for this moment, having trained relentlessly for it. A flamboyant flying ace, he wanted to blow this Wind's mind. And he did. From a dizzying height the Swedish Flyer began his aerial dive, slicing in half my peaceful nocturnal breeze. Inches from the ground in a pin-point flicker he changed course, flew at lightning speed into aerobatics I never imagined possible! Jack cheered loudly as Viggo Vespa broke his own speed record, defying all radar echolocation, the pings of which I knew by heart. For all intents and purposes, Viggo soared into invisibility. It was an astonishing display of skill, wit and downright panache! I laughed like I hadn't laughed in years at the little bat's daring do – and oh did it tickle!

"Ha ha, Viggo! Show yourself, you daredevil insomniac!"

I chortled.

A moment of quiet – then Jack's elfin ears heard Viggo's little heart pounding like a jack hammer. He knew Viggo was hovering above his head and held out his left arm as he had so many times before. Viggo alighted so softly that had Jack not seen him land, he wouldn't have known it. Viggo Vespa bowed deeply and brightly greeted us, his old comrades.

"It must be Winter Solstice! Or am I dreaming?" asked Viggo, his little black ears twitching and turning in sonar scan.

I blew through Viggo's fur adoringly, in a great tender Wind hug. "Oh to feel you fly through me again!" I sighed lovingly. "Some sensations are delicious beyond description. No one navigates my currents like you, Viggo! You make me feel like art."

Jack brimmed with joy. "A bit of insomnia Viggo? You never could sleep through Winter!" he teased.

Viggo stretched out his bat wings, all of a few inches across, and shook little ice crystals from his fur. He looked up to the sky to the *Great 88* pensively.

"Each year I tell the King: *"This Winter Solstice, this'll be the one! You'll see! The North Wind will return; the Northern Knights and the Northern Lights will serve you once more!"* And each year we both hope, and wait, and Winter Solstice passes in humdrum black night and deafening, depressing silence. Funny, I decided not to say it this year. It seemed cruel to raise his hopes one more time. He stills trusts me to be the first to bring good tidings, as I once did," sighed Viggo.

"And you will again tonight, my friend!" I exclaimed.

CHAPTER THIRTEEN

At first Viggo didn't understand. It was all so sudden that he didn't yet grasp the full meaning of our return.

"But Windham, our Kingdom is in tatters, most of our Knights melted in battles against the Fire Witch. We've tried everything Winterly possible," grieved the little bat.

"Viggo, know this: Winter's underground is stronger than ever," Jack tried to reassure him.

We Winds know there's only one cure for a battered bat: protocol. "Baron von Vespa! I bear important tidings for His Majesty the King from far off lands!" I proclaimed in regal voice.

My royal tone struck Viggo and Jack like sun strikes shade. So ingrained were eons of Royal Winter Court etiquette that their postures shot bolt upright automatically – with huge smiles!

Viggo saluted me and in courtly Winter decorum declared, "Your Excellencies Sir Windham and Sir Jack, follow me to His Majesty the Winter King who most happily shall welcome you and your glad tidings at Court!"

Viggo felt like a new bat. And Jack peeled off his own dingy outer layers as crystal by crystal little sparkling lights twinkled to life on his royal white livery. And as it came alive, Jack came alive, feeling truly warm for the first time in years.

"This way!" chimed Viggo, launching from Jack's arm.

I blew Jack's sleigh, easily keeping up with Viggo who merrily looped-the-loop chirping, *"O roar, Aurora Borealis! Light our path unto the palace!"* which his ancestors helped compose. To this day, all Swedish Northern Bats learn the descant from birth.

Then Jack began to hum, surprising himself and vibrating me.

Long forgotten lyrics formed on his lips. *I haven't sung in years,* he mused to himself. *I've had no reason to sing till now!*

We drew near the Palace and I intuitively searched for an open window, my favorite entrance. And there, on the third floor, I saw it, as if beckoning me, the gentle billowing of fine woven ice-curtains leading into my favorite room, the Snow Ballroom.

"To the ballroom v'ee go, Viggo!" I howled joyfully.

No one else spoofs Viggo's name like I do and oh, how he laughed. I cherish that sound, his little laugh. It sparkles like wind chimes and is so contagious it made Jack and me laugh, too.

INSIDE THE WINTER PALACE

Deep inside the Winter Palace in a cozy, but lonely, bed chamber, the Winter King stood in front of large ice mirrors. His crystal-crusted trunk lay open with rich white ice fabrics and jewels spilling out. Inside a blue-ice wardrobe, his crown jewels glowed longingly. His tired aging frame still had the distinct bearing of a larger than life legend. As he donned his Constellation Crown and resplendent robes, a shadow passed across his face.

"Hum. Behold a legend no one speaks of or remembers. Does that void my legend status?" he mused. But tonight something stirred him to open his wardrobe and trunk. Perhaps memories, perhaps boredom. He had not done this in such a long time that he forgot when it was he last wore the crown jewels. Curiously, he felt a warmth envelope him. His regal garments seemed to sparkle, as if each ice thread were waking from a deep sleep.

"Ah, memories again … or am I imagining things?" he quizzed his garments. Of late he was always cold. Of course lighting a fire was out of the question for he and the palace would melt. And the Fire Witch would see it, for she was in every fire everywhere now. She was on the verge of global dominion, but for the Winter King at the North Pole and Aunt Arctica at the South Pole.

"Aunty, I miss you and your pranks …" the King rued to a blue–ice snow globe of Aunt Arctica in her younger robust days as Earth's queenly ice continent. He chuckled as he flipped the snow globe, surprised by the sound of his own laughter. Winter's last visit with Aunt Arctica hadn't gone well. Actually, it was a disaster. Not only was she losing things, she'd suddenly simply fall apart. On this visit, she lost a big ice shelf and lost her cool. Much colder than the Arctic, she had once been cutting edge in calving spectacular artisan icebergs. As the world's most prolific ice sculptor, she held Glaciologists (her biggest fans) spellbound and nurtured Icemakers (ice-carving prodigies) whose imaginicings rivalled her own. But she had her De-Icers (nasty critics) whose frost bite (really bad reviews) stung. How could anyone see icebergs as "abstract art without technique or meaning?" So much was riding on sea ice, not just hitch hiking seals. Aunt Arctica was a proud being who stood by her iceberg-craft. Everyone knew her trademark: underwater, where a berg's ballast is tested and approved for floatability and self-defense, one could always find her proud stamp, an elegantly carved $S.P.$ for South Pole.

The King took two Emperor Penguin ice-sculptures off his crystal mantle. "Ha ha! Dressed for dinner?" he asked them like old friends. "Always wished we'd had penguins up here in the Arctic!" He turned the statues in his hands, twinkling their sunny yellow and orange shades of colored ice. "You know, Aunty painted you bright colors to remind you all Polar Night long that the Kingdom of Spring was on its way with the Sun." Everyone also knew that Aurora Australis' purple, pink, yellow, green and red night lights were messages of *Hang in there!* to Emperor Penguin fathers huddled for months brooding their eggs, wind-whipped by my Acrobatic Katabatic cousins to keep their heat-huddle tight. The King placed the penguins back on the mantle and whizzed his fingers around them in a sparkling frosty halo so they'd feel at home.

But it was Aunt Arctica's pranks he loved most. Yes, pranks! What a prankster ice can be! With her 'herds of bergs' she was notorious for her polar mirages: phantom *Fata Morganas* playing tricks on centuries of human sailors in icy waters. Her naughtiest pranks, however, were on her own icebergs, usually when playing their favorite game, Ice Breakers. Like human bumper cars and dodgems, icebergs played rough and tough. In Team Ice colors of blue and white, hulking colossi rammed each other in heavy seas, scoring points for how many baby bergs they cracked off big bergs. Into this rowdy mix, Aunty would sneak in mischievous *Spyce*, Spy-Ice decoy floes, slipping behind enemy lines to steal the other team's *Salty Seal*, the coveted Ice Breaker trophy. After a whomping bang-up match, bergs big and small chilled out in serene glass seas of floating ice as if nothing ever happened.

But that last Winter, there was no Ice Breaker match. The Southern Ocean had drunk Aunt Arctica's last little bergs like melted ice cubes, or so we thought. More about that later.

"If only you could pull off one last prank against Frostine, your naughty niece – your favorite till she …" he shook off the bad memory. "Anyway, here's to you, Aunt Arctica!" the King cheered, toasting two ice goblets together, smashing them in a shimmering shower of diamond dust.

The King caught his reflection in the ice-mirror and thrust out his chest as a wistful smile formed on his white lips. He thought he heard hints of the *Solstice Carol* wafting in the air and he huskily hummed a few notes, "*Raise a frosty chalice!*" He laughed warmly to himself.

"I haven't sung since the night my beloved Crystalline – no! Not tonight. I won't dwell on what I don't have!" he scolded himself.

To his credit, in all his grief at losing his wife and son, the King never stopped enjoying his own company. That was something, at least. He tried hard to be his own best friend, knowing that's how his wife and son would treat him. "I think I should like to walk in the Snow Ballroom tonight," he decided. A brief thrill of his younger self quivered through him. He donned his Solstice dancing slippers without thinking, then noticed their curious luster. "Are my slippers getting younger? Hum!"

In his full regalia, the King exited his chamber and was greeted by a large white dog, a female Tibetan Mastiff who bowed, astonished to see the King in such resplendence. He noticed her awe, deeply appreciating that she always wore her sparkling sash of high office. Her size and furry lion's mane, her breed's trademark, always made him feel safe.

"I should like to visit the Snow Ballroom, Midori!" he commanded.

"Indeed, your Majesty!" she answered, happy at this surprise break from their routine.

Midori led the proud solemn walk to the Snow Ballroom, her thick white tail sweeping the floor behind her for the King to step without slipping. Ice crystals grew and broke now with more frequency as Arctic temperatures fluctuated, so maintaining the palace's frozen floors was a palace-wide job.

Midori and the King promenaded the ornately carved ice halls and passed the few faithful staff still in service. Midori's mind went back to the night Prince Cerulean lit the Northern Lights – his first, and last, time. She had been much younger then and fondly recalled how popular she had been among the palace animals. When the King's guard was melted by the Fire Witch, Midori became the first Tibetan Mastiff at Court and was proud to guard His Majesty so closely.

They ascended the Grand Ice Stairs and approached a wall of ice so thick and so tall that it shimmered distant chasms of glacial-blue ice as if it held eternity. High above the King, hundreds of merry carved statues of Winter Faeries, sparkling wings fanned out, cast snow and frost upon the King and Midori. Not Gate Keepers but Skate Keepers, they were not to be trifled with. To these Guardians of the Snow Ballroom, dancing was and is a highly evolved art form, and in the Kingdom of

Winter, given the ballroom's ice floor, everyone *skates* the great court dances. Now, Skate Keepers' sole responsibility is to match Skates with Skater according to personality. On the few occasions they've gotten it wrong, usually with a non-Winter Faerie sneaking in disguised, it's been disastrous. Say you're a Spring Faerie and your personality is a Rain Dance, but you don skates for a Winter Volta with leaps and lifts, you're in for quite a ride – all night! Skates don't come off until the Royal Family dances the last dance, usually in the wee hours of the next morning. And all of this assumes you can ice skate, of course!

The King raised his scepter and recited an ancient strophe to the Glacial Wall:

O ancient ice of glacial blue
Sky held frozen inside of you,
You know my secrets, I know yours:
Hide no more my ballroom doors!

The King knew from experience that no one could pass beyond this wall if it wasn't courted properly. So His Majesty bowed deeply in reverence. The Glacial Wall had an enormous ego and was always hungry for an homage to its ancient Arctic ancestry. Saturnalian Ice was always stealing its thunder, for it traveled from the Solar System to Earth; while Glacial Ice, like this, did the heroic work of Earth's daily survival.

The Glacial Wall yielded to the praise. Its blue inner ice core quickly transformed into spectacular doors, each one bearing the likeness of the Winter King and the Queen in such fine detail as to look lifelike.

Midori stepped aside as the King entered the glorious Snow

Ballroom. It truly took one's breath away – first, because it was so frigid inside and second, because its resident Faerie Ice-Sculptors continually carved. Not one inch of the ballroom was without décor or filigree of some kind. The room was lit entirely by reflected moonlight magnified by thousands of ice crystal sconces, chandeliers, mirrors, icicle-abras and a ceiling that perpetually snowed enormous snowflakes that sparkled and caught light in prismatic ways. Sometimes it seemed like a miniature Aurora Borealis wafted above, for snowflakes competed to see whose one-of-a-kind hexagonal shape could catch the widest prism of colors.

The King majestically promenaded down the center of the ballroom toward his throne. As he did so, he swore he heard it again, strains of the *Solstice Carol*. Instinctively he held out both arms, closed his eyes and began to sway, as if in imaginary dance with the Queen. She always enjoyed the *First Waltz of Winter*.

That exact same moment, Viggo and I sailed into the ballroom through the open window. And there I saw him, my King, dancing by himself, humming softly and broadly smiling with his eyes closed. I rapturously encircled my dear old friend, lifting his magnificent robes in billowy lightness. The King opened his eyes, as if this sensation took him by surprise.

"Are my memories so powerful as to evoke an indoor wind?" he asked the empty room.

Then I blew directly into the King's face, stroking his aged features tenderly, surrounding him in great love. The King welled up with such sudden emotion, tears crystallized at his eyes.

"I dare not believe this! It's too good to be true!" he huskily whispered.

I spoke, sensing the King's doubt. "Your Majesty, it is I, Sir Windham, at your service. I bring you good tidings from distant lands and have much news to tell. I see I find your Majesty well – and dancing!"

"It can't be …"

I shot over to the Musician's Balcony and blew wind chimes, tubular bells, struck the harps and silver bell trees wildly. It was a jubilant clashing, bells-a-ringing-clanging fanfare!

"It IS you, wild Windham!" the King cheered, waving his arms. "Play on! Play on!"

Viggo Vespa circled the King, excitedly chirping, when in walked an aged elf in brilliant royal white livery. The elf bowed deeply before the King. "Sir Jack Frost, your Majesty," announced the animated bat proudly.

The King squinted, confused, not recognizing his son's best friend who was far too young to be an old man. But up close, it was impossible to discount the truth. "Jack? Jack Frost? Your eyes still grieve, as do mine," said the King. "My boy, welcome home!" The King embraced Jack dearly.

"Your Majesty, there is news, solid reliable news, that Cerulean lives!" Jack whispered urgently.

The King so faltered at these words we had to steady him. "He – he what?? Cerulean lives? Where? How do you know?" he gushed breathlessly.

"Shh, let us retire to your privy chamber where we can keep private council," I whispered. "Our tidings are of the greatest import."

Our party made its way through the palace quickly and silently, Midori leading us through secret passages so Jack wouldn't be seen. Without any Northern Knights standing guard, there was no telling what spies the Fire Witch may have planted. Viggo's ears were on constant alert, as were my air vibration sensors.

To Cook's dismay, the King requested an unusually large dinner. "'Ungry as a walrus, eh lit'le bat?" she teased Viggo. She laid out what was left in her depleted pantry from the Winter garden: permafrosted sweet beet root, tundra-dried sea weed, pickled herring, glazed berries and ice-crusted pine cone chips with cinnamon sorbet, the King's favorite. "I freeze-dried some oak acorns that showed up from 'oo knows where. You'll like those, a rare tree-treat up 'ere!" she beamed, trying to make the most of the meager meal.

"Cook, your wonders never cease!" the King complimented her. Upon her exit, Jack and I emerged from our hiding place. During dinner we told the King our news and he told us his, mostly Winter Warrior defeats, but also much fun gossip about the other Seasons' Royal Families. It was like old times. Out of habit I frosted each spoonful of the King's sorbet with crunchy puffs of frigid air.

"Your Majesty, you are cordially invited to a secret Solstice Costume Ball at the Castle of the Seasons! Might we entice you to mount glorious Winter one more time?" I asked, carefully gauging his expression.

But the King didn't hear me. He was far, far away in thought and memory.

"… Cerulean? His Chrysalis?" I ventured, trying to read his mind.

The King nodded slowly, his face dawning in awareness. "I've mulled that moment over a million times: we were in the cabin, and Cerulean was quite taken with that forest girl," remembered the King, casting his mind back in time, searching for any missing detail.

"Her name is Lily, your Majesty," I added. "I know her well."

"I vaguely recall that when she and Cerulean were pulled apart, I saw a flash of light pass between them. I thought it was a rogue fire ball, they were exploding all around. But if he gave her his heart, his chrysalis, it would have flashed, passing from its owner to another soul," the King reasoned.

"If Lily has such a treasure, she's never worn it, revealed it, nor spoken of it," I said, certain that Lily would not keep such a secret from me.

"Sire, your subjects in hiding would give their very lives to re-ignite the Northern Lights and restore Winter," Jack proffered. "In a matter of hours we could assemble your Court."

"Aurora awaits your slightest signal," chirped Viggo, "She'd put on the show of a lifetime!"

We all held our breath and waited. And waited. It seemed his silence would never end. I saw a lifetime of thoughts cross the King's face. Then, with the spontaneity of a crack that triggers an avalanche, he gave the command! "For Queen Crystalline and Prince Cerulean!" he beamed. "I hereby command The Grandest Winter Ever!" I watched His Majesty grow younger and radiant, more like his good old self.

Winter's avalanche gained stealthy momentum. In complete subterfuge, the entire Winter Court assembled. The air crackled with the excitement of a dangerous adventure as they each cast their fate to the Wind! The Northern Lights and Northern Knights were quick to respond to the call and I made sure I knew exactly who was doing what when, where and how. Field Marshal Frescobaldi and General Yukon gathered enough troops to form a thin guard around the palace. And one Faerie Ice-Sculptor proudly restored Winter's heraldic crest on the front gate. Old Magnus eagerly ramped up his magnetic field to prepare for Aurora Borealis' performance. Never mind that he had started to switch Earth's polarities out of boredom! He did it every 250,000 years or so, why not again now? But, for tonight, he decided to keep magnetic North and South where they were and sent a discreet dispatch to the Solar Winds.

The convocation on the main floor, the Ice Shelf, was a scene out of pre-history: a Summit of Winter's Supreme Command. Each Winter Faerie received his or her orders, performing them to perfection. We each took the Oath of Secrecy, vowing to defend our monarch to the death, for were the King to die without a Queen or heir, Winter and the Royal Family's primordial DNA from the Snowball Earth Period would be lost forever.

As General Yukon trained new recruits, the King called Frescobaldi, Jack, Viggo and me aside after the convocation. "Your Majesty," Frescobaldi didn't hesitate, "might I suggest an alternate route? I have intelligence reports of Torches along the route you have chosen. The old Faerie highways are too dangerous," he cautioned.

I was perplexed by this and spoke up. "Field Marshal, I know that country well and have surveyed no activity. The old highways are, in fact, abandoned."

"Begging your pardon, Sir Windham," said Frescobaldi, "but my network –"

"Begging *your* pardon, sir, I make it my business to know everyone's business, most of all the Fire Witch's," I said.

"Yes … blown up her smoke lately?" sneered Frescobaldi.

"Why you –!" I lost control and lunged, blowing his stout chest of medals into disarray.

"Now, now! Stop it!" ordered the King, stepping between us, his white beard flying wildly. "You two have never got on, but I expect you to do so now!" he commanded.

Damn you, Frescobaldi! I swore to myself. I struggled to regain my composure.

"Ahem, your Majesty," I counseled, "your caravan will be expected to bring Winter to Faerie festivals along the ancient highways. The old infrastructure has reawakened, more than ready to protect you. Taking a new untried route, without a full phalanx of Northern Knights is not wise."

The King silently pondered both arguments as Frescobaldi and I waited anxiously on our best behavior. To have the King adopt his plan or my plan would mean one's dominion over the other. Our rivalry went back millennia to our great-great-great grandfathers when the Earth's Winds were first roused and Frescobaldi's Arctic ancestors were the founding ice-masons of Blue M&M Co., the legendary glacier Mapping & Mining Company. It was an irony: here Frescobaldi was a Spring-Summer Mixed Seasoning from generations of inter-Season marriages, yet his ancestral roots were, in fact, entirely Winter.

At length the King spoke. "Where is the Fire Witch now, Frescobaldi?"

"Your Majesty knows she is … everywhere, yet nowhere," Frescobaldi hedged. "Her unpredictable movements make pinning her down impossible." He felt credibility slip away.

"When did you last see her, Windham?" the King asked.

"At the Great Clearing beneath Orion last night, Sire. The Eastern border is ablaze. She draws near to the Castle of the Seasons –"

Frescobaldi wryly smiled to himself – a smile so miniscule few would've caught it.

"– again, I urge we take the old roads into the old lands where Autumn is barely hanging on," I insisted. A very bad feeling crept over me.

"We shall take Field Marshal Frescobaldi's advice!" the King proclaimed.

This bombshell took my breath away. I deflated in such a stunned squall that Viggo was slung off Jack's arm. His squeal echoed as he reeled in the vaulted ice-ceiling.

"It's sound advice to travel roads his spies report to be safe!" the King said.

"But – but –!" I blustered.

The King thrust his hand up in a powerful gesture silencing me. Frescobaldi's eyes glittered, relishing his moment of triumph over me. I felt dizzy and sick, on the verge of blowing up.

But the King continued, "At the Great Fork we shall follow Sir Windham down the Great Faerie Highway. There is a Solstice Costume Ball I would like to attend." The King smiled broadly.

I calmed instantly, understanding the brilliant strategy. This twist would gall Frescobaldi to no end.

Frescobaldi went ballistic. "Your Majesty, I cannot allow you to – I mean –!" he spluttered.

"ALLOW me??" the King thundered. "Allow me, *Baldi,* to remind you that there isn't a highway or snail trail I don't know! I am fully aware that the roads you suggest are the quickest, and the most dangerous. They have fallen to the Fire Witch. But I feel urgency this year and want to travel the fastest route possible. We must reach the Castle of the Seasons before *She* finds it," the King glared at him, eye to eye.

Jack, who'd been listening quietly, finally spoke. "Lighting Aurora Borealis is a bold stroke. It will get the world's attention, including *Hers*. Is it wise?" he asked.

"It's our only hope to get a message to Orion that Winter is on the move," said the King. "I'll wager that my sister's jealousy of the Auroras has not diminished. I plan to play on it."

4:12 AM, DECEMBER 21ST

4:12 a.m. on December 21st arrived exactly when His Majesty's inclinometer predicted. The Winter Palace hummed and throbbed with renewed courage and vigor. Their presence at the secret Solstice Ball depended entirely on just how savage an attack the Fire Witch would mount against them. This was it. Winter was putting it all on the line.

The King wore his finest Saturnalian Ice armor and, in a telling change of protocol he, not Frescobaldi, proudly carried Winter's blue-ice sword, *Hibernal*. His Majesty thrust *Hibernal* to the sky, east southeast, 72 degrees above the horizon. With razor sharp accuracy, he sliced the traditional ten sharp cuts in the air – those ten whistling slashes still tickled me as ever! – outlining overhead our superstar guardian, Orion. He did the same for Orion's dogs, Major and Minor, then went back to Orion and repeated his outline of Orion's bow and arrow. We all knew what his message meant: *Orion, we need your help more than ever!*

It looked to me as if Orion's stars were burning hotter than usual. And the normal twinkling in the King's Constellation Crown seemed particularly frantic. "We're not alone, Windham," the King whispered.

For Jack, the possibility of finding Cerulean stoked his martial demeanor. He had the honor of igniting the Northern Lights and lit them in his best friend's honor. Like a champagne cork dying to pop, Aurora blazed spectacularly and triumphantly! Her panoramic sheets of borealis rose, green, yellow, purple and orange lit the way for Winter's intrepid little caravan as it started across the shrunken polar ice cap.

The King was the last one out the door. He signaled the Winter Guard to close the palace's never-closed outer ice-barricade. Like two stubborn glaciers refusing to budge, the doors let out a thunderous grinding groan … and slammed shut. *Will I ever enter you again?* The King wondered at his silent home. For the first time ever, the Winter Palace was completely empty. Every last steward, ice-carver and maid had taken up the call to follow our King, even if to death. We all wondered what lay ahead: the merry Snow Ball or *Her* fire balls?

Marching on foot beside Midori, His Majesty recalled former Solstice marches on his White Arctic stallion. *I wonder what happened to him in that battle when –?* The King's reverie was broken by a sound so deeply stirring that his heart leapt and eyes misted: The *Solstice Carol* rose proudly into the night sky, carried on Aurora's beams and my breezes. We heard Viggo chirp the descant with all his heart.

"This is a lucky Solstice omen!" the King cheered. He then spontaneously sent his son, wherever he might be, the strongest thought waves he could muster: *I'm coming, Cerulean! I'm coming for you, my son!*

THE ANKLE BRACELET

8 kylar hid in brambles by the lagoon. He had never wandered this far from his cave before, but Lily and her relationship with Orion obsessed him. He crouched, listening to the woods around him. He thought he heard faint strains of music and voices, but he couldn't place it.

He also felt something he'd not anticipated: he was soaking wet. It was hot, but he wasn't sweating. While concentrating on the forest sounds he'd been engulfed by a thick mist. He tried to brush it out of his face, but the more he wiped it away, the thicker it grew. Water dripped off his face. The Mist was relentless, as if it were determined to hold him, or hide him. He took off his tattered black coat and swung it about, whipping up the mist wildly in the moonlight. But all that did was get his inner clothes wet. He put his coat back on and in spite of the heat grew chilled and angry at the forest for its primitive conditions.

He froze when he heard the twig snap behind him. *I'm surrounded! I can't see a thing!* He panicked in fear. He strained to see something, anything, and dared not move, for the Mist was so thick he feared he'd misstep and fall into the lagoon. That's when he felt it – a piercing sting around his right ankle. *Ouch!* He grabbed it painfully.

Thorns! I should have known I'd pick a bramble to hide in! he cursed, disgusted with himself for being so stupid. As he removed a thorn, he was surprised to feel something else, an ankle bracelet of smooth ovals. He couldn't see it, only feel its intense cold, and it burned his skin. He discovered that it was elaborately fastened to his ankle and try as he might, he couldn't remove it. He tried cutting it with his dagger to no avail, but was successful in cutting his ankle which made him even angrier.

He'd read of Faerie magic, but those sorts of books had been banned by schools and libraries in the Great City. At school he'd been the ringleader of the Banned Book Brigade, one of several 'crimes' that got him expelled from his school, the last straw being his one-man Dickensian *Hamlet*. When he was escorted out the gates, he was still in costume, the very clothes on his back. He rather liked how he looked in his frock coat and top hat. It was … gentlemanly, and he knew it had made an impression on Lily.

A sudden terror took hold – a flashback to the school fire. The Mist rose around Skylar like the thick choking smoke blinding him as he had tried to find his friends. "Coral! Rocky!" he called.

"Where are you?" His best friends felt like a lifetime ago. He flailed his arms reaching for them: "I can't see anything! Help me!" his voice trembled. Skylar lost his nerve, his heart pounding wildly. He turned sharply to bolt back to his cave and came face-to-face with Lily. His heart stopped.

"I see the Mist has welcomed you to our lagoon," Lily mused, noticing his wet clothes. "She's usually not so rude as to totally soak a visitor. You must intrigue her very much."

Her? The mist is a she? Skylar wondered. He kept his mouth shut tight as he admired her pretty face lit by a lantern burning a small orange flame.

"Come with me. I'll give you something warm to eat and dry your clothes. We have covert Friendly Fire here who won't harm you. Not all fires can be trusted, as you doubtless have learned."

Friendly Fire? What's she talking about? he wondered.

The Mist formed an arched path for them to walk through. The lantern's light gave the arch a luminous, billowing allure.

I was drugged by that thorn. This can't be real. Fog isn't alive! he thought.

They came to a giant oak tree with massive roots spread wide like an entryway leading under the trunk. Skylar could've swore he saw the roots move as they arrived, as if sweeping off a doorway's welcome mat! Lily led him underground into a cozy lantern lit chamber. Midst the craggy root and tightly packed soil walls, he saw a rustic wood table, a twig rocking chair, a bed of feathers and leaves and the occasional outcropping of beautiful fungi which looked like artwork on the walls. The overall effect was earthy organic, which he loved, and he assumed this is where Lily lived.

Lily gave Skylar a fizzy drink and unusually delicious food, flavors he had never tasted. He surprised himself by how much and how fast he ate. At first neither said anything. But her curiosity couldn't wait.

"I'll ask you questions – you eat and nod yes or no, OK?" Lily suggested.

Skylar nodded yes. Several Faeries interrupted her about Solstice preparations, looked quizzically at Skylar, then left. He grew uncomfortable. Lily was speaking an odd language to invisible things. He thought her to be utterly mad, which was a shame, for aside from Coral she was the most intriguing girl he had ever met.

"Can you tell me about Orion?" Lily asked him.

He nodded yes.

"You're sure he's listening to me?"

He nodded yes again. Another Faerie interruption: Solstice musicians. Would singers be welcome given the Fire Witch's singing ban? Yes. Back to Skylar.

"How do you know Orion's listening?" Lily asked.

But this was not a yes or no question and he pointed to his full mouth. Again she spoke to invisible creatures.

Life in the forest must have driven her mad, like it's doing to me, Skylar thought.

"Listen, I'm really sorry, but they need me. I've got to go," she explained, gesturing to her invisible friends. "So much to do for Winter Solstice. It's big this year. By the way, <*Hyâh 'Ooshshh-ffahh Whhújhoúhee!* That's *Happy Winter Solstice!* in Wind."

Skylar grabbed a stick and wrote:

ARE YOU A DRUID HIGH PRIESTESS?

"I don't think so – but is it fun?" Lily laughed.

YOU CELEBRATE ANCIENT EARTH FESTIVALS

"Shh, this one's secret. You can't tell a soul!" she warned.

YOU HAVE INVISIBLE FRIENDS

"You mean you don't see them?" Lily asked.

WHY LIVE IN A TREE?

"It's the last place the Fire Witch would look for me," she shuddered, genuinely afraid.

IS WIND A REAL LANGUAGE?

"<*Hh˚fweh whüüjshahh_~hsàh whøøH'hih\/* – that's Wind for, 'What kind of school did you go to?'" she taunted.

Their eyes locked, each fascinated by the other.

HAPPY SOLSTICE! Skylar wrote, smiling at Lily but sadly certain she was totally bonkers. He put down his stick and got up to leave.

The Mist awaited him as he stepped out of Lily's shelter under Coco. He placed his hand on the great oak tree and distinctly felt something. *Did that tree just touch me?* Now that he was warm and dry, he refused to get cold and wet again.

"Follow me. I'll show you the easiest path out," said Lily, leading him through the Mist's swirling opaque veils. If this path was easy, he wondered what the hard one was like.

Skylar quickened his pace. "I could swear, this mist just sped up with me," he said to Lily. A supernatural fear shot through him from his stomach up his throat to his head, stinging his tongue, ringing his ears. "No doubt about it! This mist is after me!" Panic seized him. He broke into a run, gruffly shoving Lily aside, leaving her behind swallowed by the Mist. He faintly heard her yell, "Can Orion talk?" But he refused to be lured by her ever again.

The Mist licked his ears and slid up his nostrils. It prickled and slapped his face but he wouldn't give in. Instead of being scared he got angry. For the first time, he felt panic and fear turn into invincible determination. He felt power, even greatness, sweep through him. "I'm running faster than I ever have in my life! I left that mist in the dust!" he cheered. "Maybe it deliberately egged me on?"

He was surprised to not stumble or fall. In fact, he gained an uncanny agility like a cheetah, a big cat that once lived. He bolted into his cave, then buckled in pain from the ankle bracelet's severe burning. Somehow he'd forgotten about it the entire time he was with Lily. Angrily grabbing his ankle he tried to break the icy ovals which only numbed and burned his fingers. And he was completely soaked again, this time from the sweat of fright and flight.

THE CLIMBING PUDDLE

Skylar's eyes rested on his carved wall calendar. He knew the date by the moon phases and was confused; he must have made an error. He couldn't possibly have been gone from his cave for two days – the moon's position said so, but his calendar did not agree. He'd only been gone a few hours – or had he?

"My God," he said, "I'm losing my mind." He walked to the back of his cave where there was a puddle, his roommate, as it were. No matter how often he stomped in it or swept it out, the puddle stayed full. Now he stomped into it full on! Furious! Both feet slammed down, shooting water 360° in muddy spray. The walls dripped and his pants clung to his skin. He clomped and kicked and sloshed till he exhausted himself, finally flopping down on a rock. Holding his head in his hands, he sobbed so hard he thought he'd throw up. He screeeeeeamed. He screeeeeamed again! Not even his cave had an echo in reply. His loneliness and fear had become unbearable.

As he cried, Skylar didn't notice the thin brown vein making its way towards his feet. With tremendous effort, a trickle from the puddle advanced, dipping and pooling in floor crags, skirting past stones and twigs until at last it reached his right shoe. Then the trickle did an astonishing thing: it circled his shoe.

He was wiping his eyes when he saw it. He sat motionless as it begin to climb his shoe. "Impossible," he whispered, "water doesn't flow up." The trickle headed straight for the ankle stones which he could now see, for they glowed as if moonlight was held inside them.

"What are you?" he asked out loud. And it struck him: his voice! It was calm and normal, his good ole' self. "When did that – how did – what's the deal with my voice? Is it you, puddle? Maybe I'm not crazy … what if my thinking has just been too small?"

For the first time in years he felt the sweet magic of discovery, with no Great City teachers or classmates to dismiss his wonder with their cynical logic. The trickle was determined, as if it were sentient with a purpose. It reached his socks and was absorbed.

"You're so close, you're almost there! You can do it!" he coached it like a best friend.

It heard him. It had always heard and understood the boy but this, this was too good to be true! The puddle now felt something it had not felt all its puddle life: connection. When Skylar stomped in it, which the puddle hated, its waters jumped on his clothes and tasted the usual dirty black cloth which absorbed its drops. But this time there was another taste: a taste so familiar, so imbedded in memory, that it shook the depths of the puddle deeper than any splashing boy. The puddle recognized another water on his coat. It was ancient water, highly rare, from far away. And wonder of wonders, as if answering the question *Who are you?* the puddle tasted the ovals on the boy's ankle and shuddered in ecstasy. Saturnalian Ice-crystal tears!

Whoever's tears these were, this boy was chosen to transport them. But who? A message? The puddle had to know. It had lived in this dark cave for what felt like eternity. It was too far inside to discern any daylight or Seasons so it had no idea of time. But it knew it never got cold enough to freeze, so clearly Winter was not a visitor in this land anymore.

The trickle and the ovals melded till the ovals bulged and burst, flowing down Skylar's ankle the exact route it had taken upward. He tingled with the sensation. He had never felt magic before and always wanted to believe in it. *This is wondrous! Thrilling!* Then a crazy thought came to him: *Does water have feelings? Is that even possible?*

He saw the trickle recede to the puddle, not leaving a single wet mark. Not one micro-ounce of water was left behind. Even his sock and shoe were bone dry. The puddle rippled in every direction and it seemed to him the puddle was, well, celebrating.

Then fear jabbed him: *What if whoever attached this ankle bracelet followed me? Or did it because they knew I have the starball? But how could they know? No one knows. I took it, but didn't steal it. Not really. It came to me accidentally; and then she tried to kill my foster mother while searching for it!* He still wasn't even sure what the starball was, but he knew it must be valuable. Finding it at his school fire now seemed like eons ago.

"Hey, puddle, Happy Winter Solstice!" Skylar said.

The puddle splashed him – it *splashed* him!

He thought of that old 21st century Japanese scientist's photos of water crystals that changed according to how they were spoken to. He'd never given it any credence, until now. He decided he would never stomp in a puddle again – well, he would at least ask its permission first.

"I envy you, puddle," he declared. "You're simple and know nothing beyond your cave. I bet you didn't know I'm brilliant! I'm from the Great City and I'm the most *Promising Young Astronomer* in my country. How 'bout that? Hum? And now I'm listening to myself go insane talking to you, a mud puddle … who just splashed me …"

He felt his ankle. The strand that had held the ovals was still there. He walked to the mouth of the cave and saw the strand glint golden. It looked like spun gold, thin as hair, strong as steel.

"If I were in a Faerie tale, it would be Faerie gold. Ha!" he dismissed the silly idea. "That's it. I'm officially going mad."

He looked up to the twinkling Constellations. Orion floated overhead like a Guardian Angel. Skylar reached into his vest and, for the first time, pulled it out, the softly glowing orb, the thing he took from the Great Fire. He thought he'd seen someone in the Fire, like a wild angry banshee, drop or throw it. She, if he could call the banshee a she, was wearing it around her neck as a small charm. It snapped off when the roof fell in after that second explosion. He had picked it up when it rolled to his feet. The ball of light had come to him the same way the trickle did – deliberately, as if it chose him.

He believed in synchronicity and chalked it up to Quantum Physics. The orb had no obvious power source but glowed and was gaseous and swirled unto itself. He could hold the tiny iridescent spiral in his bare hand and hardly feel the slightest hint of motion. It was, as far as he could deduce, a miniature star which often flared hot in his vest pocket right over his heart, yet never burned a hole or glowed through his frock coat.

In his nightmares the fiery banshee terrorized him. She would hunt him down but never quite catch him. She had an eerie voice that repeatedly taunted, '*Dirty hands on prints!*' What his fingerprints had to do with anything, he couldn't guess.

"All I know is that fiery banshee was at my school then tried to kill my foster mother. Talk about Unfriendly Fire! … Huh? Is that what Lily meant?" His epiphany startled him.

He froze, astounded it took him so long to put it together: there are different kinds of fire? Was it even scientifically possible? Men set men on fire, but the hatred was in the men. But this Fire was hatred and greed in and of itself and fed on itself. How the fiery banshee even found his foster home was a mystery. All at once Lily didn't seem so insane after all, and he was glad for it.

IN THE BLACK LAGOON

"He's a very strange boy," Coco mused. "Didn't hear a word I said the whole time! Typical human. But he did feel me touch his hand!" Coco tittered.

"When he speaks, he's hostile; when he writes, he's perfectly civilized. He must have quite a story," Lily mused.

"He does," chimed in the Queen mistily. "I tasted things on his clothes that spoke of arduous journeys and exposure to the Fire Witch. I hope I didn't scare or offend him, but he intrigued me so."

"He risked a lot coming here. I think he's fond of you, Lilykin," said Coco.

"But his mind is so closed. He can't speak Wind, can't see Faeries – yet he knows Orion," Lily said. She felt pleasantly perplexed by Skylar.

At that moment a breeze tickled a neighboring Pine Tree's uppermost needles. "OOH! Ah ha! Ho! Ha ha!!" the Pine Tree giggled.

It got everyone's attention.

"Ha ha! Stop –ooh!! Ho! Wha--what do you mean he's on his way??" the Pine Tree stammered breathlessly, suddenly quite serious.

My fleeting voice at breakneck speed yelled back, echoing through the wood, "Winnn-terrr!! He comes this niiii-ght! Preparrrre! Haaaap-peee Solllll-stiiiice!"

"It's the Wind! He's back! That was Sir Windham!!" I heard voices shouting behind me as I flew over, for I was gone as quickly as I'd blown through, pressing on to spread the news.

In an instant, every needle of every Pine Tree whispered the news. The Pine News Nexus picked up the story and broadcast a 360° symphonic whisper: *WINTER COMES!!* Few trees enjoy Winter more than Pines.

"He did it? He did it! Ha! Ole' Windy!" exclaimed Coco. "I knew old Windbag still had it in him!" she laughed, dropping acorns into the lagoon.

Lily lifted her arms to the sky whispering to me, ">WHüa'ih-Háaîoh\/ <" *Thank You* in Wind.

"My dear, the time has come. Yours and mine," the Queen informed Lily, enveloping her in refreshing mist.

All around them the wood became engulfed in merry panic, as Solstice Eve should be.

"Coco, will you watch over me? What if –?" Lily said.

"I'm right here, child," said Coco, lovingly extending a

craggy root Lily held in both hands. "Do exactly as Her Majesty tells you."

Lily hung her pretty pouch of herbs and seeds on one of Coco's branches reaching over the lagoon, just as they had all agreed. "I hope the mix is right," Lily said. "Thank heavens I was able to convince our visiting shamans to leave me some herbs I can't find here. I put in Rose Hips for generating new skin cells, Rosemary to enhance memory and thinking, Comfrey for tissue regeneration and repair, Lavender to keep headaches away, Turmeric for pain relief and Ginger to prevent nausea."

"Mm, sounds perfect. And yummy!" Coco said, trying to not sound too nervous.

"A pine cone, if you please!" shouted the Mist to a Pine Tree. "To the girl! Toss one to the girl!"

The Pine Tree chose a perfectly shaped pine cone and airily dropped it into Lily's right hand.

"Now remember what I told you," the Queen whispered to Lily, thickly cloaking her till she was completely hidden from view.

Lily started to take off her leafy frock then froze. Now it hit her: this could all go terribly wrong and she could die.

"What's the matter, my dear?" the Queen misted.

"I-I'm feeling the last moments of being me," Lily stammered, "in case I don't come back – if your magic doesn't work and I –" Lily started to panic.

"You've earned it and you've learned it," the Queen assured Lily. "Now it's up to you and your thoughts. Whether you think you can or think you can't, either way, you're right."

"I can do this and I'm ready," Lily breathed confidently.

Lily continued to take off her leafy frock, but first she secretly removed from the inner sewn pocket her most treasured possession, Cerulean's chrysalis. Her right hand covered its glow and she held it close to her heart. In her left hand she clasped the pine cone and slowly entered the lagoon's soft, cool black water. Her feet felt lovely in the soft silky sand and the water felt like satin on her skin. She wasn't scared one bit and even felt a euphoria, as if she were visiting an ancient, familiar place inside herself. The water quickly lapped up to her waist, her elbows, her shoulders, up to her neck, finally touching her lips.

"Do not drink even a drop," the Queen cautioned her.

Lily pursed her lips tightly. She felt her long golden hair float freely behind her then realized she no longer felt the lagoon's bottom. She began to tread water and instinctively relaxed, floating on her back, feeling the cool water cover her head as she fanned out her arms and legs. As she stared up into the night sky she saw Orion twinkling. Did he just wink at her? Her wet body glistened in the moonlight, for the Mist surrounded the lagoon but left the center clear. Lily's thoughts drifted to Cerulean and she wished he could see her as did the night sky. She gently released the chrysalis. It floated from her hand across her body just above the water. Orion began to twinkle wildly. *Did Orion just look at me? Wait, he moved!* Her reverie broke when she thought Orion might actually be listening or watching and she quickly hid the chrysalis.

"When you are ready, let yourself sink beneath the surface. See the image you want to change into. See it in every detail as

I've described it, how you feel, what you're doing as me, the way I move, how I speak, the sound of my laughter. Surrender yourself to me," said the Queen in a mesmerizing enchanted voice.

As Lily stared at Orion, she began to visualize her image of Queen Crystalline and it thrilled her. Her heart beat in anticipation of the Solstice Ball, of snow, of the return of Windham with the Winter King and please, yes, with Cerulean.

She heard Faeries drumming Winter's beat in the distant Underground. It was an old ritual and a primal beat she knew in her bones. Every Season had its distinct rhythm which Faeries taught their children. She recalled how crickets and bees used to sing Summer's rhythms when there were crickets and bees.

"Your Majesty, I am ready," Lily said. She took a slow deep breath and sank beneath the surface, dropping her feet, letting her weight pull her down, down, down. She felt the silky water rise over her lips, her nose, until the very last thing she saw was Orion's twinkling frame, and she could swear he turned his head and smiled at her. She smiled to herself and surrendered to the bliss, the euphoria now permeating her entire being.

The black water covered her closed eyes and forehead as the lagoon swallowed her, only a ripple lapping where her last strands of golden hair had been.

No sooner was Lily gone, than the Queen gathered her misty self over the middle of the lagoon, completely enshrouding Darwina at the center of her web. The Queen hovered briefly, seeming to take one last look, then, as if she were the lagoon's private rain cloud, she showered her billions of droplets into the black water, funneling eagerly after Lily. To Darwina's amazement, not even a trace of a drop of mist was left either on her web or a single hair on any of her eight legs.

Coco perfectly timed her release of the seed pouch Lily had hung from her branch. It fell gently into the lagoon's funneling black water, and the single white daisy Lily had lodged into its opening floated free, just as it was designed to do. The pouch's interior started to glow. As it was drawn down into the water, its golden shafts of light spiraled round and round, fading into the depths. Afterwards, the only sign something momentous had just happened was the swirling little daisy looking up at the starry sky.

Descending ever downward, Lily clutched her hands tightly and began to feel drowsy, sinking deeper and deeper into the lagoon. She'd not expected it to be so deep. The Winter drums faded until all she could hear were her own thoughts. She focused intently on her image, trying to fight the increasing drowsiness. The deeper she went, the sleepier she grew. It felt like a long time and she curiously wasn't running out of air. In fact, she discovered she was breathing quite normally. What manner of lagoon was this? Was this water made of air? She yielded to the descent in a gentle freefall. Her thoughts turned to how much she loved … *My Cerulean ... snow ... don't fall asleep ... Wind home soooon .... my immmmage ... beautifuuuul ... Ceruleannn ..... sleeepeeee,'* she drifted off listlessly.

All went silent. In a dreamy sleep she sank deeper and deeper into the watery depths.

PHAETON'S FATE

T he Fire Witch never slept. She'd get hungry, yes. But tired? No. Fired up after a full night of rousing blazes, she was now closer than ever to the Castle of the Seasons. She knew it, for the Faeries here fought with great valor. She torched and tortured their villages, yet none would give up or betray their invisible, and so far invincible, bastion. She pondered this as she hungrily gnawed on dried carved mahogany, a delicacy from pillaged human homes, and her flaming lips smacked in pleasure.

The first indication that something was wrong came at 4:24 a.m. on December 21st. The little Aspen root broke through at her feet and greedily eyed her flames, jealous of the mahogany getting so much personal royal attention.

"My Queen! I bring you urgent news!" shrilled the little

sapling, for to be heard over the Fire Witch's noisy noshing was difficult.

The Fire Witch, a master of surprise, was rarely taken by surprise, but in a flash she flared, realizing she'd been startled to her diaphanous core.

"What's so urgent that you interrupt my midnight snack?" she sneered angrily at the root.

"Forest fire, my Queen! The Arctic Aspen Corridor is ablaze! The Chieftain Pando and his grove are laid waste!" he declared in thrilled panic. An audience with The Queen was something every little sapling aspired to, no matter the dangerous circumstance.

The Fire Witch was stunned. She'd not given those orders. She was deliberately withholding fire from the Quaking Aspen Chieftain to teach him a lesson. She flared in fury, "WHO HAS BETRAYED ME??"

"Some say it was the North Wind! He did it with sparks from the Coho and stoked a vast inferno. He's being hailed as their liberator," the Aspen root reported proudly.

This news shook the Fire Witch. "Windham? What's HE doing up there?" she asked. "How far have you traveled, little Aspen root?"

"From Lake Baikal, my Quee– " he scarcely replied.

WHOOSH! TSSSS!! The root was smote by a hissing fire ball, sizzling him in a flash. The Fire Witch hated receiving bad news, but he earned a good fiery end, unlike Pando. Giving Fire was as big a gift as withholding it. An unsettled feeling seized her and she gnawed her mahogany which soothed her like a drug.

The second indication of trouble came seconds later by Smoke. Smoke was outdated, an ancient emergency language that hadn't been used for centuries. There was so much air pollution that Smoke messages merely blended with smog, so she banned its use. Besides, it was unreliable, especially if the Wind was around. *Windham loves befuddling Smoke messages – but I've not felt any Wind in days,* she realized anxiously. *Of course not. He's up north starting fires!*

The Smoke spoke. She jolted in recognition – it was Field Marshal Frescobaldi. *I'm not in the mood for him! Of course he'd use Smoke, he's in love with me and thinks it's romantic! I loved you once, but it's all different now!* she thought disgustedly.

"My Queen! The Kingdom of Winter has risen and comes this way!" he smoked urgently.

The Fire Witch dropped her mahogany, stunned. She dimmed, almost going out entirely. It was as if he dumped ice cold snow on her.

"You're only telling me NOW??" she spewed. "How can this be? Don't my spies have eyes? Or fears, ears?" she screamed ferociously.

"It happened so fast – and the Wind won't let me out of his sight!" he spluttered.

"Where are my armies??" she fumed.

"In position! Winter will walk into our ambush soon!" he assured her.

Now she burned hotly, erratically. Her brother was walking into a trap. Good. Very good! Her destiny was at hand! But an old doubt crept in: *first my brother broke my engagement to Frescobaldi and broke my heart, then kept him as Field Marshal even after banishing me! Did he really think Frescobaldi would just forget me? Ignore me? Not help me … get revenge? Or come to power? There's something very odd about this whole business,* she thought warily.

As Frescobaldi floated patiently in the Smoke, a twin pair of Pixies announced their arrival by a spray of flint sparks. Pixies believe flint sparks keep them safe from forest spirits (and they generally do.)

"You Pixies, step forward! What mischief is afoot? " the Fire Witch scowled.

They gingerly stepped forward, holding their flints before them, ready to deflect any impromptu fire balls. They spoke in the lilting duet-harmony for which Pixies are prized:

"Our Queen!" they bowed deeply. "We humbly report …"

They've lit Aurora Borealis
And her twin, sweet Australis!
Sir Windham's blown monster holes
In your smog to reveal both Poles!

The Fire Witch glowed whiter than white hot. The Pixies, knowing her predictable unpredictability, beat a hasty retreat.

"Quaking Aspen? Winter on the march? The *Auroras?* How could they have organized ALL THAT without YOU knowing?" she exploded at Frescobaldi. "You SABOTAGED me, you incompetent fool!!" she roared in venomous fury.

"NO, NO! My Queen, all's not lost! You still have – you have *Phaeton's Fate!* Just say the words and I shall implement it, your Final Pollution! To silence Winter forever!" he blurted out rashly.

Yet it thrilled him. It was an unconscionable mandate no one dared believe she'd use. He was the original architect of The Plan and could not stop himself, starved for her approval and her triumph. Then an idea seized him: what if he ignited her to it? *ME! I'd make history! For once, I'd be bigger and braver than the Wind!* Everything inside him surged and he went for it before she could read his thoughts, for reading Smoke was second nature to her.

"My Queen, you are Legend! Man's Goddess of Greed! They worship you! Thanks to you, birds and beasts are nearly all extinct…" Frescobaldi coaxed her.

"I only sped up what Man started," she replied in mock humility.

"They poisoned themselves on their own food!" he enticed.

"No more rain forests, no more medicine," she snapped her fiery fingers.

"Even the rats fled their cities!" he smoked.

"My *Invisible Fire* collapsed their financial markets! Families! Governments!" she gloated.

"Ice soon gone forever …" he escalated.

"The fools never colonized space!" Her eyes glittered.

"Their technology failed them and *still* they've not figured YOU out!" He swirled wildly.

His fevered frenzy aroused her – and he felt it. The Auroras flashed into her mind: *How to outshine them? This would do it!* Her jealousy ignited her fuse and she surrendered to it.

Frescobaldi heard her breathing hard and moved in, stoking her fire. "YES! Your master stroke: infecting Man with *Invisible*

Fire! The ultimate pollution!"

FLARE!! Whoa!! She blazed larger than life in staggering beauty!

"And Man's master stroke? Some lunkhead chopped down the last surviving Mother Tree in the last surviving forest!" she shrieked in hysterics. "The MOTHER TREE!!"

"HAAAAA!" they both guffawed in uncontrollably insane laughter.

The Fire Witch's sides split and gushed like molten lava. She could barely catch her breath. "Chopped her down for … for *mo–ney!*" she mocked in a sneer. "The one last tree that held it all in the balance! Her seeds, her wisdom, the last keeper of the Underground WWW! Hear this! The Wood Wide Web is NO MORE!" Smug and victorious, she launched into the evil *Torch Scorch Mantra,* which Frescobaldi joined jubilantly:

> *Say your goodbyes to Soil's allies!*
> *Dust to dust is dirt's demise!*
> *The prize lies in Fire's reprisal:*
> *Kill off all the Mycorrhizal!*

"Who's having fun now, fungi?" she swirled and dove under a dead stump's roots blasting out the other side any fungal network that may have been hiding out. "The tree world fell on its own! I didn't have to do a darn thing! Just send it up their crummy chimneys in thick black smoke! Hee hee!!" she flung herself backwards, doubled over in a shower of sparks. She rollicked on the ground, kicking and slapping the Earth. "I fueled their wars! Burned their children! Starved their bellies! Blackened their skies! How much more can they take?" she bellowed greedily.

TSSS!! TSSS!! Fire balls hissed in a riot of fireworks. She thought she'd never loved herself so much.

"Earth is yours for the taking! They missed their chance!" Frescobaldi fanatically boomed as she, in a sensational back draft, sheered and plumed up into his thick sooty cloud.

The two rocketed upward in blazing rapture on a path of no return: *"PHAAAETON'S FAAAATE!!"* they shrilled together into the night sky.

It was their atomic bomb. Fires around the globe heard The Call. By the hundreds of millions, loyal suicide arsonists extinguished themselves, globally plunging Man into blackest night. Without *Visible Fire*, Man would die; with *Invisible Fire*, he would die horribly.

Frescobaldi was euphoric. He had done it! He stood on the stage of greatness, with her, his one great love. He dreamily watched her calm from their moment of bliss.

"All mine," she moaned distantly, imagining her imminent future.

"What's left of it," he chuckled, unaware he had just laughed his last laugh.

"What do you mean?" she asked suspiciously.

"The Winter Palace and the Arctic shelves will melt! What dry land is left shall be yours and our enemies forever destroyed," he casually mused.

"Why is Winter your enemy, Frescobaldi? Our families go back 300 million years." She wanted to know.

"Not Winter!" he declared. "The blasted Wind! Now I know something HE doesn't know!"

His words deflated her. She hadn't considered me, the Wind, dying. Here it was, her life's dream to impress the Witch Head Nebula by controlling her own planet, yet she felt empty. Losing the Wind on top of Winter took the whole sport out of it.

Humans were no fun – they never graduated beyond Fear, so they never rose to what they were capable of. *What a goof, the human experiment!* she mused. *The Earth gambled and lost with that species! Who could've guessed they'd massacre their own kind?*

But the Wind, he was a gratifying adversary whose cunning she admired. He kept her sharp and creative. *Well, maybe the Wind could be spared,* she decided to herself. *Sir Windham lights my fire!* The thought brightened her embers as she grew dangerously silent.

At last she spoke. "Phaeton's Fate, eh? To do it right, and be historically correct, I require a horse and a chariot. I'm closing in on the boy Skylar who stole the Prince's soul from me. He comes from the Great City. I've seen horses and chariots there." Her frenetic mind jumped back to Winter. "I assume my brother will change course at the Great Fork and follow the Wind. It's what he always does. Let us meet him at the iron works," she commanded. "I do not want one hair on one Winter Faerie's head touched until then. Cancel your ambush."

Frescobaldi hovered, stunned.

"WHAT?" she raged. "You doubt my tactics?" she flashed, reading his smoke-filled mind.

"No! No! But I fear you underestimate Winter's power. He has the support of the Little People," he warned, thinking how he had yet to conceive a weapon to disembowel the Underground.

"Then conceive a weapon to disembowel the Underground!" she smirked, her voice laced with ridicule at reading his naked mind.

He felt shame's sickly tingle strip his euphoria.

"Leave before my brother suspects you've betrayed him!" she ordered hotly. "Or stay! Declare to the world your love for me! Your loyalty! Now *that* will gall all four Kingdoms of the Seasons! Especially my brother! Choose <u>now</u> … *Baldi.*"

He reeled at her using the nickname he hated. Worse, did she really expect him to expose his carefully cultivated treachery on the eve of his greatest triumph? The eve of his sweet revenge? Ever since that night at their glittering dinner in the Winter Palace when he and Frostine announced their engagement and the King flew into a fury forbidding their attachment, Frescobaldi had been plotting his personal revenge. He would destroy the King just as the King destroyed his happiness. When Frostine took things one step further by destroying the Queen, Frescobaldi took that as a sign of her eternal devotion to him. It inflamed his ardor. His years of maniacal planning came down to this: in the ambush when at last the King would be alone, defeated, brought to his knees before the entire world, he, Frescobaldi, would wrest *Hibernal* from His Majesty and deliver the final fatal blow.

But now his beloved had just stolen his finest hour. Wasn't she on his side? Didn't he just ignite her passion? Fulfill her dream? The lights went out on his stage and he saw her for who she was. Fire's opportunistic caprice burned him inside and out. Like dawn breaking after a stormy night, he saw in vivid clarity the wreckage, the countless words and deeds he had forced himself to ignore: the frightening yet enticing changes in her. He had thought it was all an act and that he alone knew the real Frostine underneath the Fire Witch. All he ever wanted, all he clung to, all he believed in were his memories of the princess he almost married. If smoke could throw up, he was about to. For the first time he realized he never really knew her and he was terrified.

"You know my loyalty is to you, my beloved Queen," he vowed. "I will – " he halted, cut off by her flare.

"There's only one who'll ever play with fire and not get burned – ME!" she hissed. POOF! She was gone.

In the following seconds of dead quiet his mind went blank. Then he thought fast. He'd show her just how clever he is. All he could think of was what history would say about him … which, of course, she would write as Queen of the World with him as her Consort.

ORION'S ARROW

Skylar donned his top hat. From his cave, he stepped out into the night air, certain the Great City was in the direction he was heading. He'd made up his mind: he'd rather starve there than go insane here. He'd miss his Angel, but he put her behind him. His mind was closing after opening just enough to scare him.

He walked by dim moonlight for about a mile when, on a scorched barren clearing, a camp fire appeared, startling him. He slowed his approach. There wasn't a soul about: no camping equipment, no foot prints, nothing but a warm, lovely fire. He cautiously crouched, warming himself, for his clothes were soaked from his puddle and its water now curiously chilled him.

Unfriendly Fire attacked my foster mom, he thought. *Is this*

Friendly Fire? He stared into it. *At least it's not talking to me!*

But something else was talking to him. He felt it, the starball in his vest surged hot against his chest. He feared taking it out because he had found it at a Fire. He backed away from the blaze and the pain eased. He stepped closer and it jabbed, as if in warning. *The starball is connected to the Fire. But how?* he wondered.

He circled the Fire, noticing its flames didn't burn the wood. That defied his scientific mind more than any trickle of water climbing up his ankle. Then he did something he'd never done before: he spoke to the Fire. "You burn, yet do not burn," he said, posing a riddle.

"You live, yet do not live. Is that not the same thing?" retorted the Fire, in an eerie, husky voice.

The voice from my nightmares! His stomach lurched in panic. The starball pulsed, like electromagnetic waves in his physics class, harder and harder against his chest. Something in the night sky caught his eye. To his astonishment, he saw Orion in a lightning swift move crack out of his celestial pose, leaving a massive empty black frame. Pulsing in sync with the starball, Orion bent on his knee. *He's aiming his bow and arrow at ME?* Skylar stared horrified. The starball pounded. Skylar's heart pounded. The Fire sensed the shift in energy.

What happened next defied any astronomical phenomena Skylar knew: Orion let loose his arrow. It sailed at the speed of light through the night sky, brighter than any shooting star or comet, growing in sound like a rocket, and soared right into the heart of the camp fire. But just before the arrow struck, the Fire vanished without a trace.

Skylar was enveloped in a euphoric, protective cloud of dazzling starlight. He felt a thrilling union with Orion as his childhood dreams of being a Constellation rekindled and flooded him. He felt the starball calm and cool, which calmed him. Then all went silent but for a lovely, indefinable sound, an ancient haunting music. His ears were ringing, again, like they had often in his life, but louder than ever. And this time, for once, he actually understood the ringing, loud and clear. *Do our ears ring because Constellations are communicating with us?* he wondered.

The message from Orion was clear: "*Stay the course to Chelsea! You'll be shown the way.*"

He was nowhere near Chelsea, yet before he knew it his legs were racing across barren landscapes, bearing his starball cargo like a gazelle. He knew Fire was not to be trusted and was hot on his tail. But he also knew Orion was now protecting him. A rush of joy came over him like a runner's high. He was part of something monumental he did not understand, but his deepest instincts told him he'd been preparing for this all of his fifteen years of life. He had studied galaxies, planets, astronomers, even astrologers and their zodiac to unlock every possible secret of the stars. And here he was, a mere human boy, in the middle of what appeared to be a cosmic feud.

His mind re-opened and embraced the thrill of it all. Starving in the Great City could wait. He pressed on towards Chelsea.

At dawn, he found himself at a stream in a field of maple stumps. He tasted some old dried syrup on one stump and remembered his mom making pancakes on Sunday mornings. *You were a good cook, mom,* he thought sadly to her spirit, hoping she might hear him. Unfortunately, someone else heard his thoughts.

Instead of a camp fire, the Fire Witch ignited a thicket of rosemary mantled in lavender florets, giving off a delicious aroma. She spoke through her Smoke. "Why do you fear me? We both seek the same thing," she coaxed alluringly.

Skylar closed his eyes, giving in to memories the rosemary awakened in him. His mother's ancestors had come from Italy, from beautiful Venice, long since lost to the sea. They used to cook spaghetti with beef and tomatoes, but now both cows and tomatoes were virtually extinct. It was the rosemary and garlic, which grew everywhere like an anachronism, that had made it all taste so good. No one knew what to do with them without oil, butter or water. Olive, peanut, safflower, coconut and other 'oil' plants were either gone or the people who knew how to extract their oils were gone. He imagined his mother smiling and giving him a taste of her delicious spaghetti sauce. He smiled back, swaying in the fragrance which coiled around him like a transparent blue serpent.

"You don't know what I seek," Skylar answered telepathically.

"I seek what you took from me," the Fire Witch coaxed.

The starball heated in warning and sent a clear message, for the first time, by thought: *GET OUT!*

But Skylar felt too drugged too move. The starball started to panic. It shot a piercing stab, jolting Skylar out of the Smoke, now coiled thick around him. Skylar intuitively jumped into the stream thinking, *Fire can't get me here!* He was right.

CHAPTER TWENTY

This infuriated the Fire Witch. He had just upped the ante. *Well you cunning boy! Why I ought to – uh oh! UH OH!* She felt that old *I'm losing control!* feeling kick in, a behavior she despised in herself. A whiff of regret rose to her consciousness, for when she lost control she seized every temptation in sight, often missing the real prize. *I have to get the Prince back or the Witch Head Nebula will disown me!* For the first time in her fiery existence, she remembered her former self as Princess Frostine and the many times she got what she wanted by using self-control instead of giving in to instant gratification. This new goal demanded a surprise tactic, something no one would expect from Fire.

Forget the boy, for now! she decided. She flexed in the thicket and extinguished herself without a trace.

"Are you giving up so easily?" Skylar inquired, with a hint of false bravado.

"Just because you don't see me doesn't mean I'm not around," the Fire Witch retorted.

A fearful queasiness wilted Skylar's bravado. Fire, as far as he knew, couldn't be invisible.

It's working! she congratulated herself. *My Invisible Fire is working!* There was a rustling retreat through the rosemary thicket and she was gone. In the morning sunny sky Skylar couldn't see Orion, but he looked up anyway, trusting what he could not see, and saluted.

SKYLAR'S STARBALL

Skylar decided to walk in the stream for safety. It wasn't cold, so it didn't numb his feet. But it was dirty, which messed up his shoes and pants. With no plants to filter runoff, streams looked like stale tea you didn't dare drink. He pulled a rare late season apple out of his pocket which he'd found in an abandoned orchard. That was when he heard the voice.

"*<Hyâh 'Ooshshh-ffahh Whhújhoúhee!*" it said.

Skylar stopped dead still. He vaguely recognized the phrase from his visit with Lily: *Happy Winter Solstice* in Wind. There were no birds, no animals, no Wind – who had spoken to him? He swallowed hard and repeated it back, struggling to remember the syllables.

"*<Hyâh 'Ooshshh-ffahh Whhújhoúhee!*"

The starball lurched forward and thudded back so hard on Skylar's chest it knocked him and his apple backwards into the dirty water. He gasped, "Ugh! Soaked to the skin again!" But he didn't get up. He said it again joyfully, louder: "*<Hyâh 'Ooshshh-ffahh Whhújhoúhee!!*" He heard himself pronounce it perfectly this time.

The starball thudded more gently, as if it knew its power and wanted to be polite.

"Why now? You speak to me now?" Skylar whispered into his vest.

"You're in water. Now you can hear me! I've been speaking non-stop since you found me, but only in water can we meet like this," said the starball.

"But why didn't you say something in my cave puddle?" Skylar asked.

"What? Be heard over that temper every time you stomped around?" the starball teased amusingly. "Stand up and I shall dry you!" it commanded.

"It was you! You're the one who's been shooting off at the mouth – my mouth, I mean!" Skylar accused.

"Most humans don't think before they speak – it's easy to hijack your mouths," the starball continued. "And I've been suffocating in your vest! But when you found your courage against the Mist, I admired the change in you. I almost said something then, but kept quiet. I wanted you to experience water's magic before we officially met. And I needed to know how much you would let your mind open. Now for a proper introduction. You may rise."

"Who are you?" Skylar asked, as he stood up and felt heat spread over his body. His clothes not only dried instantly, but looked cleaner.

"I am starlight, the soul energy of every living being," it answered.

"Then you *are* a star!" Skylar whispered in joyful amazement. "I knew it!"

"Yes, and I thank my lucky stars you're the one who found me. Most humans have forgotten their origin and wouldn't recognize their own light if they saw it, let alone someone else's," it sighed.

"Someone else's? To whom does your light belong?" asked Skylar.

It was silent, struggling to answer, "I…I am … uh, I'm not sure who I am," it confessed. "This is only a part of me. I also had a chrysalis, like everyone, and don't remember where it is or how I lost it."

"I've never heard of anyone having a chrysalis, except butterflies, but they're extinct," Skylar said.

"It's the heart of a being. Your chrysalis is your heart. Who and what you love reveal who you are. Let us walk downstream," it commanded.

Skylar did as he was told, for the starball had an authority which warranted obedience.

"You have no idea who you belong to?" asked Skylar, eager to help. "Are you an alien from outer space?"

It shot back, "What kind of crazy question is that? An *alien*? Starlight that makes it all the way to Earth stays here. This is home! Here's what I remember: colors. White, silver, blue, sparkling. I think I had something to do with *snow*. Do you know what snow is?" it asked hopefully.

"Of course I do!" Skylar replied. "I've read about it in books. It doesn't snow anymore. It's not cold enough. There's an old human legend about snow: clouds used to gather on Winter Solstice to snow for a festival called Christmas Eve when a jolly fat elf in red brought toys to children. The festival is long gone. Men worship only Fire now. Have you heard of Saint Claus? His '*Ho Ho Ho'* made him famous. His sleigh took flight with some kind of flying deer that also went extinct."

"What *do* you believe?" the starball asked.

"That I'm imagining all this and I'll go extinct" replied Skylar wryly.

"That's what I believed until you found me," it replied.

"Well, if you speak in water, maybe you were a fish or a water lily or a whale. What I'd give to have seen a real live whale –" his voice trailed off.

"What did you say??" the starball demanded, startling Skylar who stopped in place. "Keep walking! And talking! Say it again!" it insisted.

Skylar obediently stepped forward, bewildered, trying to remember exactly what he'd said. "I said I think you might be a fish or a water lily or –"

"Water lily! Yes, something to do with me, it's vague. It grows in water you say?" it asked.

"If I see one I'll show it to you," Skylar offered. "Frogs used to sit on water lilies, when there were frogs. Maybe you're some kind of Faerie Frog Prince!" Skylar mused. "Another legend, and I will NOT kiss you!" he joked.

The starball did not find this amusing. "I am no frog! … But a Prince?" it drifted off. All this talk of water lilies made Skylar miss Lily, which surprised him, and a new deep emotion began to settle upon his heart, like what he had felt for Coral.

Simultaneously, deep emotion overtook the starball as old memories began to stir. It concentrated hard on catching each one. Soon it was engulfed in spectacular visions. It watched its old life start to flash before it. In a sting of shock, it recalled the Fire Witch's words: *I strip you of your Princely pride!* Princely! It pulsed in heated flares of joy at rediscovering what it knew beyond any doubt: he was a Prince.

"Ouch! Stop it! What are you doing that for?" Skylar cried out, grabbing the hot starball out of his vest. What his ears heard next was neither human nor earthly.

"I AMMM WINNNTERRR!" Prince Cerulean boomed in a stentorian *ring Ring RING!*, echoing through the wood, vibrating through Skylar's hand and body hotly. The sound pulsated in waves so massive they crackled in his ears like static, hitting his face in hot puffs. *Can it be? Is this the elusive language of Star? And if so, how is it I understand it?* Skylar wondered in awe.

Then he froze. He could swear he saw the stream stop flowing upon hearing *"I Am Winter!"* He grew nervous that he had a psycho in his hand, or worse – someone *really* important.

Too hot to hold, Skylar gingerly tossed the starball between his hands. "Winter, you say?" he hesitantly asked. "Winter who?"

Without warning, out of nowhere, I gusted Skylar so hard he

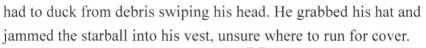

had to duck from debris swiping his head. He grabbed his hat and jammed the starball into his vest, unsure where to run for cover.

ꟾꟾꟾꟾiSS THAAAAᴀᴀᴀTTTT YYYOOOUᴜᴜᴜ??????? I howled wildly, whizzing past like lightning.

Was that the Wind? Is he talking to me? Skylar's thoughts raced, terrified, exhilarated.

I howled in his face, ᴡᴡWHHHHOOO AARRRʀʀEEEE YYYOOOUᴜᴜᴜ?????????

There was no mistaking it. *The Wind is talking to ME!* Skylar was exultant. His face and hair stretched in my head-on gale. If he thought Orion shooting an arrow was astonishing, what happened next left him changed forever.

"Windham! It is I! Prince Cerulean!" shouted the muffled voice inside the vest.

I turned in midair so hard I spun Skylar in place, screwing him into a watery stream bed hole up to his knees.

ʟʟʟʟʟʟET MMMMEEEᴇᴇᴇEE LLOOOᴏᴋ ᴀᴀAAAT YYYOOOUᴜᴜᴜ!!!!! I howled, trying to match voice with face.

ʙʙUTTHꟾꟾꟾSS IꟾꟾSSSꜱɴɴNNN'T YYYOOOUᴜᴜᴜ!!!!!

I whisked and tugged Skylar's black clothes. I was so flummoxed I breathed in a hurricane strength ᴡᴡHHHHHOOOOOOOOO?????

"No, no! Inside the vest!" shouted Cerulean. "Skylar, let us not keep Sir Windham waiting!"

Mid-air exhilaration … anticipation … I huffed … I puffed … scarcely able to believe it … and then I – I saw him! Skylar gently removed the starball and raised it on lifted palms to me, invisible breathless-in-winderful-wonder me. The starball rose lightly above

Skylar's hands, hovering, emitting iridescent starlight. Neither it nor Skylar flinched in the sudden dust cloud when I down drafted, kneeling in loyal obeisance, in awe and such joy as I'd never felt.

"Your Majesty, I'm overblown to see you again!" I gushed ardently.

"Rise, Sir Windham, let me feel you!" Cerulean commanded in his now manly voice, a new vibration I memorized happily on the spot. I breathed softly on the starball which wafted and rolled over and over in place.

"Ahhh Windham … you … the Winter Palace, my father – I am remembering you all! You know, I thought I heard my Father today … *"I am coming!"* It was so real. I remember the Castle of the Seasons and Aurora and – *Her.* How long has it been since she kidnapped me?" the Prince asked, afraid of the answer.

"Many, many thousands of Seasons, your Majesty. Ahem, I believe your friend and I need a proper re-introduction," I suggested.

"You two have met?" asked Cerulean.

"I hope his language has improved!" I grimaced, ruffling Skylar's hair teasingly.

"Better blame that on me, I'm afraid," said Cerulean. "You can't imagine the horrors I saw while imprisoned in that pendant of hers around her neck! You see, it was a fire proof see-through pendant, so the Fire Witch could always see me. And what did I see? It's what I heard and felt: her evil soul, her savagery, her wicked glee eating things alive and worst of all, the endless screams of life's last searing moments. The human and animal screams were bad enough. But the trees, oh Windham, you know the horrifying shrieks of burning trees! It takes a long time for a tree to surrender to fire. They can't do anything but stand there listening to her demented crackles and feel her flames lick their bark off from bottom to top like they're blazing lollypops.

"I tried to fight the feeling, but before long her anger infected me. It grew in me because it's all I heard. I forgot who I was as she became all I knew. Then one day the pendant snapped off in a school fire. I felt myself fly through the air and crash on the ground, the pendant shattering apart. I felt myself expand briefly in freedom as I rolled and rolled on the ground – right to Skylar's feet. Next thing I knew he scooped me up and stuffed me into his vest! There I was imprisoned again – an angry confused starball just wanting to explode!"

Skylar was dumbfounded. He had spoken with Fire, a starball, and now he could understand the Wind? His mind was so open he felt like he could fly.

"Sir Windham, meet Skylar of the Great City. Skylar, meet Sir Windham the North Wind of the Kingdom of Winter, most trusted friend to my father, the Winter King," Cerulean proclaimed.

"A very great honor, Sir Windham," Skylar said to me in a courtly, sincere bow. Why he even donned then tipped his top hat to me like a proper gentleman!

"Windham is my favorite prankster – you sack of penguin fish breath!!" Cerulean hurled the insult with exquisite timing.

I LOVED it! I giddily shot up to the sky and plunged back down, driving Skylar deeper into the stream bed. "The years haven't changed youuuuu!! Ha Haaa! Skylaaar, an honor to meet the Prince's bodyguard and so braaave a Knight! Might I suggest we seek shelter?" I urged them.

"The Fire Witch is on to us! Were it not for Orion and
this stream, she'd have recaptured the Prince," Skylar hushed
urgently, incredulous at his lips forming the wondrous words of
Wind.

"Orion? He's made contact? Brrrrrilliannnnnt! Well of course
he has, he's Cerulean's Guardian Constellation. Is he brrrrringing
the dogs?" I bubbled.

"The dogs –? Guardian Constellation?" Skylar asked.

"Everyone has a Guardian Constellation. But long ago Man
forgot all but the Zodiac Twelve while the rest of nature grew to
rely on all of the Great 88," I blew. "There's a farm nearby where
we can hide. This stream goes right to it. Follooow meee!"

I forged the stream's dense thicket of brambles into a vaulted
archway, the leaves of which waved and bowed as Cerulean passed.

"Make way for His Majesty, Prince Cerulean of Winter!
Prepare your feasts! Your secret Solstice Balls! Winter is nigh
upon us at last!" I windily proclaimed.

Skylar perceived millions of bits of movement in the
undergrowth. He thought he heard music and singing erupt.
Now and then he glimpsed colorful flashes, like dragonflies in
costume. It was as if his eyes were developing new vision and his
ears new hearing.

Skylar dared address the Prince hovering on his palms, "Your
Majesty, I apologize if I offended you, the frog joke and all –"

"Are you kidding? And call me Cerulean! It is I who owe you
an apology for endangering you. You saved my life, my friend,"
said Cerulean gratefully.

"I could say the same for you," Skylar replied. "Hey, d'you feel that –?" It was something brand new: cold air. He'd only ever known warm and hot, not cold, and never outside.

"You can thank Sir Windham!" Cerulean cheered. "What you're feeling is Winter. Father must be getting close!"

"And the clouds are different, they're not smoke, but –?" Skylar noticed, looking up.

"The Snow Delivery Corps, persnickety perfectionists if ever! The conditions have to be just right or they simply refuse to snow," bragged Cerulean proudly. "You've no idea what goes into pulling off a good old fashioned blizzard. Cold air's just tip of the iceberg!"

Skylar thought of Orion beyond Earth's clouds. "Where am I that I can see Constellations move and understand the languages of Star, Wind and Fire?" asked Skylar, certain he was dreaming.

"On Earth, silly," answered Cerulean.

"Yes, but where? In the Great City no one speaks Star, Wind or Fire – they don't even think such things are possible." Skylar thought of his school chums. "Except for my best friends Coral and Rocky. Of all people, they would've loved you and believed all of this is real."

"Let's go find them!" shouted Cerulean.

"They died in the school fire – at least I think they did. Hey, is it safe for you to be out in the open like this?" Skylar quickly changed the painful subject.

"Spokennn like a truuue bodyguaaard!" I breezed, eavesdropping on the two new friends getting to know each other. "A bodyguaaard whoose body iiis shivvvering, I miiight aaadd!"

Cerulean took the cue. "Invest, please!" he punned. No sooner did Skylar tuck the Prince inside his vest than toasty starry heat enveloped him. *Love ... home*, Skylar thought wistfully.

True to his Winter nature, the lower the air temperature dropped, the more powerful Cerulean grew. *Home ... love*, he thought eagerly and glowed brighter.

"Welcome to the Real World, Skylar, the Natural Realm, where all is visible and understood. Humans believe *What you see is what you get!* so that's all they get, and they don't see much. In the Real World *What you believe is what you get!* And you see so much more. It's a much happier way to live. That puddle in your cave was one of us, a Winter Faerie, trapped long ago when Winter failed to return. Whoever gave you the ice ankle bracelet was another Winter Faerie reaching out, recognizing the puddle's taste on you. That's how it is in the Real World: we live to give," said Cerulean warmly.

"And the Fire Witch?" whispered Skylar cautiously.

"Did you notice Orion doesn't fear her? She's helpless against stars. But on Earth, not one single human has ever escaped her *Invisible Fire*: FEAR. She ignites it in their minds, their hearts and bellies so they burn out of control with it. That's how Fear reinvents itself, inside them, by habit, with their blind permission, generation after generation, artfully sabotaging their every good dream."

This plunged Skylar into deep thought. *With Coral and Rocky I was never afraid. Maybe best friends are Fear's biggest fear? I think I won't mention Lily. She's my special secret. When this adventure is over, I'll find her and love her for the rest of my life. I won't lose her like I lost Coral.*

CHELSEA

The farm was an abandoned, lonely place and held an aura of misery. Before leaving the stream, Skylar emptied his boots so the water could stay in the stream. Cerulean found this a touching gesture. Skylar mused to himself, *I never thought I'd be considerate of water.* He was cozy warm and Cerulean's heat dried his boots within seconds of stepping onto shore.

I led the boy and Cerulean's essence down a winding bridle path. The smell of horses was in the air, reminding Skylar of the Great City Park. At length we came upon a dilapidated stable which, upon feeling my breezy greeting, swayed and creaked in a relaxed friendly welcome, like a comfy old shirt glad to be worn again.

I blew slowly, nudging open the large stable door. "Ennterrr,"

I hushed, then just as quietly closed the door behind us. "I'll fly in and out through the rafters up there," I added. So relieved was I to have gotten them in a safe house, I didn't realize I'd plunged Skylar into pitch dark. He groped around looking for something.

"Something you need?" I asked.

"A lantern might be nice," Skylar joked.

"And invite the Fire Witch? As far as I'm concerned ALL Fire is Unfriendly these days! Why not let His Highness light up a room as only he can!" I suggested merrily.

"Of course!" replied Skylar, who gently produced the starball, swirling brighter than ever.

Instantly the stable glowed in changing stellar colors. I circled the Prince lovingly, then scooped him up, supporting his swirling energy on my undulating current. I sensed Skylar feeling the love and trust among our three beings and a feeling of nobility rising within him. The boy was growing.

A startled snort and shuffle of hooves broke our reverie. We all turned toward the back of the stable, but saw nothing.

"Sounds like a startled horse," Skylar surmised.

He grabbed a fist full of old dirty hay and pulled out another apple from his frock coat. He spoke softly, as one might to a frightened child you don't want to surprise. Approaching the furthermost stable he slowed. A spooked horse could kill him with one kick. He decided to have a look over the neighboring stall first. He stood on a barrel and hoisted himself up. He peered over the edge and looked directly into the deep blue-violet eyes of the most magnificent horse he ever beheld, an enormous white stallion.

At first he was stunned by the direct eye contact, as if the horse had anticipated his move and wanted to shock him. He knew horses demanded respect. They read everything in an intuitive instant. What he couldn't figure out is how such a huge horse couldn't be seen over the stall wall.

"I'm going to have a look, all right?" Skylar asked the horse.

The horse snorted, gave a great nod and turned his head away so Skylar could look in. At first Skylar couldn't believe what he saw.

"Is the darkness playing tricks with my eyes? One moment, my friend," he paused. "Cerulean, may we have a light?"

I floated the Prince to the stall and golden light fell upon the horse. Skylar's eyes had not lied. Lying on its side, this extraordinary white horse's four powerful legs were bound with thick rope and black iron chains. In its attempts to break free, the horse had repeatedly gashed itself. Skylar thought fast and with his dagger, gingerly removed the coarse rope, careful not to irritate the already torn flesh, speaking gently to the horse in a most unusual way.

I realized then that the boy was what men called a Horse Whisperer. *No wonder he can speak Wind, Star and Fire,* I thought to myself.

The horse relaxed with Skylar's skillful touch and allowed him to work, though it hurt terribly. His leg wounds were bad enough, but the pressure sores from lying on his side were infected and burned. Skylar removed the chains with great effort.

"Whoever bound you meant to kill you by slow cruel starvation," Skylar said while offering hay, which was practically inhaled. He then offered the apple, a second peace offering. Again the horse stared him in the eye. The horse's lips eagerly snatched the apple from his hand.

"I have more!" said Skylar. "I stuffed my pockets at a lone apple orchard and you are the beneficiary. Have several while I fetch you more hay and some water."

The horse let out a raspy neigh of "Ttttttthankkkk Yoh."

"Ah," said Skylar, "you're a hoarse horse! You've yelled long and hard for help, yes?"

The horse's big violet eyes blinked yes, relieved to be understood, wincing in pain.

Outside it was twilight and thick blue-grey snow clouds blanketed the sky. My pre-blizzard sentinels blew leaves everywhere and Skylar loved the refreshing new feeling that blustery cold air stirred in him. "I think Winter's my new favorite Season!" he said happily to the air, hurriedly filling the bucket and returning to the warm, cozy stable. Within an hour the horse was well fed and watered, its wounds tenderly dressed. Skylar helped him stretch his powerful back legs as if discovering them for the very first time.

"How is it you, a city boy, knows horses so well?" Cerulean asked Skylar.

"In the Great City I lived by a park and after school I'd help the coachmen tend their horses in the park stable," he reminisced. "They were hearty souls – the horses, I mean – city dwellers who saw it all. They endured overweight tourists, impatient taxis and grueling hours in terrible heat. They didn't live long, breathing fumes all day. I aided them in dying more than in living. I'd see new arrivals come and within weeks their noble spirits were broken, dreams shattered. Many horses dream of being a fashionable Carriage Horse. I'd love to know this horse's name and his story," Skylar said, brushing the stallion's magnificent white mane.

"Chelsea …" Cerulean whispered in awe. The horse's violet eyes opened, locked in a distant, far away stare recalling his former life in happier times.

"What?" asked Skylar, astonished. "*Stay the course to Chelsea* – this is Chelsea?" he asked.

"Yes," said Cerulean, "I was stunned, too. When you went out for water just now, we learned his rider was killed. All he remembers is being brought here, some man restraining him and leaving him to die in the dark."

"He's been here over a thousand Seasons," I added, softly wafting Chelsea's mane.

"A *thousand* Seasons?" asked Skylar.

"He's a legendary horse from the Kingdom of Winter," said Cerulean. "My father's horse."

Eyes closed, the horse listened, yet wasn't asleep. He'd been through too much to trust sleep. He reveled in being groomed and feeling clean again, but remained suspicious of men.

Skylar brushed Chelsea's mane in quiet awe. "The Winter King's horse …?" he wondered aloud in Wind, amazed again by the sound. "What does all this mean, Sir Windham? How is it that I –?" Skylar didn't know how to finish his question, there was so much he didn't understand.

I looked at Cerulean who, in an instant, flared in two small bursts. I understood his approval. "Here's what it means," I said to Skylar.

"Everyone knows that Fire barely tolerates humans. How long can you stand in a fire before it gets angry and burns you? But we Winds, we love Love LOVE YOU! Yes you, dear boy and all your kind! We love your foibles, your humor, your incessant trying. You cheer our windy old souls, for you humans are creative companions who share with us and rely on us for your kiteboarding, sailing, windmills, windsurfing, wind farms, airplanes, parachutes, flags, balloons, kites, even drying your hair and laundry! Why do we love it all so? Well, I confess, your contraptions wintickle us! And when we break wind – I mean laugh, well, you know – 'tis true, we Winds make some embarrassing noises.

"But more embarrassing, for all our sport and play and weather together, how is it our families, Human and Wind, still can't understand each other? Is it the language barrier? I breeze, whistle, even storm in your faces and ears, day and night, even knocking off hats and lifting skirts to get your attention. But oh the names you call me! You've invented over 6,800 languages, yet humans miss all the good jokes that long-nose monkeys and birds, especially ducks, tell. You're the one animal locked out of all of nature's languages … as we're locked out of all yours. Yet we all live here. Together.

"Optimist that I am, I knew one day a human mind would open and understand me, which is all it ever takes for a new idea to become known by everyone. I also knew that you, and all humans, more than any beings in the Universe, have a unique unlimited mind designed for an auspicious collective destiny, in spite of your fears. "Someday you will know the other side of fear," I assured him. "It's freedom."

"But how is it I'm speaking to water, fire, stars and to you, in Wind?" asked Skylar.

"You speak the language of horses. As you already know, communicating is more about listening than talking," I answered. "And you are a very good listener!" I said.

Skylar took in my words as sleep overtook him. For the first time in weeks he felt himself relax. He yawned, utterly exhausted, and rubbed Chelsea's neck. "You'll be good as new, my friend" he said. "I think we all will be."

"You two get some rest. I'll check the Night Sentinels and be right back," I blew, ascending through cracks in the roof. My upward swoop added to the whistling of the gathering storm.

Skylar fell into a deep sleep on a bed of straw beside Chelsea's stall in case he was needed during the night. Cerulean dimmed his light, darkening the stable just enough so Chelsea wouldn't know total darkness again. Hearing the boy's rhythmic breathing in deep sleep, the horse twitched his ears, a familiar signal.

Cerulean quickly, silently set to work on the wounds. He floated over each gash, cut and sore and applied himself with meticulous, artful care. He hadn't used his healing cryo-arts since his capture and it rejuvenated him to meld his energy with a powerful Winter Faerie.

Chelsea shakily stood on his four famous legs which felt like four long lost friends having a reunion. He limped quietly to the stable doors just as I blew back in.

"Let me feel Winter's chill, Sir Windham," Chelsea murmured longingly.

I swung open the stable door and Chelsea walked out into the frigid windy air. He shook his mighty mane and then, to our astonishment, reared up on his hind legs spectacularly in a joyful, grateful *"Neeeeeighhh!"* to the Sky, as if releasing all his pent up despair. *I'm rescued! I'm alive!* Chelsea couldn't believe it, his front legs landing sure-footed as ever. And with his hooves fell Winter's first snowflakes! I couldn't believe the timing. A few deep horse-breaths of clean snowy air and he turned, and re-entered the stable. I gently blew the door shut.

In a corner where cold air was seeping in, Chelsea nestled. We three spoke long into the night starting with favorite tales from shared Winters long ago. Then things got serious.

"You know, your disappearance is the stuff of legends," I told Chelsea.

"It didn't feel legendary," Chelsea snorted quietly. "I remember I was dizzy from the blazing Sun and the battle was wiping out our side mercilessly. Next thing I knew, the Fire Witch's fire balls knocked my rider off, a Northern Knight called Knighthawk, and a lumberjack of a man called Papa jumped on, rode me here and bound me in chains. A monstrous girl called Kir took away all the food and water. I tried to communicate with her in case she had The Gift. I saw that she recognized my Faerie blood, but it's as if she despised me for it! I've never smelled such evil in a youngling before."

I wondered if Prince Cerulean remembered Papa and Kir, but

he said nothing, so I said nothing. Instead, I galed the details of the Winter King's triumphant return happening at that very same moment. And I told them of my Secret Project in Machu Picchu and how it was undermining the Fire Witch. But best of all, we three marveled at the sleeping boy. At long last, one young human and one old wind had met and somehow, after 200,000 years, the language barrier between Man and nature was broken forever.

A HORSE, A PHAETON, A DRIVER

Through the night Cerulean hung on every word of our stories, piecing his memory back together. All he needed now was to find his chrysalis. We planned our journey to the Castle of the Seasons to meet the Winter King, eager to maybe even catch the end of the Autumn and Winter Courts' elaborate ceremony for the Changing of the Seasons. Both Courts would be on high alert for any signs of the Fire Witch.

"The boy," Chelsea said dreamily, nodding off. "I will break my *No Humans* rule and carry him." With those historic words, he drifted off into a deep welcome sleep. Nothing could wake him, not even …

"Flurry Freeze Tag! YOU'RE IT!!" I hurled the Prince across the room.

"Bring it on!" cheered Cerulean. "Hide me in this!" He dove

into Skylar's battered top hat.

I toppled the hat on a rising current and out we flew into the First Blizzard of Winter! To me it felt briefly like the good ole' days as I tossed that hat bearing my beloved Prince. But Cerulean's laughter felt forced, even though I knew he had always loved my *snowllercoaster* swoops as a boy. I sure didn't disappoint this night. In a moment of rest, I nestled Cerulean in a snowy pine bough. "My Prince, I sense melancholy. A round of Lost 'n Found?" I asked.

"Lost: my youth. Found: Winter. Lost: my mother, my chrysalis. Found: Skylar and Chelsea," Cerulean replied. "And you? Your play has an edge to it, rather brutish I'd say!"

"Lost: trust. Found: a traitor at Court whom your father seems intent on trusting," I riskily ventured knowing my news would shock him.

"A traitor at Court? That's quite a charge. The Winter Court never knew betrayal until my aunt killed my mother. Given her dominion, I'm not surprised another has surfaced. Whom do you suspect?" he asked, not sure he really wanted to know.

"Let us speak inside, lest the wrong ears overhear," I whispered. I spirited Cerulean back inside the stable. We settled in an upper rafter and spoke low.

"Whom do I suspect? The one I'm sure had a hand in your mother's death: Field Marshal Frescobaldi," I stated flatly. No amount of tact could've softened the blow. The Prince's light wavered. He still mourned the Queen. Though an infant when he lost her, she was large in his mind, for no mother is replaceable.

"Ancient rivalries aside, why him?" Cerulean asked, doubtful but intrigued.

"His obsession for your aunt. His ambitions to marry her were well known and forbidden by your father. Ever since then, she has only inflamed Frescobaldi's ardor. There's nothing he won't do for her and, it seems, she for him," I warned. "Last night my Pixie spies caught him in her Smoke. He did the unconscionable. He wooed her into implementing *Phaeton's Fate*, their Final Pollution toward global meltdown."

"Phaeton's Fate?? She thinks she can drive the Sun's Cosmic Chariot with his team of immortal wild horses and not lose control like Phaeton did? Her?? HA!" Cerulean laughed so loudly that the boy and horse stirred.

"She told Baldi she needs a horse and chariot," I said.

"Then let's give them to her!" said Cerulean. "We have a driver, a horse and carriages a plenty. Come morning we shall lay the bait and foil her fate," the Prince plotted.

I felt a long forgotten feeling, relief. A smile warmed over me. Before me was indeed the long lost successor to the throne.

"Your years of captivity have made you fearless, your Highness," I extolled.

"No Windham," said Cerulean, "they made me a patient strategist. I devised thousands of escape plans, just one of which worked with the right boy in the right place at the right time. I think I'll rest now. Please tuck me in his vest, will you? His breathing and heartbeat calm me."

Careful not to wake Skylar, I gently rolled Cerulean under the blanket into the vest. The stable went dark and I kept Night Watch over Winter's future King, a legendary Arctic-White stallion and the bravest human boy I had ever met.

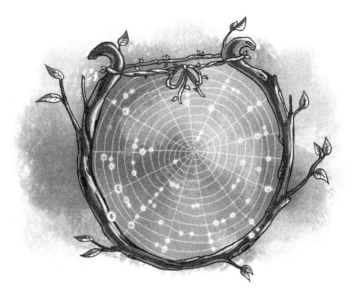

CERULEAN'S HAUNTING MEMORY

Inside the vest, Cerulean's mind swirled with a memory he dared not share with anyone. It was a distant memory that gripped him irresistibly: Lily, that one little word triggered an avalanche of unfrozen feelings. *Water Lily*, two little words proving he and she belonged together. He marveled that in his first taste of freedom his thoughts had turned to a girl he'd known for only a few minutes. But those minutes had rewritten the history of Earth. He had given her his chrysalis the night his aunt condensed him into starlight, chaining him around her neck in a glass-prism prison.

But Lily was part human, so she might be long since dead. This didn't bode well for finding his chrysalis. Yet, it might have kept her alive all this time if it could live without his starlight! And if it were alive, where she might have put it, if she even kept it, would be impossible to know. Countless human generations had passed. He well remembered that she had The Gift, so Faerie folk might know of her fate.

Am I chasing a memory, a phantasm, an impossibility? It haunted him in a lovely aching way. *Lily is my special secret and when this adventure is over, I'll find her and love her for the rest of my life. Lily's the one thing I most cherish.* A tingling feeling overtook him. He was in love.

The Prince fell into dreaming starry dreams, the one part of his gaseous nature he did like, for stars dream big, bright, bold dreams. They have no natural enemies, but for Dark Matter, and are emboldened by the billions of nightly wishes made by humans and Faeries. He dreamed that he wished upon himself, and granted himself his own wish, to find Lily.

LILY WHITE LIKE SNOW

I could barely contain myself as dawn broke on Winter Solstice morning. My consciousness was so big that one minute I was in the Arctic launching Winter and setting Aspen on fire, and the next minute I was rollicking with the Prince in a blizzard! I felt young being my good ole' self again. I knew that Time was relative, my relative, and we traveled infinite parallel paths together. Trillions upon trillions of events happening at the very same moment and I the Wind, like light and love, was present in all of them, all the time. And no matter where I was blowing, I could always hear Lily sing, even if quietly. I was startled by how much I missed her.

Inside the stable, the Sun's early rays filtered through dusty cracks as the Prince, Chelsea, Skylar and I cemented the plan to sabotage the Fire Witch. In the back of the barn with Cerulean's light, Skylar inspected several old carriages in various states of disrepair.

"That one's missing a wheel. Broken axel on this one. Neither of these will work. Hey, what's that one over here?" Skylar pointed to a dark corner. Cerulean lit the back wall as I blew the dust off an old black carriage that looked like it hadn't been used in a century. Skylar shook the wheels and spokes, they were solid. He checked the old harness and bridle, the leather was intact. He inspected the shaft.

"It's all a bit ancient, but I think it could work," Skylar said. "If I'm not mistaking, this is a vintage Phaeton carriage from the 19th century! In fact, it's the kind of carriage Charles Dickens would've – "

I cut him off in shock. "What did you say?" I gusted in his face. "It's what kind of carriage??"

"A Phaeton. I'd say 1850's," Skylar replied.

"An actual Phaeton to foil *Phaeton's Fate?*" Cerulean beamed. "Now it's starting to feel like the Kingdom of Winter! Serendipity abounds! It's meant to be!"

"As long as the old Greek myth doesn't come true," Skylar joked nervously.

"Nnnnot a channnnce!" Chelsea neighed. "I promise you won't lose control of this phaeton's horse!"

"Come here, you!" Skylar clicked to Chelsea. "Time to put on your disguise."

Skylar smudged dirt all over Chelsea to darken him while

I blew his mane and tail into two filthy gnarly messes to make sure the Fire Witch wouldn't recognize her brother's faithful and mighty stallion.

It was hard for the Prince and me to leave Skylar and Chelsea to brave their challenge alone, but the Fire Witch was furious and held me responsible for Winter's rise. I was sure she had some revenge in store for me – she always did. We four friends wished each other "*<Fwoöhazh Qh'Whooff!*" (*Good Luck!* in Wind) and parted company. I blew open the stable doors. There before us lay a freshly fallen mantle of new snow sparkling in dawn's sunlight. Skylar and Chelsea hit the trail heading southeast to the Great City riding an antique coincidence too big to ignore. Astounded by Chelsea's miraculous recovery, Skylar felt pride in how he had dressed the horse's wounds. Astounded by Skylar's manner with him, Chelsea felt safe in allowing himself to be harnessed. The relationship between horse and boy was balanced, equal in respect and cooperation. And in this case, equal in valor.

In the opposite direction, northwest, at a very high altitude, I whisked Cerulean away to the Castle of the Seasons. In the blinding glare of sunlit clouds, Cerulean's light went unnoticed. I found a few freezing air currents which made him grow stronger and brighter.

As if on cue, the Fire Witch appeared before Skylar and Chelsea, just as they had hoped. Their carefully rehearsed charade began. Chelsea pretended to bolt at the sight of Fire. Skylar reigned him in, yelling harshly and whipping hard on his flanks. The horse calmed, snorting loudly, shooting a glance at Skylar, who stood tall on his phaeton, very much in control.

"I thought I was done with you!" Skylar yelled to the Fire Witch.

"Not until I'm done with you!" she fired back at him, hissing and sparking malevolently. Her tone threw them slightly, as they had expected her to be more ingratiating. After all, they had what she wanted.

Skylar suddenly feared she knew their plan. Chelsea, sensing Skylar's fear, bolted with a loud neigh, breaking Skylar's thoughts and any attempts the Fire Witch might make at reading his mind. The distraction worked and Skylar remembered he had to control his thoughts around her.

"I think you are in a bad mood today, Fire. And you're upsetting my horse," he toyed.

She took the bait. "I'm not used to this bitter cold. I hate it, in fact! It puts a strain on my resources when men get cold," she snapped. "How much for your horse and carriage?" she asked.

"They're not for sale," he answered.

"Everything's for sale," she shot back.

"Everything but my horse and carriage." Skylar loosed the reins and rode past her.

The Fire Witch was stunned by the boy's arrogance and fearlessness. She did not expect this kind of greeting, for she had never met a human who couldn't be bought. She tried a different tactic.

"Please might I borrow your horse and carriage? I promise to take excellent care of them," she asked with as much forced gooey courtesy as she could muster.

But they rode on. Skylar did not look back and was beginning to wonder if she had given up when at once he felt a searing heat from behind him, onboard his phaeton.

He turned around and there, on the cracked leather seat, perched the red-hot-orange-glowing banshee of Fire from his dreams. She radiated a wall of heat with audacity and fearless power. For a moment Skylar thought her beautiful and awe inspiring. He memorized her face, diaphanous and ephemeral, as she locked him in her brandishing stare. Most of all, he held her in his thoughts as a business deal to avoid. She liked that, for she indeed read his mind.

"I could take your horse and carriage and leave you hanging from a tree burnt to a crisp, you know!" she threatened.

"But you won't, because fire can't drive a carriage," he said manipulatively. The power shifted between them and it made her furious. It was all she could do to maintain her new self-control.

"Why do you need my horse and carriage?" he asked.

"To … impress some friends. I imagine this horse can go very fast," she said.

"He can fly like the wind," he baited.

She brightened, leaning forward, sprinkling sparks on the ground. "Fly? Like the Wind? Why, that's exactly what I intend to do!" she said, her eyes glittering.

"Wasn't the Wind obnoxious last night? You hate the cold; I hate the Wind," Skylar said. "Maybe we're meant to be a team?" he carefully offered.

The Fire Witch was silent. Chelsea plodded along, stepping quietly so to hear every word with his finely tuned Arctic-White ears. He thought, *This boy is restoring my faith in Man.*

"The last time I partnered with a man I was cheated out of my reward!" she sparked. "My payment was to be a girl, *Lily white like snow!* she mocked in a high scratchy voice. "The stupid girl vanished," the Fire Witch ruminated.

Skylar felt it stab through him. He couldn't believe his ears. *Lily?* It had to be her! He instantly banished her from his mind so not to betray her to the Witch.

"The last time someone I know partnered with Fire, my friends and favorite professor died," Skylar said.

Not one to play games with a cunning adversary, the Fire Witch did not deny this one. "Yes, you were at the Great School blaze that day. You stole my charm when it rolled to your feet. I only sought my charm – your professor and friends got in my way," she hissed hotly.

"We were experimenting with stellar gases when something went wrong. The explosion blew me out my classroom window onto the grass. I came to, and I saw the building in flames and heard them all screaming – they were trapped. And you, dancing like a banshee, celebrated our horror, dodging the Firemen's hoses – laughing! I ran to the building determined to help them. That's when you shot up through the roof. It was a horrible accident."

"There are no accidents," the Fire Witch hissed. Was there a hint of remorse in her voice? He doubted it. "There is a purpose behind my Fire. I destroy so you can create. Surely you've heard of Alchemy?" she said. "But I'm vilified for my best efforts! I'm an artist and my art transforms everything it touches!"

Skylar regarded this magnificent dangerous being in his carriage. Here he was having a polite conversation with the infamous Fire Witch. Every scientist dreamed of understanding fire more intimately, yet none ever got as close as he was right now. He had to ask while he could, "Men hunger to know your Secret. What is it?"

"The real question is would I tell you?" she retorted.

"Now you have something I want," Skylar bargained.

Oh the Fire Witch warmed to this clever boy. It even crossed her mind not to destroy him when this was all over. During the course of the conversation the Fire Witch did not notice that Chelsea had changed course. They had curved slowly back on themselves, now heading northwest to the Great Faerie Highway where Winter would soon arrive at the crossroads where her headquarters, the iron works, puffed and belched its hideous plumes of toxic black smoke. So engrossed was she by the conversation that she also didn't notice that the millions of Faerie folk along their route were quickened to life by the coming battle. But Chelsea noticed them, and they were heartened by the sight of him, the Winter King's legendary stallion pulling an unaware Fire Witch to her final doom. It was history in the making and new Faerie tales were being spun as quickly as pointy little ears could transmit them.

"I will tell you my Secret if you and your horse do my bidding," the Fire Witch lured.

"You are notoriously capricious, your Highness," he said, bowing his head slightly, which greatly stroked her ego. "Dare I trust you?" he asked.

"Fair enough. My Secret has two parts. I'll tell you the first part now; the second after we've accomplished my task, if you survive it," she said.

Skylar felt a rush, then remembered the screams of his professor and friends being burned alive. "How can I know you're telling me your true Secret? I've heard many versions," he pushed her.

"I'm the ultimate celebrity! The more outrageous I am, the more humans are obsessed with me, want to be like me" she glowed. "Look how much *you* want to know *me*," she dodged his question.

Remember who you're dealing with, he reminded himself.

"Yes, do remember," she goaded, invading his mind. Her words slapped him hotly. Too much was at stake to be weak like that again!

"I accept your offer!" he declared, cocking his top hat to her in lieu of a hand shake. There was no hand to shake. Then she made a gesture, just like his professor. He felt nauseated realizing that as his professor burned alive, Fire had absorbed his traits, his mannerisms, his essence.

His anger flared. "Why kill my professor, my friends, burn down my school? Why not just leave them and come after me if you knew I had your damn charm?" he lashed out.

Chelsea quickened at the outburst. Things were heating up. "Would you be here if they were alive?" she taunted.

This surprised Skylar. What kind of question was that?

"You were marked for a greatness, they weren't. I've merely carved your destiny, cleared away the weeds," she darkly persuaded. "I enjoyed your friends the best, for they loved you the most. The first part of my Secret? *I feel love only when I'm burning it!* the Fire Witch whispered into his ear. Her hot breath singed his hair and left his cheek and ear sunburn red. The smell of his burnt hair almost made him vomit.

This Secret was believable, he'd just seen proof. "OK, where to?" he asked.

No answer. He turned around and the Fire Witch was gone, utterly vanished without a trace, though she did scorch the leather seat. He leaned back and read a message burned into the cushion:

Lily white like snow.

Skylar couldn't breathe. Everything spun. *She saw through me all along and played me! Now she knows!* he panicked. A Master Vibrationist like the Wind, the Fire Witch had sensed instantly that Cerulean was not in Skylar's vest. But why didn't she kill him? Why the charade? Was she after Lily?

"Hyah, Chelsea! Hyah! Make like the Wind! She's onto us!" Skylar yelled, unhitching the phaeton and jumping onto Chelsea's back. He realized at once he didn't have to grab the reins or even hold on, though he did. Chelsea knew the way or the way kept opening before them. It was happening so fast that Skylar surrendered to the ride and took in the incredible sights: thousands of miniature villages were saluting them, waving banners, playing music, toasting them with raised mugs and flagons of mead. Women and girls tossed them mincemeat, berry and pumpkin spice tarts which Chelsea easily, and eagerly, devoured. Skylar smelled wafts from all the delicious foods and tried catching tarts for himself without any luck.

"Close your eyes, use your nose!" neighed Chelsea.

It worked! As soon as Skylar closed his eyes, his nose and hands synchronized as one. He caught flying tarts a plenty and wolfed them down. He marveled at how flavor is so much more intense when you taste something with your eyes closed. But he couldn't resist opening his eyes, and found he was now a pro at this. As he ate he heard Faerie carolers singing merrily in a language he recognized, Russian. He saw them singing door to door for treats wearing animal costumes and scary masks to ward off evil spirits, mimicking nature's death in Winter. Then he heard something he didn't recognize at all.

"What on earth are those sounds?" Skylar asked.

"You've never heard throat singing?" Chelsea whinnied. "Female Faeries from Greenland sing like Inuit women! Ooh, and that sound there, that's yoiking, singing Sami style! They're all welcoming Winter! The Sami people, herdsmen of Earth's reindeer for thousands of years, now they know about magic, elves and witches. These good tidings mean the Kingdom of Autumn has departed! And the Kingdom of Winter's Court is at the Castle of the Seasons! *Neighhhh!*"

Skylar tingled with the vibrations of Chelsea's thundering Pegasus-sized neigh. He also shivered, realizing he was freezing cold. Chelsea's speed had intensified the frigid wintry air. As it grew cooler, the one thing Skylar didn't see anywhere was fire – not one burning yule log or lantern, not even a candle in the Sami Faerie kotas (wooden tee-pee shaped huts.)

"How are they staying warm without fire?" Skylar asked, his teeth chattering loudly.

"Solstice is a worldwide secret! And who keeps secrets

better than Faeries? There's Winter rime rum a plenty to warm any out-of-Season Faeries staying awake to see what happens!" Chelsea replied.

Skylar was numb with cold. But quick as he knew it, some last standing trees ahead wove remnant Autumn leaves into a thick coat, scarf and hat which flew down onto him as he passed. He was surprisingly toasty warm in no time and he marveled at the growing feeling that this forest loved him. His coat, scarf and hat's rich smell of Autumn leaves reminded him of Lily and her leafy frock. That made him feel warmer than ever.

CHAPTER TWENTY-SIX

UNDER THE POLAR ICE CAP

*I*s *there no bottom to this lagoon?* Lily wondered as she woke from her sleep and was still descending. That was when she felt the first change come over her. It began on her head. As if several coiffeurs were at work, her hair was combed, swirled, curled, pinned and crowned. Next she felt smooth cool jewels on her neck, ears, wrists, fingers and ankles. The jewels sparkled brightly, like moonlit ice, enticing her eyes to open underwater just as a pair of soft sparkling silver slippers slid onto her feet.

The undersea panorama took her breath away as she gently touched down on the white sandy bottom. She was in an aqua-blue ice-water kingdom. She had arrived on the sea floor under the floating North Pole and Winter Palace.

She looked at the rings on her fingers and bracelets on her wrists and was shocked to see someone else's hands. She touched her face and didn't feel her familiar features, but instead someone else's cheek bones, chin, lips and forehead. In fact, this costume wasn't just clothes and jewels, it was an entire body. She was Lily on the inside and, it dawned on her, Queen Crystalline on the outside … a taller, regal, older woman. The transformation had happened.

Lily was in a mirrored boudoir of ornate blue ice and saw in hundreds of reflections that she wore an evanescent silk underdress shimmering every shade of blue imaginable. On her wrist hung her pouch of herbs, now transformed into a drawstring pompadour purse of woven blue satin-ice, sparkling snowflake lace and ribbons and a twinkling prism tassel.

But it was the face reflecting back at her that held her spellbound. There she was, Crystalline, Winter's legendary Queen and Cerulean's mother. And there she was, Lily, growing more curious by the minute as to what the Queen and I had in store for her and how she would get back to her own body and be with Cerulean as herself.

From behind her, several white Beluga Whale ladies-in-waiting came forward, mantling her in an ornate white and silver gown, shaved-ice cloak and white gloves soft and light as powdered sugar. Her slippers were covered by embossed knee-high ice boots that somehow warmed her skin. The crystal laces glittered and the carved heels made her feel elegantly regal. She was handed a mirror which bore the name *Crystalline*. She turned the mirror and saw a black cloth covering its face. She looked at her attendants and they all nodded at her. She slowly untied and lifted off the black cloth and gazed into the mirror.

"Huh?!" Lily gasped. The flash of recognition stunned the mirror. Lily felt a tingling sensation vibrate her hand holding the mirror's handle. She and the mirror held their gaze breathlessly, beholding the wondrously beautiful reflection of Queen Crystalline, now a gracefully aged woman with twinkling blue eyes, flowing white hair and elegant bearing. Then Lily was jolted by a scary thought: *How can I possibly pull this off? After all, doesn't everyone think the Queen is dead?*

An attendant took the mirror and handed her the pinecone, which she had completely forgotten about. It was now covered in iridescent crystallized frost and was on a sparkling diamond chain. It clicked open like a purse and glowed brilliantly, for it held Cerulean's chrysalis which she also had forgotten about, much to her chagrin. But it was safe, she was resplendent, and she found herself speeding back up to the lagoon's surface.

She barely had a moment to catch a last look of that brilliant deep sea wonderland and felt a pang of longing to stay there. Her speed slowed as she approached what she thought was the lagoon surface. But the lagoon was gone! She drifted in a cocoon of hazy fog, Arctic *sea smoke*, before she felt her feet touch ground again. Beneath her, a stair illuminated and beside her a Faerie squire offered his arm to help her ascend the bank of the dried up basin.

The instant she felt the top of her head and ice crown break through the sea smoke, Lily felt a surge of regal dignity. She remembered what the Queen had said, *You have earned it and learned it.* She decided to play the part with every regal fiber of her being no matter the outcome. She had to – the feeling of being a genuine queen was indescribable: utterly foreign, very adult and spine tinglingly exciting! Robed in splendor and crowned with millions of years of history, she imagined this must be what peacocks and wisteria vines feel in Spring: metamorphosis beyond their wildest dreams.

Lily adjusted her posture as her head and shoulders rose into regal bearing. She noticed it made her breathe differently, confidently. When her eyes broke through the sea smoke's haze, she saw a vast panorama of brightly lit lanterns twinkling all around the hollow. She looked up and saw that Orion was not only watching her, but had changed position, leaving a gaping black hole in the sky. He was poised on bended knee, bow and arrow in hand, as if ready to shoot straight at her. But he winked instead! Yes, that was definitely a wink. And she knew he was watching over her and protecting her with great love. But it was the Winter music that most comforted her … ancient drumming and singing which suddenly stopped, but for one lone Faerie fiddler who didn't see her momentous arrival. There arose a collective gasp among the hundreds of thousands of Faeries gathered.

THE CHRYSALIS

The sound of a Faerie gasp is often inaudible to other Faeries, for it can be rude. The sound of hundreds of thousands of Faerie gasps is the same sound as light traveling from the sun. It is the sound of colors, radiant and joyous. Only one language has a word for it, Wind: >*Høzh'höwœhh!* And one must inhale (>) as one says it. Lily saw two attendants gently lift her gown's luminescent front trim for her to step onto the path strewn with … what? Could it be? Her path was strewn with frost sparkling in the moonlight! Such visceral joy welled up inside her that her eyes teared.

Lily looked around. She saw Coco and Darwina, but not the Mist. "Mist? Where are you?" Her voice cracked. *This isn't my voice!* Lily thought in dismay, then caught herself. She wanted to hear it again to make sure she connected with it as fast as possible. "Greetings, Mother Tree," Lily said deliberately slowly to Coco. Oh, the Queen's voice! How elegant, eternal, musical – the kind of voice you want to hear telling stories at dinner and reading to you at bedtime.

"The Mist has gone, your *Majesty*," Coco answered formally.

"Majest--?" Lily caught herself again. She must play the part, the Queen had warned her. She cleared her throat and started again.

"Gone? What do you mean gone?" she asked Coco in a regal tone.

Coco spoke deliberately so all could hear: "When Mistress Lily descended into the lagoon, the Mist and its water followed her. They have yet to return, but I am certain they will. And you, your Majesty, Queen Crystalline, have miraculously returned to us this Winter Solstice night!"

In the distance there was a commotion: an approaching sound rather like a freight train. It sent deep sonic vibrations throughout the wood. Lily glanced at Coco who remained utterly calm and coyly waved a tiny oak twig as if to say, *All is well.* The sound grew in intensity, encircling them. Lily recognized the sound's signature with relief: *It's Sir Windham, in one of his tornado twisters!* She knew it had to be an urgent high speed delivery for such a dramatic entrance. *Could it be? Could it be…?* Lily's heart pounded as an even more thrilling thought occurred to her. As far as she could see down the frosty path, Faeries crowded to catch a glimpse of my unexpected arrival.

On the opposite end of the path, as far as I could see, the coast was clear for Cerulean and me to fly over the massive assembly straight to Lily. And we flew! At first Lily couldn't make out what we were. *What's Windham got there? Something bright floating on his current,* she wondered. I weaved the Prince's starball in and out over the path, over the Faeries, all of whom swayed in his direction, oohing and aahing, none quite sure what they were marveling at. The closer we grew, Cerulean's light brightened, intuitively feeling the electromagnetic attraction pulling him stronger and stronger. I slowed our wind speed.

Lily felt the first sweet kisses of my breeze on her forehead, cheeks and lips and I gently billowed her gown. She glanced up at Orion, who burned more brightly than ever. The floating Princely light gave a sudden start when he came upon her. Was he scared?

"Your Highness, are you alright?" I whispered to the starball. But Lily thought I addressed the question to her.

"We are well, Sir Windham," she answered, "and pleased with your safe return." She dared not asked about the floating starlight, for fear it was something a real Queen would understand, and she didn't.

I breezed in Lily's ear loud enough for just her and Cerulean to hear. "Now listen carefully. Strong Winter Solstice magic is at work. Lily and Cerulean, neither of you is quite yourself at the moment," I said. I heard each of them silently gasp the other's name. Cerulean's starball flared in disbelief. Follow my lead – all must believe Lily is Queen Crystalline. Lily, on my cue open your pinecone purse."

She nodded slightly, smiling in stunned pretense to the massive assembly, which had quadrupled in just the last few minutes. Had she really just heard me address her and Cerulean? For his part, Cerulean wondered what wondrous magic had melded his mother with Lily and why? My omnipresent windy voice broke the silence with a grand false proclamation, hoping it would work.

"Your Majesty, Queen Crystalline of the Kingdom of Winter, I am overjoyed, as are we all, to see you alive! But none more so than your beloved son." The crowd's gasp interrupted me, but I forged on. "Your son, Winter's royal heir, His Royal Highness Prince Cerulean, who is rescued from the Fire Witch!"

There arose an ear splitting chorus of cheers. I felt Lily sway at the news. I perceived two strong vibrations, euphoria and anxiety, rise inside her. She held up her hand and the crowd instantly silenced. This shocked her, for she had never seen Faeries behave so well, nor take an order silently. She heard herself form the words, hoping she was a convincing queen and mother. "My son? My Cerulean?" she could scarcely contain her wild joy inside. "Where is he, Sir Windham?" she breathlessly asked.

I gently bore the starball of swirling gas up to the Queen's face. She could feel heat emanating from the orb and closed her eyes to breath it in. Now it was Cerulean's turn at breathless pretense.

"M-Mother?? ... It is I, your Cerulean! But only part of me, Orion's part, my starlight. I gave my heart, my chrysalis, to a girl ... *Lily*," he said with all the love in his heart, hoping she would feel it. She did. "But I can't return to my myself until –"

"Now Lily!" I hushed.

Lily opened the pine cone purse. A blinding light shot out like a super nova. She whispered urgently, "Cerulean! Here's your heart, your chrysalis! Return, my love, to yourself and to me!"

In a flash of silver-blue-white fireworks, Prince Cerulean's heart and soul flew to each other and reunited as his chrysalis and starball fused. The Prince was transformed instantly into a tall, handsome teen in royal Winter attire. Cerulean and Lily barely had a moment to marvel at his new form.

Whether Orion's arrow hit first or the Fire Witch's fireball exploded first, every Faerie tale tells it differently. It all depends upon where you were standing at that historic moment when Time stood still. For even Time couldn't make out what happened and had to think about it. Coco, being an unusually tall Oak, had a bird's eye view, so her account is generally accepted as the most historically accurate. But one thing was certain: after that thunderous kaboom lit up the sky and the glittering smoke settled, the Fire Witch was gone. I was gone. Lily and Cerulean were gone, having been transported at the speed of starlight by Orion's arrow to the Castle of the Seasons. And Orion and his two celestial dogs, Major and Minor? Gone. All that remained were hundreds of thousands of Faeries, stunned motionless, wondering *What will happen next?*

A TORCH ON ICE

"Your Majesty, I beg you, please! Cease your snow now! It'll only increase the Fire Witch's wrath!" Frescobaldi pleaded with the Winter King, hoping his revenge would now unfold exactly as he had planned.

"You never could take the cold, Frescobaldi!" the King mused. "Bad form for a Spring Faerie, wouldn't you say?"

The Winter caravan was drawing near to the Faerie crossroads and for the last several hours Winter had put on an elegant, loving snowstorm which spanned thousands of miles. Puffy powdery snowflakes floated in the air, drifting in carefree amazement at themselves. Winter's sound of silence, hibernating land, spread in a peaceful panorama. Ice froze over ponds and lakes while exhausted trees gratefully fell asleep under the blanket for a long overdue nap. Already the few remaining beasts and plants reset their body clocks and irritating pests and blights were frozen off. Earth was cooling off at long last.

Along the route, the Winter King was hailed by millions of jubilant Faeries, and not just Winter Faeries. The Seasons were so discombobulated that Autumn, Spring and Summer Faeries were also making merry, for they knew their Season, in time, would be restored to its rightful place, too. The King joined in their songs as he passed, with Cerulean heavy on his mind, both in memory and in anticipation.

Jack Frost and Viggo Vespa rode at the front of the procession. "So far so good," Viggo said, perched atop Jack's arm. "But I can't believe *she* hasn't attacked yet."

"She will. I just wish Windham would gust some intel," Jack replied, looking up.

The sky was remarkable: a sharp line of voluminous snow clouds stretched as far as the eye could see. The moonlight made it all the more dramatic: a heaven-sized wall of white encroaching on the clear, starry midnight blue sky ahead. It was an effect Jack was proud of and he made a note to compliment the Snow Delivery Corps.

It wasn't long before the first of several news dispatches arrived by my gusts. Viggo flew the messages to the King, who at once dismissed Frescobaldi from his presence.

"Your Majesty!" Viggo chirped into the King's ear. "It's Prince Cerulean and the Queen, *Crystalline* herself, they've been found! THEY'RE ALIVE!! Alive, your Majesty!" Viggo got so excited relaying this news that his little bat wings flipped him in somersaults.

The King released the longest-held breath in history, for part of him hadn't breathed since that Solstice night long ago when this nightmare began. He erupted in a paroxysm of sobs of unbridled joy. Sparkling tears ran down his venerable old beard forming baby icicles. He danced in place like a teen to his own music as Viggo held on, riding like a bronco!

"Where are they, Viggo?" the King asked in a lilting, thrilled hush. "Where are they?"

"There is also dark news, Sire," Viggo hated to add.

The King's brow crinkled and he stopped dancing.

"As a precaution to keep you safe, I'm to take you to the Castle of the Seasons where the Queen and Prince await you. But Sire, oh these words fall heavily, the Fire Witch and an accomplice, they – they have – they implemented *Phaeton's Fate*," Viggo uttered the hateful words.

"WH-WHAT??" the King gasped. *"Phaeton's Fate??"* He inhaled in alarm. "No one believed she'd really do it! Why destroy every living thing? She's sealing her own fate with everyone else's! What happens to your neighbor, happens to you!" His anger turned to resolve. "I leave Jack Frost in command. I order Frescobaldi to be put on ice! Call it MY masterstroke. Guards!" he thundered.

Three Northern Knights promptly dispatched a kicking and screaming Frescobaldi to the ice carriage. He was incarcerated in the subzero chamber, his angry yet panicked yells fading behind the King, Viggo, Midori and their Northern Knight escort, Knightglow, a brave young knight in training. As they crept across a snowy meadow, they were greeted by several Blue Spruce Sentries who let them pass.

"He was right!" the King surmised to his companions. "Sir Windham suspected Baldi was a Torch. The Wind shall be rewarded for exposing this treachery! How much further, Viggo?" the King asked excitedly. He was so invigorated and walking so fast in the snow that the others could barely keep up. With every step he felt younger and brimmed with pride in his prolific snow banks and drifts. Midori's thick Mastiff coat caught snowflakes tossed by the Blue Spruce Sentries and she romped behind the King in near delirious joy at how their lives had changed in just a matter of hours.

"Look, your Majesty! Over there!" Viggo chirped as he soared in and out of the Blue Spruces' complex and prickly security canopy. Then they saw it: the Castle of the Seasons appeared in magnificence before them.

The sight was breathtaking. The castle glistened in its Winter-style architecture. Each Season has its own unique aesthetics and building traditions. The Winter castle's shape shifted out of Autumn's giant maple leaf footprint (with cornucopia wings and pumpkin-shaped towers) into a high rise multi-dimensional snowflake structure with carved interior ice bridges and vaulted translucent ice ceilings that let in Aurora Borealis' light, moonlight and starlight. A giant hexagon, it had six wings that fanned out sporting turrets like none other: they spun upward like giant upside down icicles! The approach to the castle's ice-draw bridge, which lowered over a frozen moat filled with ice sculptures of Winter sports, was lined with rich green

Holly Sentinels loaded with bright red berries. Every thorny leaf was on high alert should trouble appear. To the King, the castle never looked more festive or welcoming.

"Ah, look at her!" the King admired. "The Castle of the Seasons has done it again! She's a galaxy unto herself! A giant Solstice present wrapped in ice-bows and tied with silver-blue ribbon!"

The ribbon he meant, of course, was the Four Seasons' trusty year-round Blue Spruce Guard whom all of nature admires and fears. If you've ever experienced the painful jab of a Blue Spruce's dense spikey needles, let alone been dwarfed by Spruces' dizzying heights, then you know why they guard our castle! On this Solstice night, every adult and sapling Blue Spruce was on duty, each in silvery blueness brightened by moonlight on snowy boughs.

Viggo raced ahead to alert the castle gatekeepers to lower the draw bridge for His Majesty. Usually there would have been much fanfare, jingle bells, ice drumming and singing of carols, but time and secrecy were of the essence. Midori walked ahead of the King, her tail brushing clear a path. As the King crossed, his every footstep radiated shafts of blue light through the ice bridge down into the frozen moat, creating a mesmerizing under-water blue glow which lit the sculptures and reflected up the castle's majestic ice walls.

Knightglow was the last to enter. As he did so, he gave a signal to the Spruce's commander and the entire Blue Spruce ribbon snapped to attention, on the lookout for *Her*.

ORION'S BELT

"We're lost," Skylar said to Chelsea. "I bet she put a spell on us! Enchanted our path!"

He and Chelsea knew the battle had begun, for they'd seen and heard a thunderous blast of dazzling light in the distance. They also noticed Orion was gone. If they saw all this, so did the Fire Witch.

"Chelsea, we're too late. They've all forgotten about us," Skylar complained.

"Forrrget youuu? Not I!" a resonant voice sang.

"Ah, Chelsea, nor I, you," Skylar warmly replied, giving his horse a warm pat on the neck.

"I didn't say anything," Chelsea answered.

Skylar recognized the other voice with a start. It had an odd accent and was musical. Just like when he'd heard, *"Stay the course to Chelsea!"* His heart began to pound, for as he looked all around he was enveloped by the darkest darkness he had ever seen. Blacker than black. All light was gone but for a few distant pinpoints that seemed infinitely unreachable. Skylar clung to Chelsea tightly.

"What's the matter?" Chelsea asked. "Haven't you ever been inside a Constellation before?"

"Inside a Constell –?" Skylar's mind raced to retrieve everything he ever learned about Constellations. He never thought he'd actually meet one! He knew them as science, mythological heroes and monsters, navigation symbols, animals real and imagined connecting stars like dots to help astronomers map the sky. But if Orion was physical, not just a concept, but an actual being or person, then that meant all the Great 88 were sentient, too! His epiphany staggered him. It was one thing to discover Winter is a Kingdom where the wind, fire, horses and starlight could talk. But to now be inside a real live Constellation, one he'd studied and often spoke to – never expecting a reply – blew his imagination even wider than it already was. This was BIG. It was the Sky, for whom he was named, inviting Skylar into its cosmic reality.

"Let go of me and see what happens!" Chelsea encouraged him. "You'll enjoy it! I'm right here if you need me."

"Let go? You mean like –?" Skylar hesitated.

"Liiiike you'rrrre flyyyyinnng!" the resonant voice sang.

Skylar took a deep breath. "Here goes nothing!" Chelsea's mane slipped from his fingers as he let go and floated into weightless black space. For a boy who loves the stars, this was incredible! How could he possibly be floating in space and breathing air? And how far away was Earth? Somewhere out there in the great stellar beyond? *I don't remember leaving Earth,* he thought to himself. But all the questions and dismay gave way to an inexpressible bliss. He did somersaults and navigated in any direction by simply pointing his two hands together and thinking it.

"Are we inside Orion the Hunter?" he asked Chelsea. "I always wanted to know what it's like to be a Constellation!"

"Nowww youuu knowww!" Orion sang back happily.

Orion's voice was one of the most unusual sounds Skylar had ever heard. Its tone and cadence were like ghostly ringing bells. Skylar and Chelsea vibrated, as if they were his vocal chords. But the phenomenal thing was that Skylar assimilated Orion's self-awareness. He felt Orion's vastness and felt right at home observing the Universe from Orion's unlimited perspective. Skylar thought, *There's no human word for this – this 'forever' feeling!*

Everything was vibrating. Skylar felt more alive and aware than he ever imagined possible. *Remember the day we learned how chairs, clothes, trees, dishes, rocks, books, you name it, vibrate?* He thought. *The whole world's abuzz! Atoms and molecules pulsating, each one at its own speed. Energy fields are everywhere! In fact, that's all anything is: energy fields. Including me! It never meant anything till now!* It was like a giant light bulb switched on in his brain.

Chelsea sang as only a horse can: "Orri-i-i-onn, my

frie-e-e-nnd, tha-a-annk you-u-u! We're n-no-t l-lo-st!"

"Morre like founnd! The Firre Witch waas comming back forr youuu so I hid youuu! She has bad intennntions for Earrth – and the Winnnd. He'd better steerr clearr of herr!" chanted Orion.

Skylar was struck by this musical dialogue and felt a pang of shame stab through him. He didn't know if he could sing. He had tried once, in the Great School's Spring Concert, and remembered loving the feeling – he sang those songs with such spirit! But the music teacher pointed at him and said, 'You, mouth the words!' Everyone laughed at him. That was the end of his singing career. But Orion seemed like a forgiving Constellation. *If I don't sing well, he may not care,* Skylar thought. Something inside him said to give it a go.

"Ahem … *Did Winndhamm and Ceruuleann make it okaay?"* Skylar sang haltingly.

"YOU CAN SING!!" Orion boomed. *"WOW!"* Orion was exultant and his jolly vibrations shook Skylar and Chelsea to their cores. *"Yes, they mmade it! Winnter's King, Queen and Prinnce arre reunited at the Caastle!"* Orion harmonically intoned. *"I stood guarrd overrhead and watched it alll!"*

"A-a-nd a-a-t the Crosss-roa-d-ds?" sang Chelsea.

"Alll quiet. Frescoballdi didn't last lonng in the ice carrriage. Whenn the Fire Witch couldn't finnd you two, she decided to attack the Winnter Caravann. But alll she founnd was Frescobaldi's lifeless body frozzzen on the grounnd. Sir Winndham and my dogs, Majorr and Minorr, stannd guard at the Caastle of the Seasonns. Jack Frost annd the Northernn Knights arre at the crossroads awaitinng orders," chanted Orion. *"And thaat's wherre we come*

in," he added ominously. *"SHE is up to sommething. She's gone quiet and innvisible, a danngerous combinationn. And we have an important errannd."*

This news wasn't nearly as important to Skylar as another thought on his mind. Still grieving his mother's death and realizing more and more each day he was now an orphan on his own, a burning question rose up inside him. *"Orion, are you my Guardian Constellation?"*

An ancient harmonic chord cluster arose, the music of Orion's old soul. It grew so loud Skylar was sure the whole Universe could hear it.

"If sou-u-nd cou-u-ld ma-a-tch colou-u-r, he's si-i-nging the Auro-o-ra Bo-o-rea-a-lis!" sang Chelsea in unbridled mirth.

"I've never seen the Northern Lights!" sang Skylar excitedly.

"You will withinn the hourr!" chanted Orion.

"Is that a yes, then?" Skylar eagerly asked.

"YES, my son, yes! I am your Guardian Constellation!" Orion sang proudly.

It was if as Skylar had just been told *I am your father!* He had found his soul's home. *So this is how Constellations communicate in deep space,* Skylar thought. Constellations sing and ring in frequencies that transmit over millions of light years. It's one big concert up there in outer space. Astronomers had known this for decades, but he was the first human to comprehend it! And sing it!

Orion broke Skylar's free floating reverie: everything at once flipped upside down and inside out. All Skylar knew is the blood rushed to his head as he spun in helpless somersaults. He kept reaching for but missing Chelsea's tail.

"Cliiiiiimb uuup meee nnnowww!" Chelsea yelled distantly, his voice distorted and flung afar.

Skylar saw the horse's tail jerk upward. He grabbed it and it flipped him onto the horse's back. He flung his arms around Chelsea's neck and hung on for dear life.

"What's happening?" Skylar yelled in panic.

"Orion is on the move! Constellations can't walk on Earth. They're multi-dimensional and photonic, and Earth's gravity muddles them, so he's climbed above the thermosphere where he's more at home," yelled Chelsea. "We're on Orion's Belt, the smoothest place to ride!" he exclaimed, so happy to be reunited with his old stellar friend again.

Skylar looked behind them and saw a grey and yellow marble sharply outlined by black space. From up here Earth's yellow-grey clouds and grey-brown oceans spoke of severe trauma.

"I'm in – sp-space?? … HA!! I'M – IN – SPACE!" Skylar couldn't believe it as he yelled it.

They trundled along in wide sweeping curves and dips out into the Solar System. Skylar imagined the size of the hyperbolas on a graph that would match Orion's sweeping heaving steps. He let himself sway with the Constellation's extraordinary power. It was very much like riding a horse, just learn its rhythm and relax into it.

"Wannt to knnow why your mother nammed you Skylarr?" Orion chanted.

"Yes, sir! Please tell me!" Skylar sang back.

"Because yourr eyes are the colorr of Olde Skye!" Orion

sang, *"That breathtaking bluue that the Winnd and I and Machu Picchu are trying to restorre to Earrth's atmospherre."*

Then Orion stopped. Abruptly. Skylar and his questions about Machu Picchu were flung off the horse. He flailed his arms and legs, trying in vain to slow his out-of-control spinning momentum. Then the sight of a lifetime rose before his eyes. Floating face to face with him was his favorite planet, Saturn. Thousands of rings of ice whizzed just in front of his nose.

"AH!!!" Skylar cried out. So overwhelmed, so thrilled was he, all he could do was yell again, "AH!!!!" Oh it was jaw-dropping! Its size was mind boggling. Saturn's many moons, over sixty of them large and small, and chunks of ice, some bigger than skyscrapers in the Great City, floated all around him. He saw the moon Titan and the Cassini Division between Rings A and B. And there at the center was Saturn himself, a hydrogen gas giant. His colors were iridescent, ever changing, a masterpiece ever repainting itself brilliantly upon brilliant!

"How'd we get here so fast? It took barely a minute to go 746 million miles?" Skylar sang incredulously.

"A hop, skip and a jummp, my boy!" Orion trumpeted. *"Youu want to zip thrrough spaace? Stick with mee! We Constellationns knnow how to get arounnd!"* Orion sang as he loaded large chunks of Saturnalian Ice into his stellar sack.

"How come I can breathe up here?" Skylar sang.

"You'rrrre wiiith meee and we'rre Saturrrrn's Guessssts!" Orion rang.

Chelsea floated over to Skylar's side. "We're making a pick up. Saturn is the bank and his rings are the vaults. He's the treasury of our oldest, finest ice in the Solar System, the progenitor of Earth's great Ice Families. Hop aboard!" Chelsea neighed to Skylar.

They took off like a shot, galloping out of Orion onto Saturn's A Ring. At lightning speed Skylar rode his equestrian champion effortlessly. The sight was so remarkable that even Orion paused to watch and could hear the boy's shouts of glee. With each bigger and higher jump Skylar impressed himself, and his horse, for as Saturn gradually increased the course's difficulty, Skylar improved with each new challenge.

A loud, eerie pulsating sound erupted which Skylar instantly recognized as Saturn's radio emissions he had studied in astronomy class. It sounded like a high pitched oscillating *Woooo-owww-woooo-owww!* and vibrated through Skylar's body. At once, Saturn's rings sped up.

"Hey, what's happening?" Skylar shouted to Chelsea.

"Saturn just gave the order: *Full Speed!* Hold on!" Chelsea neighed.

It felt as if they were flying. Skylar never knew a horse could be so aerodynamic! Saturn's nine biggest rings became an extreme obstacle course of speed traps, moonlets, gaps, giant spokes, waves, night side darkness and insane day side lightning in *Storm Alley*. At the slightest finger movement, Chelsea responded to Skylar's directional touch with uncanny precision. The boy and the horse maneuvered as one in gravity defying feats of graceful and strategic brilliance.

Saturn, Orion and Chelsea now knew, as did I, that we had at last found the first human to break the language barrier between Man, Earth and the Stars.

THE SOLAR WINDS' INSULT

"Dead? He's dead! How could old Baldi be dead?" The Fire Witch was wild with grief. She burned with revenge. All thoughts of self-control vanished on finding his frozen body laid in an ice boat, a Winter burial tradition, on a frozen pond along the Faerie Highway. She'd tried warming his body to no avail, incredulous at her brother's cruelty. Yes, she killed wantonly, but she's Fire, it's expected! But the benevolent Winter King? Had he changed so?

And, to add insult to injury, Frescobaldi had been stripped of all regalia. His sash, epaulets, medals and insignias of high office were gone, especially Winter's most distinguished medal of honor, the *Aurora Aura*. She could see on his frost covered uniform the faded place where it had hung. He had received the *Aura* for feats of bravery long before they were engaged. The *Aurora Aura's* ice mineral content was a special magnetic design that behaved similarly to the Auroras in amplitude and spectral light. It was the medal Frescobaldi wore most proudly, and the one that never failed to spark the Fire Witch's jealousy of her twin cousins, the Auroras.

A tradition among the Kingdoms of the Seasons is to honor the transitioning being's Season(s) of birth and his or her contribution to nature. As many long suspected, Frescobaldi proved himself not to be a Winter Faerie, not just in how he died by freezing but by how he lived conspiring against the Winter King. Being a Mixed Seasoning, a Son of Spring-Summer, he had it in him to withstand both cold and heat, but each only up to a certain tolerance depending on which Season pulled stronger in his blood. That Frescobaldi succumbed to the cold meant Summer was the stronger Seasoning in him. On the ice boat, an ice carved sign read:

Frescobaldi, Son of Spring-Summer
Traitor to the Kingdom of Winter

The Fire Witch stared at the sign and burned in indignation. Once a Seasoning Sign was posted there was no altering it in the Faerie Death Records. This is how Frescobaldi would be remembered for all time. It then struck her that he froze to death.

He didn't turn to coal.

Coal was always the demise of evil Faeries.

Frescobaldi had frozen.

"Perhaps your love for me spared you that humiliation?" she said to his corpse.

"My brother made it so I'd find you …" she continued, confused by her emotional state, flaring hot and cold. "Maybe he wanted me to finish the rite … or maybe he was just taunting me!" she spat sparks. She wouldn't play into anyone's plans, especially her brother's! "But this is you, Frescobaldi, you who's been iced to your core. Just this once, just for you, I will do a death rite, but I'll do it my way."

The Fire Witch clasped and pointed her arms above her head and shot a stream of fire into the sky, her signal for any nearby Torches to come at once. They appeared out of nowhere, proving how dangerously omnipresent and well disguised they were.

"My Torches! Gather wood and load it into that boat! Then push it to the center of the pond!" she ordered. The Torches vanished back into night and were gone only a few moments before they returned with dry chopped wood stolen from neighboring wood piles. They placed the wood around Frescobaldi and gave the ice boat a giant heave, sending it skating and spinning out to the middle of the pond where it at last rested. "Now leave me!" she ordered.

Faerie burial rites are richly elaborate affairs – she cut it down to two parts: *The Admiring* and *The Firing of the Departed.* She offered *The Admiring* in a hushed private voice. "Frescobaldi, we loved each other in ways no one could ever understand. I regret mistreating you. There wasn't anything you wouldn't do for me. I see that now. You were my ultimate servant, worshipper, flatterer, fuel. As far as I'm concerned, that is true love. In your honor, I now give you a fiery send off. In your memory, I will implement *Phaeton's Fate* on my own!"

She sucked in a mass of air and flared high over the frozen pond. Her red-orange-yellow glow reflected in the newly fallen snow as she shot bolts of sizzling fire into the ice boat, setting the wood ablaze. Then with careful precision, she laser heat carved a circle around the boat through the ice. She heard the ice circle crack and break away from the pond ice and float in the water now fluttering around it. "And how about this, for a bit of décor … and to speed things up?" she said as she fired dollops of flames around the ice boat, as one might add colorful sugar-flowers around a cake. The ice boat melted quickly and Frescobaldi transitioned to ash. Soon he, the boat and the ice circle melted into the pond and Frescobaldi returned to the Earth – and the Fire Witch vanished to implement her Final Pollution.

Some minutes later, she reappeared atop a steaming volcano in all her steaming fury. "You, Windham, will pay dearly!!" she shrieked. Summoning all her strength, she rocketed upward, higher and higher, then in white hot rage she plummeted, casting herself, flames streaming for hundreds of feet, into the Earth's belly invoking her *Phaeton's Fate* spell, calling on the Solar Winds of her fiery God, the Sun:

> *Empower me, Phaeton, with fiery hell!*
> *This hour doth Satan envy my spell*
> *To scorch and torch the Earth till black!*
> *Crown the art of my attack!*

The volcano was taken by surprise at tasting this new hot spice. It thought for a moment or two, by moment three it did not like the taste, for it was soaked in hatred and revenge. Volcanos aren't known for acting impulsively, but in this instance it had no choice. It took a deep tectonic breath and with all its might heaved a God awful eruption, quaking the Earth for thousands of miles. It belched loudly and rudely. The Fire Witch rocketed up into the earth's atmosphere faster than any human missile, all the while anticipating the Solar Winds welcoming her.

She landed exactly where she hoped, atop the Earth's superheated atmosphere and was elated to hear the Solar Winds approaching. She had no idea they'd come for her this fast. "I must be more important to the Sun than I imagined!" she said. Never having done this before, she wasn't sure what proper Solar protocol was. After all, Solar Winds weren't really winds, but supersonic streams of the Sun's own self, its plasma, charged particles.

"They'll crush you, Windham, in a hot huff!" she gloated at Earth below. "I wonder, does one salute? Bow? Lay prostrate?" she asked herself. "But, wait – I am a Queen!" her ego reminded her. "I'll greet them as nobles, for they are the Sun's emissaries. As for meeting the Sun, I will deign a bow, for he is a God." But then a new thought frightened her: "What if the Sun is a Goddess?" Uh oh. "No Goddess would let me shine – I'd outshine her! No – no, he's a God, he has to be! I know it." Uplifted by emergency magical thinking, she adjusted her flames, radiating magnificently and heating up in excitement as the Solar Winds drew near. "What synergy!" she cheered. "You're making me stronger already!"

"Huh??" She froze in awe. In spite of the atmosphere being a murky mess of her own creation, the Fire Watch caught sight of … oh, she couldn't believe it! Dusky and oddly small, but no doubt about it, she was sure it was he, her distant god, the Sun. She took it as a sign he was coming for her. She waved. She fanned. She even copied something she learned from humans but never attempted: she blew the Sun kisses of fire.

"I give myself to you! We'll rule together as one!" she beamed. Then, thinking no one was watching but the Sun, she let her guard down and … flirted. Like a pretty young fire just starting out in life, she flashed sparks teasingly to the dusky orb. Confident her fiery beauty would draw his fiery attention, she coyly looked for his reaction – but saw another sun! Slightly confused, she blew that sun even more flirtatious kisses. She even arched backwards like a soaring solar flare to prove her fitness and worthiness as the Sun's mate. "I've never felt so beautiful! So hot!" she gleamed, growing drunk with loving herself. But mid-air upside down she saw a *third* sun – the *real* Sun, a giant radiant sphere glowing between the two smaller orbs, her false starry suitors. She took in the vastness of their triple sun display. The small orbs shimmered bright red facing the sun and bluish-orange facing away. Her molten arms tried to wave the vision away as panic set in.

"What? Impossible! Is that a –? No, it can't be! I've been tricked! The last one to make *Sundogs* was – I made sure Aunty would never again –!" she gasped in naked alarm, cut off by an awful sound. Mortified, she looked up to see the Great 88 twinkling and ringing in hysterical laughter – especially the female Constellations.

HYSTERRRRICAAAAAL!!!!!!
WHAAAAAAT A PRRAAAAAAANK!!!

Flirting is an art among stars and the Fire Witch's display

made for one of Andromeda's best entries in the *Constellation Book of Humors* subtitled *Celestial Jokes, Jibes, Jinx & Jests*:

> *There was a Witch itching to tease*
> *With flames of a thousand degrees;*
> *To the Sun she blew kisses,*
> *No hits, only misses!*
> *That fiery flirt didn't have to get hurt –*
> *Romantic fakes are common mistakes;*
> *Where'd the fool break love's rule?*
> *In spates of hate for beasts and trees:*
> *One cannot slay then expect to play*
> *With the birds and the bees!*

In humiliated horror, the Fire Witch looked at the South Pole under her flaming feet. The sight staggered her. There, in the Southern Ocean, where today was Summer Solstice, Aunt Arctica had melted and cracked off thousands of monster icebergs in a thunderous Summer match of Ice Breakers! But this wasn't just any game. They were playing to the death, pulling the biggest prank of their lives. They exuberantly smashed each other into zillions and zillions of ice crystals, sparkling frozen *diamond dust* ascending in swirls to the atmosphere, roaring in laughter on the rollercoaster ride of a lifetime on the Acrobatic Katabatics.

"Ice?? Diamond dust?? Where did you find –?" the Fire Witch yelped at Aunt Arctica, defensively spraying a shield of hot sparks against the cold stinging crystals. Then it struck her: "Brinicles! You did it with brinicles! I should have known you'd pull a stunt like this!"

Yes. Underwater, where the Fire Witch and her Torches

didn't have eyes or ears, one of nature's undersea wonders had volunteered for duty. In countless columns, brine secretly formed under placid seas into an army of tornado-shaped ice plumes reaching down to the ocean floor. On Aunt Arctica's cue, these icy fingers broke free, joined hands and high-fived each other in icy slaps and claps adding their ice crystals to the ascending ice-cloud.

In horror, the Fire Witch watched the ice-crystal cloud rise, bending the Sun's rays horizontally. As it grew, the two side orbs glowed even brighter and the horizon halo swelled even bigger. Aunt Arctica had done it! In one last prank meant to weaken her monstrous niece, she created one of Earth's most extraordinary atmospheric phenomena: *Sundogs! ...* known to some as *Phantom Suns.* And, precision artist that she was, Aunty stretched her luminous ring around the Sundogs in a perfect 22° halo.

The Fire Witch felt her temperature drop and her beauty start to fade. "NO! This can't happen! I've come too far for you and your Sundogs to stop me now!" She heard the roar of the Solar Winds close in. "I won't let anyone or anything come between me and my sunny destiny!" she swore. She fanned her flames imperiously to greet the Sun's emissaries. "Welcome, my friends! I've been waiting for you!"

But the Solar Winds did not stop to greet her. Instead they blew right through her, practically extinguishing her. In fact, they completely ignored her and flew straight to Earth's North and South Poles and magnetically converged! In a perfectly synchronized ritual she knew from her youth, the Solar Winds joyfully ignited her beautiful twin cousins, Aurora Borealis and

Aurora Australis, as they had for billions of years. A lifetime of jealousy exploded as she watched the two beauties light up as never before. The illumination was phantasmagorical, even to the shattered Fire Witch.

Yet even more insulting was what came next, the Sun's romance dance she had been hoping for, dreaming of, planning on! At the North Pole, the Solar Winds partnered Aurora Borealis in their legendary undulating *Solero Bolero*. At the South Pole, the Solar Winds and Aurora Australis tripped the light fantastic in athletic Magnetic Balletics, the latest in electronic dance, to hail Aunt Arctica for pulling off a Sundogs for the ages. Orion's dogs, Major and Minor, barked in twinkling approval as Aunt Arctica re-assembled herself with what ice was left, energized by a Summer Solstice mash up few would soon forget and confident Winter would visit her in six months' time.

The Kingdom of Winter was officially and firmly established in the North and the Fire Witch was trapped in Earth's 2,700° thermosphere, blown to bits by the Solar Winds and utterly disgraced in front of Earth and Sky. As Aunt Arctica would later brag to baby bergs about her now legendary Sundogs Prank, "I simply pulled rank and gave her a spank!"

But it wasn't over.

"How did it go so wrong?" the Fire Witch raged. It was impossible to pull herself together, for the Earth's 1,000 mph spin kept snuffing her out. She stumbled and tumbled with nothing to hold on to. "Without me, Fire will be subdued by Man all over again!" she wailed.

It occurred to her to ask the Auroras for help, but her pride refused.

"Why do you turn your back on me, Sun? I offer you the Earth and you *ignore* me??" she shrilled. But the Sun did not answer. She was incensed by his hubris. Not to be outshone by the Sun, the Fire Witch let out a banshee of a scream so fierce she radiated ultraviolet light which turned the oxygen around her into ozone, thumping her down, down, down to the top of the stratosphere where ozone is abundant. That put her much closer to the Earth.

Still not a word from the Sun.

The atmosphere's layers regarded this intruder disdainfully. She was negative energy. She was also responsible for much of the toxic junk they absorbed around the clock around the world. But the Fire Witch was a pro at reinventing herself and liked her new niche. If she couldn't wreak havoc on Earth, she'd use the Sky. No one turns down the Fire Witch! If the Sun wouldn't partner with her willingly, on his own, she would trick him into helping.

I'll poke holes in the ozone layer and the Sun's ultraviolet rays will char them dead! It was a brilliant strategy. A masterstroke. "Ha! The Witch Head Nebula will laud my ingenuity!" She knew it for certain.

FAREWELL, SATURN

C helsea's Arctic-White ears heard it first. *"I think the Fire Witch is in trouble!"* he sang.

"She turns trouble into opportunnity!" chanted Orion. *"She'll reinvennt hersellf! Counnt onn it. It's no seeecret!"*

Skylar had completely forgotten about Fire's Secret. This morning felt like eons ago. *"Orion, why did we come here?"* he sang euphorically, happier than he'd ever been.

"To bring gifts of ice to the Winnter Court! Saturnn and I have alwaays celebrated Winnter Solstice with each other annd Earrth. Now, do you know the Solstice Carol?" Orion chimed.

"I know 'A Christmas Carol' by Charles Dickens, my favorite author!"

"Ah, Dickens. Monoceros the Unicorn is his Guardiann

Constellation!" Orion chimed. *"Chelsea, teach himm the Solstice Carol! Off we go! Thannk youuu, Saturrrn!"* Orion sang, loping back to Earth on his well-worn stellar path.

"Good bye, Saturn!" Skylar sang with deep affection.

"Happy Winter Solstice, Childe o' the Skye!" Saturn warmly answered in his ancient dialect.

"Did you hear *THAT*? Saturn spoke to ME! What'd he mean, Childe of the Skye?" Skylar asked.

"He recognizes your understanding of the stars!" Chelsea answered. "Now repeat after me. Even Saturn knows this carol by heart: *O Roar, Aurora Borealis! Light our path unto the palace…"*

It was the most beautiful tune Skylar had ever heard. Sung in Horse, to boot! The poetry of the lyrics turned Skylar's thoughts to Lily and he memorized the music of space in space. He felt one of those fleeting moments of eternity, when joy bursts inside so big that one's awareness effortlessly slips into a bliss rarely glimpsed. He wondered what and where this good feeling-place is and how he could stay there, live in it forever. He knew it had to do with gratitude, and he had never been more grateful or more open in his entire life than right now.

INSIDE THE CASTLE OF THE SEASONS

As reunions go, the Castle of the Seasons had never witnessed one like it: tears, looks of stunned recognition, long lost kisses and never-let-go father and son hugs were exchanged. Cerulean and his father walked arm in arm sharing each other's trials as they awaited the return of the real Queen Crystalline at any moment. The hush in the usually high-spirited Throne Room was at last broken by wind chimes and bells as the ornate ice doors opened.

Lily, still in costume as the Queen, entered, followed by Jack Frost and Viggo, escorting a large sparkling cloud. The Mist floated and fluffed herself regally down the aisle, glistening effervescently. How she had dreamed of and waited for this moment. The entourage stopped in front of the Winter King and

Prince.

"Your Majesties," Jack Frost bowed, "We have reports that the Fire Witch was hurled into the Sky by a nauseous volcano she tried to poison. Her suicide arsonists have fallen, her Torches are unable to reignite without her. We thus proclaim Friendly Fire is re-establishing itself in all realms worldwide!"

A deafening cheer arose inside and out of the castle. The news spread like fire over the PNN as Friendly Fires came out of hiding by the trillions: candles, bonfires, lanterns, bar-b-ques, stoves, fireplaces, yule logs, all behaving in their proper place and happy to serve humanity again in peace.

As for me, I successfully consoled the victimized volcano and gathered its noxious spew from the air. Other winds joined in and helped me swirl it into pumice lumps and dump it where some humans we knew would make good use of the rich rock.

Inside the castle, Jack and Cerulean stared at each other, two best friends racked with guilt, eager to rekindle their friendship.

"My Prince, I let you down all those years ago. I failed in my duty. It's haunted me every single day," Jack tried to apologize.

"No Jack, it is I who let you down! Sir Windham told me how you've suffered, all because that night I wanted –"

"To help Lily" Jack answered. He presented a parcel to Cerulean and continued. "Now is a moment you can really help her. Only you can reverse the spell on your mother, since you were there in your cradle that night. In freeing her, so shall you free Lily."

The Prince stepped forward, receiving the parcel.

"Do not open this until I tell you," said Jack. He snapped his fingers in the air and music began, played by the Hot Toddy Teddy Bear Band, the Queen's Court Musicians. They played her favorite Winter Waltz and the Mist swayed to the beat. Viggo alighted on the King's shoulder as Jack spoke.

"The Fire Witch cast a double spell: she condensed the Queen to Mist and poisoned her mirror by showing it death and ugliness. My face is one of its victims, aged before its time. Mistress Lily freed the mirror only halfway, for mirrors also remember thoughts behind the eyes. Cerulean, unwrap the mirror and hold its face to the Mist."

Cerulean lifted the black cloth off the mirror's face and raised it into the sparkling cloud.

The Mist enveloped the mirror and Lily. Ice cold water started dripping down Cerulean's arm, for the mirror was crying. It had seen such horrors, such cruelty, and now the joy of seeing its mistress alive finally broke the spell. The Mist gazed into its reflection, at first hazy sparkles. Then slowly a beautiful woman's regal face appeared, Queen Crystalline. The Mist absorbed herself into Lily and spoke in the Queen's voice as Lily felt herself slip into a place of bodiless weightless limbo.

"I release you, Mistress Lily, from the lagoon's enchantment and welcome you, my friend and royal sister," said the Queen.

A glow radiated from the pompadour purse containing the medicinal herb mix Lily had prepared. The purse's ribboned drawstrings loosened magically, releasing its contents into the Mist.

">Fweezh'rahh, Hhehyü'hü/\ <Hhehyü'hü, fweezh'rahh/\"
Lily chanted in Wind. Upon hearing the ancient healing verse,
"To heal is to love and to love is to heal", the herbs' essences
poured out in a golden fog of healing balm. They channeled
energy to Lily as powerful magic set to work in separating her
from the Queen. Lily raised both her palms and turned them
inward toward her chest, summoning the heat her healing hands
radiated. The heat started melting the air's ice crystals into water
which attached to the Queen's face, arms and dress and quickly
iced into a living statue of Queen Crystalline.

Lily felt herself pulled backwards out of the Queen's body and
emerged bedecked in Winter's finest raiment. Her gown fluttered
and shimmered, fashioned in countless thin layers of finely
shaved ice, each hue subtly prismatic and reflective. Lily had
never seen or worn anything like it and its graceful flow made her
feel like an angel. And there on her wrist was her faithful pouch,
empty but glistening in frosty elegance.

Bells, chimes, gongs, trumpets and cheers heralded, *Hail
Queen Crystalline!! Hail Mistress Lily!!* The joyous sound
resonated out into the night beyond night out to the stars.

Tears of joy streaked the King's face as he passionately
embraced his dear wife, each kiss feeling like a dream.

Lily took in her surroundings. She wondered if Coco and
Darwina missed her and the Mist? The Mist was right: her lagoon
changes people, forever. Lily saw the Queen give the mirror to
Jack Frost who hesitated, then looked into it. Incredibly, his old
craggy face grew young again!

"Haa! I am restored!" cried Jack. "Look everyone! It's ME!

The me you know and I love!" Jack and the mirror were swarmed and cheered by adoring friends as Cerulean high-fived Jack in familiar camaraderie.

Cerulean and Lily saw no one but each other. He took her hand and led her up the steps to an ornate cushion and helped her kneel. A courtier handed the King a glittering multicolor tiara of gems shaped in the Four Seasons' symbols: a Snowflake, Flower, Sun and Maple Leaf.

The King crowned Lily saying, "Mistress Lily, for unconditional love, courage and botanic wisdom, in the name of the Kingdoms of Winter, Spring, Summer and Autumn we crown you *Healer For All Seasons*. Upon your marriage to Cerulean, you shall thence also be known as the Princess of Winter!" Lily and the King shared the happiest kind of smile, the smile of loving and being loved in return.

The Queen unlatched her Saturnalian ice necklace and placed it on Lily, kissing her lovingly on each cheek. Cerulean produced his silver flagon from which Lily drank so long ago and held it to her lips. She drank just one sip and her transformation was complete. She felt a toasty warm sensation envelop her and knew she would never feel cold again as her hair and eyebrows tinted to sparkling frost.

One last gift remained, in some ways the most special of all. Two Winter Courtiers approached, each bearing an ornate pillow made of Vicuña, the softest fabric on Earth from one of the most missed animals in all the Kingdoms of the Seasons. On one pillow was Darwina the Bark Spider, warmly bundled up in her finest silk. On the other pillow was Lily's silk-harp, newly winterized.

"Go ahead! Try it!" chirped Darwina, eager for Lily to hear it. For Darwina, this experience was mind blowing. No spider, let alone a Darwin Bark Spider from Madagascar, had ever been honored by Winter. She thought back to the scientist who set her free with his other laboratory animals when the floods came. She would've drowned, just like she would've back home when the Indian Ocean swallowed much of her island. *My life's been spared several times,* she thought to herself, *for this glorious moment!*

With newly frosted Hummingbird and Nightingale feathers, Lily lightly strummed the silk-harp's crystalized threads. The notes were brighter and much louder. Everyone, even humans, could now hear her play.

"Darwina! How on earth did you –?" Lily asked.

Darwina pointed to the Snow Ballroom doors. "We musicians stick together!" she replied.

Cerulean gave Lily his arm and led her into the Snow Ballroom followed by the courtiers carrying Darwina and the silk-harp. They approached Sammy, Conductor of Winter's famous Samoyed Swing Orchestra, who greeted them warmly.

"Mistress Lily, I take it you're pleased with your Winterized silk-harp?" Sammy bubbled merrily, as only a big fluffy white dog can.

"Indeed I am!" Lily replied.

"Our Winter Workshop makes the finest instruments in the world," Sammy bragged. "But never before have we seen a harp like this. The strength and sound of its strings, why it may start a musical revolution! Darwina, if you please?"

Darwina crawled onto the silk-harp now mounted on a pedestal in the orchestra's percussion section.

Cerulean whispered something to Sammy, who instantly lit up and announced to the thronging crowd, "In honor of Mistress Lily, the Prince commands a Volta! Your favorite and mine, *"My Borealis Beauty!"* The crowd went wild.

From any view, Sammy's Orchestra of Swingin' Samoyeds looked like rows of bouncing snow balls, each dog jamming freely in Siberian groove. Plucking and strumming thru it all, Darwina improvised to the band's delight. Musicians love new sounds and this one was a keeper!

Cerulean and Lily took to the ice and skated joyfully to oohs and ahs. The ice floor twinkled their reflection and gradually took on the colors of the Milky Way and Northern Lights above. On Cerulean's cue, thousands of Faerie couples joined them in the Volta. *Up!* went the ladies in swirls of gowns, lifted by their partners showing off their skills. Winter Faeries take pride in their ice dancing and after thousands of silent Seasons you can imagine all the pent up energy!

But then, as if a Volta wasn't enough, so everyone really knew Winter was here, the orchestra's alpine horn section sounded the intro to the *First Waltz of Winter!* We all stopped what we were doing. Even the smallest snowflake understood the gravity of the moment. This time honored tradition pulled us together in gratitude for what we shared and what made us who we were: Winter. For the first time in thousands of Seasons, we sang the *Solstice Carol* verse reserved for Solstice Night:

All hail, Orion! All hail, his Dogs
With ice from Saturn and spice yule logs!
All hail, Sir Windham! *Wh'hah-hee! Wh'hah-hoo!*
 Winter, Summer born anew!
All hail, Equator! We Seasons chime
You're who keeps us all in line!
All hail, the Sun's return to bring
And sing, ring the Kingdom of Spring!

O roar, Aurora Borealis!
Light our path unto the Palace!
Friends and loves who warm our hearts,
Raise a frosty chalice
To love for love is always in season,
Always the reason,
LET THE SEASON START!

Sammy cued a dazzling trumpet segue into the *First Waltz of Winter* and the King and Queen skated on to a thunderous roar of cheers.

"Wheee! How I've missed dancing with you!" laughed the Queen as the King lifted her high in a spin. Her gown billowed ice crystals into the air, each one popping into a sparkling sprite before our very eyes. It was as if they hadn't ever been apart. They didn't miss a step. They spoke nonstop and the King was most intrigued by her stories of how, as a Mist, she interacted with so many unusual beings from the other three Seasons.

"My love," said the King, "is there anything you want to tell me from that fateful night?"

"I remember I kissed Cerulean goodnight in his ice-cradle," she remembered wistfully. "Then I noticed it started to snow, and poof!"

"Your Solstice Kiss … it was to Cerulean! Of course! How often I've wondered how it started to snow that night without your traditional kiss to me. Now it all makes sense."

"My dear King, allow me to make up for it!" the Queen replied. She kissed him like she never kissed him before! Up went a merry cheer and down came snowflakes carved by Faeries in the ceiling. Lost in their kiss, the King and Queen skated past Cerulean and Lily, lost in memories of their own.

"I will seek you out every Solstice until I find you again," Cerulean whispered in Lily's ear.

"Your last words to me…" she whispered back, feeling her face against his. She cherished this moment as much as she did the first time. "I never forgot you. I learned to speak Star, made friends with the Mist, saw you in every living creature and every Solstice I kept watch with Orion. I knew you were alive, for your heart's light never faltered," Lily said lovingly, softly kissing his ear.

"Where did you keep me hidden all this time?" Cerulean

asked, caressing her face tenderly. She looked into his blue eyes and placed his hand on her heart.

"I sewed you into my dress here, over my heart."

They kissed, skating as if floating … until a hand touched Lily's shoulder.

The music stopped. Everyone froze. Who was this human woman breaking court protocol, interrupting the *First Waltz of Winter*? This was unheard of! Lily, intoxicated with Cerulean's sweet kiss, turned and stared into the woman's gentle face. She looked to be of fine Faerie lineage and was exquisitely dressed. A deep memory from long ago stirred in Lily. The woman took both of Lily's hands in hers.

"Lily, it is I, your mother, Gala," the woman said tenderly, knowing it would shock.

Lily was thunderstruck. *"… Mama?* But I thought you were … dead," she uttered in disbelief.

"And I thought the same of you," Gala replied. "It was the Kingdom of Autumn's Red Maple Guard who found me in the forest, lost and distraught, searching for you, my sweet new born baby. Kir had shown me a blood stained baby shirt. She said you'd been taken in the night. I was out of my mind with grief! I've no idea how long I was in the woods, but the Red Maple Guard gave me shelter and brought me here. And ever since, I have been Mistress of Ceremonies here at the Castle of the Seasons. I never knew you were alive until tonight. Welcome, my dearest darling daughter."

Lily brimmed with joyful tears and held her mother for a very long time. Then she felt another hand on her shoulder. It gripped her firmly and would not let go.

"Lilykinlichen?" the old man's voice lilted.

Lily's heart leapt. She'd know that voice anywhere! *"Zhu Zhu??* Grandpapa!" She buried her face in his fuzzy white beard bursting with joy. Through tears of joy, Zhu Zhu saw his dear old friend, the King, skate up to them.

"Sire, you kept your promise. You returned my *Lilykinlichen* to me!" Zhu Zhu beamed. "And your rime rum has me feeling like a young man again!"

"It's one promise that sure took its time!" the King mused.

"Which makes its keeping all the more sweet," replied Zhu Zhu.

Gala, Lily and Zhu Zhu swayed in a huddle hug in the middle of the dance floor. Cerulean cued the music to resume and wrapped his arms around Lily's family, looking up and smiling broadly, his eyes closed. Then the King and Queen joined them, wrapping their arms around the group. The two reunited families, soon to be one family, danced in a merry huddle, feeling the love, strength and courage each had endured to live into this dream come true.

THE WITCH HEAD NEBULA

O rion's left foot entered the Earth's atmosphere first. Generally this was friendly and effortless. Constellations constantly went to and fro through the North and South Poles, but Orion felt a new energy in the mix and couldn't resist putting the Fire Witch in her place.

She flew at him the minute she felt his big toe dip into her ozone layer. But she had not expected the boy and the horse. Orion sprinkled her with shavings of Saturnalian Ice which frosted her so severely her energy morphed and destabilized her even further.

"You big bully!" she blustered in confused gassiness.

And then she did it, the taboo of taboos: she insulted the Sky. "Don't you dare look down on me, Sky! That's all you Skies do, look down on Earth! Yet they all look up to you – but do *you* ever look up? Do you know what's on the other side of you? Huh? I do! It's where I'm going! And when I'm through with all of you, you'll *have* to look up: to ME, Queen of the Universe!" her ego shrilled, convinced her big thinking would threaten. But no one thinks bigger than the Sky. And it knew its Multiverse neighbors on the "other side" were peaceful companions in eternity. The Sky reacted the way any Universe would: it relied on its Constellations to take care of business.

In Orion's left foot is the Blue Super Giant Rigel, the bright star illuminating the blue Witch Head Nebula, a vast cluster of young stars. As soon as Orion's foot landed in the atmosphere, the Nebula's Supreme Witch Counsel tuned in and heard the Fire Witch's diatribe, aimed at Skylar:

"You, boy! We had a deal! Now I'll never tell you or anyone the Secret of Fire!" she shrieked.

Orion quietly signaled Skylar, "*Shhhhhhhh…!*"

"I was tricked! Earth was nearly mine! But the shifty Wind shifted! Just when I needed him most! Winnnnd-hammmm, I will have my revenge!!" she thundered, rippling the atmosphere. "*YOU,* boy, and your horse delayed me so the Prince could unite his heart and soul! *YOU*, Orion, shot your arrows – and missed both times! Ha ha! And *YOU!*" she screeched at the Sun. "You are my sworn enemy! You turned your back on me, now I turn mine on you! I'll show the Witch Head Nebula who's the greatest Witch of all!"

This was too, too much and three Star Witches in the Nebula piped up immediately.

"Young lady, mind your manners!" Star Witch #1 sang.

"Do be still, you'll wake the babies! We're a stellar nursery, after all!" sang Star Witch #2.

"What do you take us for? We're <u>good</u> witches, Star Witches!" sang Star Witch #3.

"The Sun didn't turn its back on you: it <u>never</u> <u>heard</u> <u>you</u>! In fact, it's never heard a single word you've said!!" crooned Star Witch #2.

"WHAT?" the Fire Witch asked huskily, flabbergasted, mortified. She knew only one thing burns hotter than fire: Truth. It seared her inside and out.

"All because of your Seee-cret!" Star Witch #3 teased.

"Which is no Seee-cret at all!" chimed Star Witch #1 mischievously.

"No! No! No! No Secret at all!" the three Star Witches blended in hip rhythm and harmony.

"NO!! Stop!" the Fire Witch barked, scorching her throat, covering her ears, refusing to hear anymore.

But the Trio was joined by Orion singing bass, making a perfect stellar quartet:

Lucky for Earth you can't evolve
Beyond the flaw you can't resolve:
In every land the thing you banned
Would've given you full command!
Your snap-crackle-pop cannot offend:
'Tis noise the Sun can't comprehend!

The crescendo that followed holds the record as *Loudest Musical Moment Above Earth.* In one fateful chorus they blew the lid off what holds the record as *The Most Obvious Thing in the World:*

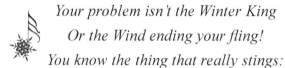

> *Your problem isn't the Winter King*
> *Or the Wind ending your fling!*
> *You know the thing that really stings:*
> *You cannot swing, or ding-a-dong-ding,*
> *Or play like a string, a babbling spring,*
> *A crystal ting, a sonar ping, a bell's ring!*
> *No, your Secret is, the problem is and always was*

FIRE CAN'T SING!

It echoed throughout the Universe. The most far flung Galaxies heard it and nodded for they, too, had un-evolved beings wreaking havoc. In fact, it was a Universal Problem.

For a fleeting instant, awareness sickened her: *Every being on Earth, even the crazy Wind, can hum, howl, buzz, chirp, purr, neigh, sing! Hissing doesn't count and I've always resented it!*

"*But we can teach you!*" eagerly chimed Star Witch #1, reading the Fire Witch's thoughts.

This jangled the Fire Witch. Her mind cracked open. The intimacy of it threw her, scared her, for never ever had *anyone* read Fire's thoughts. But rather than rise to the magic of the moment, her ego and anger robbed her of her shining opportunity and slammed her mind shut.

"*YOU* teach *ME*?!" the Fire Witch roared. "Everything I burn, I learn! I AM OMNISCIENT! For everything burns, even you stars! And I shall outlive you all!!"

With supreme, ferocious bravura, she flexed her being, now so massive that she lit night skies high above Earth with an eerie glow. She made up her mind: "This time you've gone too far! I'll show you!" she flared. Summoning her last reserves of fire power, she hurled herself wildly at Earth below shrilling, "*Phaaaetonnn's Faaate!*" As she fell away from them, her voice trailed off in fateful paradox, for she'd begun singing and hadn't even noticed – or had she?

Orion gasped at the sheer audacity of it all. Was this the last stop for the unstoppable Fire Witch? For a moment everyone held their breath, listening. In the far distance a slightly muffled crackle was heard, then silence. The Constellations stopped singing, riveted in suspense; both Auroras held back their ribbons of light, wondering what might happen next. Time, however, ticked on, tickled by the spectacle, for the Fire Witch had chosen very bad timing: the first day of Winter.

It was an ironic comeback on the atmosphere's part, for the

Fire Witch impaled herself atop Earth's frigid troposphere, the master weather-maker and vapor storehouse. She literally turned to ice. Yes! Fire froze. Unwittingly she returned to her original state as a Daughter of Winter. To this day, Fire Rainbows (or *circumhorizontal arcs* for all you meteorologists!) can be seen when the Sun refracts her ice crystals in cirrus clouds.

It was over. For now. He whom she served was still out there.

The Constellations burst into song; the Auroras fanned their colors; the Witch Head Nebula returned to tending their baby stars. But most dramatic of all was the reaction of Earth's troposphere. Caught off guard by the Fire Witch's crash landing, it did what came naturally when it sensed a pollutant: it cleaned house. Its team of *don't-bring-dirt-into-my-house!* neat freak hydroxyl radicals kicked into atmosphere self-cleaning mode. An army of gazillions, they were so hyper they even shined Orion's giant sandal and buffed his toenails!

"Here's to you, Orion! Well done!" saluted Captain Droxy, the radicals' gruff rebellious commandant.

"Hi, Droxy! Oooh! Haa haa!" giggled Orion. (Who could've guessed our cosmic warrior has ticklish feet?) He then dipped his right foot into the atmosphere and it, too, got the equivalent of a cosmic pedicure.

"The more toxic junk the Fire Witch spewed into the Sky, the more impossible our job became. Some witch she was – we're the ones with the brooms, cleaning up after her! But too much of a good thing, I mean us, and well, you know: ozone overdose. She may be gone but *he's* still down there on Earth," Captain Droxy warned. "But today we celebrate! With the Sun's help, we'll get on top of this mess, scrub the air clean … perhaps a return to Olde Skye blue, hum?"

The reaction was astronomical! Every star in the Sky twinkled for blue was, and still is, the Sky's favorite color.

"Wee leavve it inn yourr raadical hannds, Droxy!" chimed Orion.

In a single loping bound, Orion stepped out of the atmosphere down onto the Faerie Highway Crossroads where the gritty, grimy black iron works stood alone.

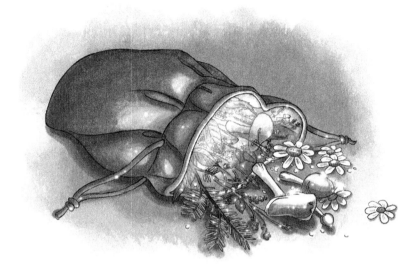

AT THE IRON WORKS

A supersize white footprint crunched the snow, jolting the chimney's dying coil of smoke.

Orion sang, *"Onne laast taask: dismaantle herrr shrinnne to Unfriennndly Fiiire and rre-openn the Faerrie Hiighwaay Crossrrroads to the Fourrr Seasonns!"*

A whirling dervish of snow arose in the moonlit distance. I soon engulfed them. "Waaait forrr meee!" I howled merrily.

Skylar recognized my voice. "Happy Solstice, Sir Windham!" he shouted joyfully.

"Happy Solstice to youuu!" I chortled.

I gave Orion a congratulatory slap on his stellar back. Have you ever heard the sound of Wind hitting a Constellation? Few have. Orion's weightless vacuum is a vast echo chamber, so when my airborne particles ricocheted off his stars and clusters, they vibrated pitches high and low, stacking one on top of the other until a massive vibrational tone cluster tickled Orion silly. He laughed in loud heavenly harmony!

"Wind Chill!!" oohed Orion. *"That's whaat I'll call this new muusic for Winnter Solllstice!"*

"Ha! Ha!!" I laughed. I knew how to get a rise out of my superstar friend. But, as merry as we were, we all remembered the serious unfinished business at hand.

"I'll stannd guarrd while you three cleann house," chanted Orion, poised directly over the iron works. *"The Firre Witch may have beenn destroyed, but unntil her headquarters arre demolished, anythinng cann happenn."* Fire's element of surprise always irritated Orion. He stood firmly, bow and arrow at the ready. I slowly blew open the heavy, whiny iron door. It seemed to moan at the effort, though I was doing all the work.

Skylar, Chelsea and I entered the iron works cautiously. The curling wisp of blue chimney smoke outside meant someone was inside. I wafted into the room, scouting ahead and saw them first, an old man and a middle aged woman, both with sunken ash-grey features and forbidding black eyes, the kind you're afraid to look into. I recognized them at once, as I never forget any person's vibration. The man grabbed his gun, but its metal was so cold it burned his hands and he dropped it in pain.

"Who are ya'? Whaddya want? We don't got no food!" Papa shouted defensively.

This caused a coughing fit so violent that he fell onto his hands and knees coughing up black liquid clumps from his lungs.

Skylar and I saw Chelsea bristle in revulsion, laying flat his huge white ears and showing the whites of his eyes. He snorted and reared onto his haunches. I smelled rage erupt hotly in Chelsea and quickly wrapped the horse in a powerful, calming wind hug. "My friend, they cannot hurt you now or ever again," I gently whispered. Skylar, too, laid a calming hand on his friend, realizing who these people were: Chelsea's torturers. At the same time, the man and woman, upon seeing the horse, exchanged a glance of alarmed recognition.

"The Fire Witch is dead. This building is condemned. Pack up your things!" Skylar ordered.

The woman, a badly aged Kir, raised her head in wonder at his voice.

"Lovely…" she whispered. "Lovely! … I've not seen a young man – ever! That old witch only let old men work here, afraid I'd run off with a young one! I would have! … Are you *real?"* She lifted her shriveled hands as if to touch a vision. "Or another trick of that hag?" she rasped the words hopelessly, as if she'd been tricked out of her voice as well as her dreams.

Skylar approached her and could see she had once been pretty, but never beautiful. Her eyes told all: envy and grinding resentment seethed behind her soul's two dark, shuttered windows.

"They're not budging. What should we do?" Skylar asked me in Wind.

"What'd you say?" the woman yelled, as if stricken. "I know that language! You're speaking her language! That gobbledy-gook of my insane little sister! *Who are you?* This is all her fault!

She-!" Papa viciously slapped Kir down and yanked her hair.

"Shut up, you stupid girl! She got away – we didn't! She tried to tell me, but I listened to *you*, the *pretty* one. The stupid, selfish one! *Do it daddy, do it!"* he mimicked, gruffly shoving her. "You got no one to blame but yourself and you know it! Day in and day out we swallowed the Fire Witch's lies! For a while she kept you young and pretty, like you'd find a husband; and me, strong and fit, like I'd get money and respect runnin' her damn iron works. A pack o' lies, ALL of it! All to keep her evil empire burnin'!" Papa spat bitterly. "I knew it was over when it started snowin'! You gonna' be mean to the end?" he asked her disgustedly.

Kir began to breathe with difficulty. "All these years of smoke and smelt! I was the prettiest girl in the whole world," she sang in a deranged lilt, adoring herself in her cracked wall mirror.

"How d'you know? You never left the forest!" Papa stung her with the Fire Witch's words.

Kir turned to Skylar, donning traits of the Fire Witch, a frightening transformation. "Is she alive, my little sister?" she eerily inquired, suspecting the answer.

Chelsea neighed, *"Don't answer!"*

But Skylar felt pity for the wretched woman. "Who is your sister?" he asked gently. She appreciated the kindness in his voice. It was new to her. It was music she thought she'd never hear.

"Lily. *Lilykinlichen*, grandpa used to call her. He never gave me a pet name!" she snapped.

"You mocked them every chance you got! Her imaginary friends, her mud mix, his talkin' animals, a hidden castle – Zhu

Zhu was a lunatic just like your mother!" Papa spat again.

Skylar was stunned speechless. He hadn't ever thought of Lily's family.

Kir feebly walked to a chest and opened a drawer. "No. Not lunatics. Zhu Zhu favored Lily because she had The Gift. She could speak gobbledy – no, *Faerie*. If she were here now she'd probably talk to your horse instead of you," she wryly smiled, showing broken black teeth.

"How dare she look me in the eye?" Chelsea grimaced, still tightly held in my airy embrace.

Kir laid a small tin box on the table and opened it. Inside was an old leather pouch which looked shiny, new and supple. She untied it and poured the contents on the table. I recognized the magical herbs and seeds, as did Chelsea, for their fresh fragrances filled the air.

She sat down with difficulty, but something in her burned and she spoke deliberately. "The night Lily ran away she clutched something glowing in her hand. I knew it was magical, from one of her invisible friends. When she struggled with Papa she dropped her pouch, the one thing she always kept with her. When no one was looking I grabbed it off the floor and hid it. Years later I opened it and discovered these were no ordinary herbs and seeds: they never aged and were always fragrant. See how the leather is so supple and shiny? Her little 'medicine chest' heals itself as well as others! I started searching the woods to find more seeds and herbs like these. I tried talking to the Faeries, asking the trees, the animals, the sky, but no one would answer me.

"You see, I did believe Lily and Zhu Zhu. Because when

Lily was born, Mama sang her a Faerie lullaby. Only minutes old, Lily sang back to her, in Faerie! I hated them both for being half-Faerie! So that night I hid Lily in the woods. I told mama the next morning that wild animals got her. I even produced a shredded baby shirt with my own blood on it. Mama, she went wild with grief and ran into the forest to find Lily. But I brought Lily back to our cabin immediately. *'Look! I found her!'* I told Papa and Zhu Zhu. We all waited, but Mama never returned. *'Dead,'* Papa told me. *'I know she died ... of a broken heart.'*

"I just wanted to stay mama's favorite!" Kir continued. "When Lily sang that faerie lullaby, she took my place. I didn't mean for it all to go so horribly wrong, Papa!*"*

"*...You??* All this time you ...?" Papa stared wide eyed in horror his daughter. "I always wondered why the Fire Witch asked me <u>twice</u> if I was giving her the right girl ..."

Kir withered into a shriveled old woman before our eyes. It happened so fast, it seemed she could die at any minute. She sifted the herbs and seeds in her gnarly hands.

"Nature saw what I had done – it always does – and it shut me out. The hatred in me isn't for Lily. It isn't for mama or you, Papa...or the Witch. It's for myself. I killed them both, mama and Lily, then slowly killed you and me rotting in this god forsaken place," she wearily confessed her wasted life.

I cut the thick air. "Should she know the truth before she dies?" I whispered to Chelsea and Skylar.

"What harm can it, do?" Chelsea replied, finding forgiveness felt better than revenge.

"Skylar, tell her that Lily, Zhu Zhu and her mother live in the

Kingdom of Winter," I said.

Skylar's heart skipped a beat hearing that Lily was alive and that she was a Faerie just as he had surmised. "Madam, may I give you some peace in knowing that Lily, Zhu Zhu and your mother are alive. They dwell in the Kingdom of Winter, a Faerie realm."

Kir and Papa were stupefied. Their eyes betrayed a flood of feelings: relief, jealousy, accusation, regret. Papa was the first to turn to coal. It happened so fast we could barely recall what he looked like. He tipped forward and his head broke off, rolling into the fire grate.

Kir could hardly speak, she was now so old her voice wobbled. "The Fire Witch threatened us that bad people turn into coal. But I knew better. Only bad *Faeries* turn into coal. We … were … ve-ry bad Faeries, and people. The magic was in us all along! It's in *you* … and *you*!" she pointed her old boney finger to Skylar and Chelsea. "But you won't find it unless you *believe* it – *in here*."

She hit her chest hard as if to punish herself. "The magic is never, ever *out there!*" she coughed, gesturing with her hands.

Kir reached into the pouch and pulled out a shredded baby shirt with dark brown stains on it. She held it up to Skylar wordlessly then stuffed it in the pouch with the herbs and seeds. "The pouch is hers. Tell her, *'Lilykin, sister, forgive me.'*"

The old woman closed her eyes, shuddered and turned to coal in her chair. She teetered for a moment then fell, cracking into several pieces. Skylar put the pouch in his vest where he had carried Cerulean. The three of us gratefully returned to the fresh night air, breathing deeply to cleanse ourselves of what we had just witnessed.

Orion wasted not a moment. *"Let 'emm go! They have their Guardiann Constelllations helllping themm noww!"* he chanted. *"All aboard – we've a Solllstice Balll to get tooo!"*

Skylar and Chelsea stepped into Orion's giant sandaled foot and floated in weightless space. They looked up and saw Orion open his jam packed satchel of Saturnalian Ice.

"But firrst, thiss shoulld doo the trrick!" Orion chanted like a stellar shaman as he plunked down a towering chunk of Saturnalian ice squarely atop the iron works. It super-froze the structure on impact and disintegrated it into trillions of crystals. Then I sucked in deeply, made a swirling crystal funnel and gusted with all my might, scattering the residue for miles in every direction.

"Thaat felllt gooood!" I exhaled with release and relief.

Orion then shaved the ice chunk over the naked scorched ground in a miniature snow fall.

"To heall the Earrth from a painnful burrn," he chimed tenderly. The site steamed at first as the ice hit the superheated ground, then it slowly blended perfectly into its snowy surroundings. *"The Grreat Faerrie Crossrroads is restorred!"* Orion caroled to the Sky.

Skylar saw the heavens twinkle in response. The Great 88 heard Orion's historic announcement, assured of their astronomical duties for Winter above and Summer below. I took off in a gleeful gale. "Seee youuuu therrre!"

Skylar and Chelsea floated up onto Orion's belt. The deaths of

Kir and Papa left Skylar uneasy, stirring memories of his mother's death. It made him wonder, *What if mom actually became a star when she died?* He decided to ask Chelsea, knowing Orion would hear.

"Chelsea, what happens to Faeries when they die?" Skylar asked.

"We don't die, we just keep changing form into other natural essences," Chelsea replied.

"You mean you can turn even into stars?" Skylar asked.

"Evennn innntoo starrrs!" chimed Orion.

"Can humans become stars, too? My mom died last year," Skylar said. "What if her soul is in space, like right here in Orion?"

"For us, the life and death cycles of humans is knowable only to but a few Faeries … our mediums, the *Autumn Mystics.*" Chelsea said. "Unless a human drinks one of our elixirs and becomes at least half-Faerie, I'm afraid they are mortal. But what happens to their souls, therein lies magic beyond what any of us know."

"So it's possible? I mean, she could maybe possibly actually like – be here? Floating somewhere around us? And see me?" Skylar desperately hoped.

"Humann soulss go wherre theyy belieeve they'lll go whenn theyy leavve theirr morrtal bodyy. Yourr motherrr's Guarrrdiann Connstelllationn wass Cassiopeiaa," rang Orion. *"Yet yourr motherr isn't there, for she didnn't knoww Cassiopeiaa, or me … but shee knew youu, annd is innsiide yourr hearrt and parrt of the myssterry of the Unniverrse."*

The mystery of the Universe, Skylar thought to himself. On a deep level he knew that whatever place he imagined his mom being, she was ok and would share his life forever in his heart … and, for now, he would keep believing his mom could very possibly be a star … a fabulous blue-giant star watching over him, for blue was her favorite color, too.

"Holld onn! Herrre wee go!" Orion chimed.

Skylar and Chelsea swayed in Orion's sweeping right turn, landing them squarely at the doors of the Castle of the Seasons, which appeared before their very eyes.

FOUR LIVING LEGENDS

Major and Minor, were waiting at the doors of the castle. They barked and wagged their starlit tails at seeing their master arrive. Skylar had never heard dogs bark musically, and true to their names, they barked in celestial major and minor tonalities, vibrating the castle's Stellar Portal, a special entrance for Constellations and Winds. Viggo Vespa was next to greet us, flying headlong into my breeze, heralding the arrival of Winter's *Four Living Legends*.

Viggo landed on Chelsea's head, right between his ears, chirping, "Old friend! Wonder of wonders! Make for the doors so all may see you!" Chelsea took his place just inside the vestibule, whereupon tens of thousands of faeries strained to get their first glimpse of history in the making.

"Announcing Sir Chelsea, Champion Arctic-White of the Royal Stables! Sir Windham the North Wind! Master Skylar, the Bravest Boy on Earth! And His Stellar Eminence, Orion the Hunter!" Viggo Vespa announced, his voice carrying brightly on my currents.

The orchestra trumpeted us with regal fanfares as we four friends heard the thunderous cheers and applause of the Solstice Snow Ball guests. Skylar took it all in: the spectacular snowflake castle, the music, the starlit ambiance, the Faeries. "Huh? I can see them! And hear them!" he realized excitedly. He breathed in holiday aromas of pine, cinnamon and spice.

"Look where I am now! Look!" Skylar told himself. And look what he was, a hero! He had helped save the Kingdom of Winter. Who could've ever imagined that? He wondered if old Kir was right and if he had The Gift all along and just never knew it? Did that mean all humans have The Gift and don't know it? And if so, what awakens it?

Now for us Winds, there's an extraordinary naturally occurring phenomenon that happens only inside the Castle of the Seasons: Wind is visible. Skylar had never *seen* me, only heard and felt me.

"The Wind is a handsome fellow!" Skylar mused to Chelsea, as he watched me grandly sashay down the aisle, blowing caps off lads and rustling girls' curls and feathered fascinators.

Skylar felt a change in air pressure, turned and saw the gravity-defying moment: Orion squeezed himself through the Stellar Portal, shrinking from colossal multi-dimensions into 3-D Earth size. Skylar remembered from physics class how stars and black holes collapse. "Of course a Constellation can collapse! I wonder how he does it?" he asked himself in awe.

Orion was, without question, the most magnificent being Skylar had ever seen. And I would have to agree with him. Against the crystal and white of the Castle, Orion's midnight blue figure was theatrical and epic. He was studded with pulsating stars of every color: red giants, yellow dwarfs, blue super-giants, orange-green nebulae, pink clusters, white-dwarfs, purple-rose spiral galaxies. The sight took everyone's breath away, even mine. And Orion knew it.

He sang a call to his dogs, "*Major! Minor!*" each in the right tonality, of course. Both dogs came bounding in, also shrunk to midnight blue, star-studded magnificence. Each let out excited musical barks like puppies let out to play and getting treats.

"Orion's dogs give *Best In Show* a whole new meaning!" Skylar mused to himself.

Chelsea received the lion's share of adulation. Faeries strewed frosted pine garlands around his neck and magically wove ornaments into his tail and mane as he majestically strode past them. Jingle bells were fastened on his four massive hooves and Viggo rested squarely atop Chelsea's head, proudly holding on with his bat wings stretched ear-to-ear.

All at once, Skylar realized his black Dickensian clothes and top hat were gone. He was now wearing ornate, white fur-lined attire reserved for the highest nobility – Winter 'fur' being the softest, and rarest, spun ice. He wore a baronial sash of white peacock feathers flecked with gold faerie dust. Something hit his thigh as he walked. It was a full length carved sword in an ornate crystal scabbard hewn in Saturnalian ice, he knew, for he recognized the embedded rich blues from Saturn. He laid his hand on it and he felt the sword tingle in reply. He momentarily froze. "Will I ever get used to talking horses and sentient swords?" he asked himself. The sword tingled again. He smiled in amused wonder.

But the main thing Skylar searched for he couldn't find: Lily. He wasn't sure where to look, but he knew she had to be here. "Somehow I'll find her," he assured himself. His heart raced at the thought.

The Procession of Heroes wound its way through the Snow Ballroom up into the Throne Room. At last, in the distance, Skylar's search ended, though not the way he expected. Prince Cerulean was first to greet him, rushing to Skylar and embracing him in joy. It was a shocking moment of discovery: Skylar took in the Prince's handsome features and strong bearing. He'd only known Cerulean as a floating starball of luminescent gas.

"Skylar! Bravo! I name you the Prince's Champion of Winter Solstice! Here he is, everyone! The brave Knight who rescued me!" shouted Cerulean.

Cheers resounded and Skylar felt his throat and chest tingle. Praise was a new feeling and he liked it. Several ladies, young and old alike, fainted from the overwhelming sight of so many Winter luminaries in one place. Cerulean, Lily and Skylar were overnight stars, the new teen idols of Faerie maidens and lads everywhere. Not only had their courage and wit set them apart, they were the faces of hope for a young generation inheriting a badly injured Earth.

Ballads and epic poems were already being written and new recipes named and cooked, for the highest Faerie honors come through music, poetry and food: *Lily Chili, Skylar Skillet Scones, Prince Praline Pretzels and Chelsea Cheese Chews* still top the *FFF List (Favorite Faerie Foods).* Also popular to this day are *Crystalline Eggs in the Snow*, Winter Wings* and *Arctic Ale.* Faeries love their after dinner sweets and cordials when gathered 'round the fire telling Faerie Tales. But it's after Faerie Tales when the old timers really cut loose and break out their thousand year old flagons of *Borealis Brandy* and *Wind Wine!*

(*Meringue custard floating in vanilla cream!)

A MAN FOR ALL SEASONS

"C 'mon! I want you to meet the brave knight who saved my life," Cerulean said, grabbing Lily's hand, leading her down the steps. Skylar and Lily locked eyes as they walked toward each other.

"*You??* You're who saved my beloved Cerulean?" Lily beamed with joyful eyes.

"You two have met?" Cerulean asked in surprise.

Skylar's heart sank at Lily's words *beloved Cerulean.* "Your Highness," he replied, bowing slightly and fighting disappointment's burn in his eyes and cheeks, "just days ago I wandered to a black lagoon and found myself trapped in a thicket of brambles in a very heavy mist. You could say Mistress Lily rescued me with delicious food – she's a really good cook!"

"Skylar, brace yourself – the Mist was my mother," Cerulean said, indicating the Queen who joined them.

Skylar had not anticipated this twist at all. "Your M-Majesty?" he asked the Queen, dumbfounded. *"You* are, uh were, the – the Mist?"

The Queen took his hands in hers, as a mother would her own son's. "Yes. I affixed those ice-crystals around your ankle when I tasted our ancient water on you," she said warmly. "I recognized one of our own and had to send a message of hope. It is our tradition. All water is kin, no matter the color, mineral content, source. Snow or tea kettle's steam, salty sea or mud puddle or fog or swimming pool, we're all the same and remind each other of our common heritage."

Cerulean added, "No one's ever honored a puddle as you have, my friend!"

"Nor fled a forest with such agility!" the Queen teased. "I hope you didn't mind my egging you on – I wanted to see what you were made of." She smiled with a hint of mischief.

"As did I, your Majesty," Skylar agreed in good humor. He paused, then turned. "Lily, I bring you a token from your past." He reached into his top coat and found the leather pouch, curiously in the same pocket he'd placed it in his old black vest. He handed it to Lily, now joined by Gala and Zhu Zhu.

"Skylar, I'd like you to meet my mother, Lady Gala, and my grandpapa, Zhu Zhu," Lily said.

"At your service," Skylar bowed to them, noticing they bore no resemblance whatsoever to Kir or Papa. Each radiated warmth and love with that twinkle in the eye of those who've who lived

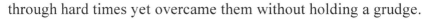

through hard times yet overcame them without holding a grudge.

Lily handled her old pouch with a forgotten familiarity as childhood memories flooded her mind.

"I remember that pouch," said the King. "You had it the night we found you."

The Throne Room fell quiet and Lily, inspecting the pouch, looked inquiringly at Skylar.

"From your sister Kir, who kept it all these years. She and your father operated the iron works. When the Fire Witch was defeated, they aged suddenly and horribly, turning to coal before our very eyes," said Skylar.

"Coal?" asked Cerulean.

"They had Faerie blood?" asked the Queen.

"Open the pouch, go on," I puffed to Lily.

"Kir said to tell you, *Lilykin, sister, forgive me,*" said Skylar.

"She said *Lilykin*?" Zhu Zhu gasped.

Lily poured some herbs and seeds onto her palm. As soon as they touched her hand they turned into fluttering Summer Faeries, who, feeling the cold, instantly frosted themselves into Winter Faeries. Hundreds upon hundreds of glittering magical beings flitted around us gaily as she poured out the entire contents.

"I remember gathering these for you, grandpa, to make your herbal tea," Lily recalled, enchanted by the airy sound of the glittering sylphs' flutters.

"There's something more in there," urged Skylar.

Lily felt inside the pouch and pulled out the blood stained shirt. Lily's mother let out a cry.

"*Huh?* Your baby shirt! That's what Kir showed me when she

said wild animals got you!" Gala exclaimed. She was overcome and began shaking with sobs as Queen Crystalline held her in that comforting universal embrace unique between mothers.

"I see we have many stories to share, happy and sad," said the King. "It's a good thing this is the longest night of the year – we'll need it! But first, some important Solstice business. Orion, my ancient friend, thank you for bringing us Saturn's greetings and much needed stellar ice. We shall deposit it at the Winter Palace for long overdue repairs and revitalize our permafrost at Summer Solstice.

Orion beamed. *"A happy and healthy Winter Solstice, your Majesty! The Great 88 join me in singing galaxies of joy at the return of the Prince, the Queen, Chelsea and you, dear Winter!"* Orion bowed deeply and as he did so winked at Lily, just as he had before from the sky. She felt herself blush hotly and her hands flew to her cheeks. She tried gracefully to recover as she recalled floating in the lagoon staring at Orion and the night sky – was that really only a few hours ago?

"Sir Windham!" the King declared. "What reward can I give you? What can match your acumen, your loyalty, your bravery, dear friend? Ask anything, and it is yours."

I didn't have to think about this. I knew right away. "Your Majesty, my Queen, there is one thing … I should like very much to visit … well, your mirror," I softly, timidly requested.

"Why Windham, but of course!" the Queen answered. "Bring my mirror to the Wind!" she commanded.

Jack Frost carried the mirror, holding its face out to all. It reflected thousands of beautiful shining souls. Jack raised the mirror to where I hovered, where everyone could see me, but me! A lovely hushed intake of air wafted through the room as I caressed the mirror and beheld my billowing self. I was most taken by my size – and this mirror somehow captured most of me! I promised myself to remember that moment always, and I have.

"I give you, Sir Windham, my mirror as a token of my heartfelt gratitude. You never gave up searching for me, you pursued every rumor I started, and then never gave away my misty identity once you discovered me ... though you did blow me to bits a few times!" the Queen laughed.

"To maintain your anonymity, your Majesty, I assure you!" I gusted.

The King lovingly turned to his magnificent horse. "My faithful Chelsea, you are hereby restored to your legendary and rightful place as King's Stallion, the King beamed, feeding Chelsea his favorite cinnamon iced-apple treats.

Chelsea gave several loud snorts which erupted into a jubilant neigh as he reared on his back legs, hoisting his front legs high into the air. The mighty horse turned slowly in a complete circle, something which had always delighted the King. He neighed twice, shook his ornamented mane and roused a deafening applause. He gracefully landed his two front legs then, turning to Skylar, regally lowered himself in a deep equine bow. Chelsea held the bow until Skylar whispered something in his ear, and both ears twittered back and forth playfully. The horse rose and nuzzled Skylar's face.

"And you, brave Master Skylar, approach," commanded the King who unsheathed his ice sword, *Hibernal,* as Skylar knelt on a white cushion. "Skylar, Son of Spring, you have been deemed fit for this high estate by Earth and Stars. Do you now swear by all that you hold sacred, true, and holy that you will honor and defend the Winter Crown and the Kingdoms of the Seasons?"

"I will," Skylar answered.

"Do you swear that you will conduct yourself in all matters as befits a Knight of the Seasons, drawing your sword only for just cause? That you will enshrine in your heart the noble ideals of Winter, Spring, Summer and Autumn to the benefit of Earth and her inhabitants?"

"I will," Skylar answered.

"Then having sworn these solemn oaths, know now that We, the King, Queen and Prince of Winter by right of Winter Water do dub you with Our sword, *Hibernal,* and by all that you hold sacred, true, and holy ... Once for Honor ... Twice for Duty ... Thrice for Chivalry …"

As the King, Queen and Prince laid *Hibernal* on Skylar's shoulders, he felt extraordinary sensations suffuse his body.

"Arise, Sir Skylar!" declared the King.

Skylar stood as Cerulean produced a silver flagon and the Queen produced a Constellation Crown and Constellation Chain with 88 midnight-blue charms, each twinkling with life, each in the shape of its namesake. The King produced the most incredible saddle Skylar had ever seen: woven crystalice with embedded Winter etchings.

The King smiled warmly. "We offer you, Sir Skylar, life in our realms, in the Royal Households of the Four Seasons."

Skylar breathed in disbelief, his breath forming a cloud that hung in the air, for it was sub-sub-sub-zero in the castle.

"Two sips from Cerulean's flagon and you shall become one of us, as has our Lily," said the King.

"One sip this night; and in time a second sip, when you wish, and our ancient blue ice will course through your veins," added Cerulean.

Skylar nodded to Cerulean in inexpressible joy. Cerulean, equally moved, approached Skylar. "Brother, I welcome you into the Kingdoms of the Seasons and promise to teach you our ways and to learn yours," said Cerulean, offering the flagon to Skylar's lips. Skylar drank one sip, closed his eyes and felt a delicious coolness radiate warmth through his body. There appeared tinges of frost on his hair and eye brows and his feet were suddenly warmer than the ice floor.

The King placed the Constellation Crown on Skylar's head. "From Orion and the Great 88 you are hereby given the power to communicate with and visit any Constellation any time you like. Simply choose a charm from this chain and off you go!"

The Queen placed the Constellation Chain on Skylar's shoulders. It was lighter than he expected and he felt vibrations emanate from each twinkling charm. He recognized them all, his lifelong Constellation friends.

I'm wearing our Galaxy! he thought in astonished wonder.

"We grieve the loss of your dear mother, and offer ourselves as father, mother, sister and brother," said the King.

Skylar was caught off guard by such affection and through misting eyes regarded them in deepest gratitude, with a love he had not felt for anyone but his mother, Rocky, Coral and Orion.

The King signaled to someone behind Skylar to step forward and Skylar heard the familiar clop clop of hooves at his side. Cerulean then placed the etched crystalice saddle on Chelsea.

The King continued, "We honor you, Sir Skylar, as Master Equestrian. You not only passed the course trials on Saturn, but exceeded all expectations! We now offer you our stable of Arctic-White thoroughbreds. They are eager to meet you!" he chuckled, as did the entire company, for all knew how finicky Arctic-Whites are about their riders.

The King saved the best for last. Two courtiers presented a pine bough with pine cones on a rich burgundy velvet cushion to the King who raised it for all the court to see. Its rich warm color stood out against all the silver, blue and white.

"The Pine is the universally acclaimed *Tree For All Seasons*, growing everywhere on the Earth in all Seasons. Evergreen and ever true, these journalists, once trillions strong, transmit up to the moment news with their ceaseless whispering in the Wind." That was my cue, and I breezed forward beside the King.

The Royal Family and I announced in unison: "In the name of the Kingdoms of Winter, Spring, Summer and Autumn, with this pine bough we proclaim you, Sir Skylar, Son of Spring, the first ever *Man For All Seasons!"* The King handed the bough to Skylar. "With this bough comes the most sought after prize in all of nature."

A tremendous gasp interrupted the King. Skylar thought at first it was me, but then realized it was thousands of Faeries.

"Ahem…" said the King, his hands trying to quell the crescendo of murmurs. "Yes, the most prestigious post in all of nature –"

Everyone knows that Faeries adore one thing almost as much as music and dessert: surprises. Good surprises, that is. And this crowd simply could not bear the suspense. They erupted noisily, drowning out the King, in collective rapture. Delighted with this long overdue excitement at Court, the King signaled me to make the grand announcement over the din. I let loose a mighty melody,

ooooOOOrRRRRRRIIIIIONNNN, IIIIIIFFFFFFFFFFFFF YYYYYYYYYOOOOuUuUu PLLLLEEEEEASE!

I howled, blowing over more than a few surprised Fairies, for howling is my favorite way to sing.

Every head turned to the Castle's ornate Stellar Portal where Orion stood with his dogs. Right on cue, their three midnight blue frames began to grow in dazzling size, and as they did so, the entire castle simply vanished. The assembly found themselves standing in the heart of the Blue Spruce forest in fresh powdery snow, surrounded by Aurora Borealis in resplendent undulating panorama. Aurora had specially lit up a clearing, where the Cosmic Sun Chariot was majestically parked. Its sheer enormity took Skylar's breath away.

Why, it must be ten or twenty skyscrapers tall! he thought in stunned disbelief.

This chariot was more elaborately ornate than any jewel-encrusted treasure anyone had ever beheld. It glistened, it radiated, as if it knew the astonishing impression it made. It was a stellar being unto itself. And not until tonight had it ever parked on Earth.

"Sirr Skyllarr and Sirr Chelllseea, apprroach!" sang Orion. By now courtiers had fully outfitted Chelsea in his new livery of high office and the horse seemed to grow in size.

"Skylar, let's break in this new saddle!" Chelsea neighed.

Skylar mounted Chelsea and the whole forest rang out in rustic farm bells and raucous cheers. Banners were raised, the Blue Spruce Guard hurled crystal confetti from their branches, the orchestra played triumphant Winter Fanfares and beasts of all families gathered to watch the historic moment. Skylar didn't have to urge Chelsea to trot or canter, for the horse broke into a powerful gliding stride, as if skating.

The immensity of the Cosmic Sun Chariot took on even more mind boggling proportions as they drew near. As soon as they got there, Orion harnessed Chelsea and then, in a grand gesture for all to witness, formally handed Skylar the reins. The Winter King raised his scepter and the crowd went silent. He then addressed Skylar.

"The highest calling on Earth, Sir Skylar, is now yours. It takes 365 days for Earth to ride around the Sun. Speed, altitude, spin, orbit, axis? They're now all up to you and Chelsea. You and the Sun shall become great friends and help restore the Seasons to their natural rhythms. You have earned the Earth's trust, the very first human to do so."

Skylar looked around in wonder and joy, memorizing every detail of this precious spectacular moment. From the glittering fresh new snow in silver moonlight to the golden torches of Friendly Fire, he could hear the hushed whispers of the Blue

Spruce Guard as they reported the live breaking story worldwide through the PNN. And he saw Lily with tears in her eyes, gazing at him in deep admiration.

Orion's voice brought Skylar back to the moment. *"Yoou'll mmeet the Suunnn in the morrrningg!"* he sang.

"How do I greet the Sun?" Skylar chanted to Orion.

"How youu greet any Yelllow Dwaarrrf Starrr! Sinng yelloww songs!" Orion chimed playfully.

The King gave Skylar his first official orders. "Every three months on the Solstice and Equinox, when a new Season holds court, you and Chelsea will be honored guests. Magnetic North or South, you can enter and exit the Earth's atmosphere at the Poles. The Twin Auroras will illuminate your path whenever you need them to. Chelsea will now take you to the Royal Stables at the Winter Palace where your horse team awaits."

Skylar and the King embraced tightly. "Thank you, son, thank you," the King choked with deep emotion. His gratitude was visceral, illuminating him as only blue ice does when charged with powerful feeling. A wave of cool blue energy engulfed Skylar. It was scintillating and empowered him to step into his greatness.

"Thank *you*, Sire," said Skylar, equally moved, glowing with his own young blue light, to his amazement.

The King gave his blessing and sprinkled Winter's good luck snow-powder on the horse and the boy. Viggo Vespa, not one to miss anything, landed squarely between Chelsea's ears in time for his dusting, too.

Skylar suddenly felt he should say something profound. His

mind raced for appropriate lines from *Hamlet.* He muttered to himself, "*To be or not to be? … Arrows of outrageous fortune? … Traveler to the undiscovered country …* What do you say when you've been given things beyond your wildest dreams? Maybe it's more like, *To believe or not to believe, that is the question.*" Standing in the Cosmic Chariot, he felt his Constellation Chain vibrate, illuminating one of the crystal charms. I felt its vibration, too, and blew to Skylar's side. Chelsea and Viggo pricked up their ears as the King stepped closer. The Great 88 knew an important ceremony was in progress, so it was odd one would interrupt it.

"Which of your new friends is ringing you?" the King asked.

"Sire, it's coming from the Sky's *Sea Region*," Skylar replied. "What men call 'The Heavenly Waters' where many Water Constellations live. I think it's … Cetus, the Sea Monster."

"Cetus? A whale of a fellow! I wonder what he wants?" the King asked.

"Let's find out!" I puffed to Skylar. "Go ahead, see if you can translate his message."

Skylar looked totally lost. He had no idea how to communicate with Cetus. He glanced at the King anxiously. With a twinkle in his eye, the King nonchalantly brushed his hand alongside his own crown.

Of course! My Constellation Crown! Skylar remembered. The moment he touched his crown while holding Cetus' charm, he instantly heard a message.

"I can't make it out, Sire," Skylar said. "It's quite garbled."

"Let's have a listen. Cetus speaks a very old Stellar dialect," the King answered, touching his hand to his Constellation Crown. You'll get to know their voices and odd quirks of speech. "Ah, here we go. *Happy Winter Solstice!* he says. And, oh wait … I see … it appears Winter's return is affecting an ocean … his exact words are '*I found a live coral*' …" the King said.

"Huh?" I gasped. "But coral has been extinct for ages."

"What good tidings from Cetus! We'll leave rebirth to the Kingdom of Spring! It's curious, though, that you'd receive this as your first Constellar communiqué … very curious indeed," the King wondered, looking up at the Sky.

Skylar was speechless. Good news? It was great news! His heart pounded as the words sunk in: *Alive Coral.* It could only mean one thing and it was totally meant for him. Somehow, somewhere on Earth, Coral was alive! Coral the oceanography whiz, Coral who said yes to going out with him … and now Coral who somehow is connected to Cetus the Sea Monster in the Sky.

Then a second charm vibrated. It was Orion, standing right there.

"Time for you to head home?" Skylar sang.

Orion nodded, just as he had the first time Skylar saw him.

"I can visit you anytime?" Skylar asked.

Again Orion nodded.

"And meet all your celestial friends?" Skylar sang excitedly.

Orion suspected there was something more to this. *"Is therre sommethinng I cann do forr yoou beforre I go homme?"* he sang.

"I get to meet Perseus? And Pegasus? And Draco?"

"yessss Yessss and YESSSS!"

"I could use some pointers from Auriga the Charioteer! And

both compasses, Circinus and Pyxis, and Sextans the sextant!
They'd sure come in handy! And – and –" sang Skylar, breathlessly.

"… Annnnd?" sang Orion.

"Herrrcuuuleees …!" Skylar belted out.

Orion burst into gigantic, sonorous peals of laughter all the while burgeoning into his vast super stellar size. He whistled and clapped to Major and Minor and pointed to the Sky. Both dogs supersized and bounded out into the galaxy, rippling Earth's atmosphere.

With Orion standing tall and his giant stellar feet melting the snow around the Cosmic Chariot, we all held our breath. But for whispering Pines and Blue Spruce, the only sound was the progressive awakening of Skylar's Constellation Chain as Perseus, Pegasus, Draco, Circinus, Pyxis, Sextans and Hercules transmitted their eager invitations to meet the brave young Man For All Seasons.

"Huh?" gasped Skylar, in awe of his cosmic phone callers. "Orion, wait! Look! It's them! It's –" Skylar was so excited he couldn't catch his breath.

I whispered in his ear, "It's time. Now, Skylar!"

And with that Skylar tightened his hold on the reins and shouted, "Hyah, Chelsea! To the Winter Palace! Tomorrow, we greet the Sun! In three months, the Kingdom of Spring!"

Orion lifted Skylar, Chelsea and the Chariot up above the atmosphere. The Chariot suffered the same surface-gravity woes as Constellations, but in its 365-day orbit around the Sun, it was a dynamic high tech marvel.

"Happy Winter Solstice to you all!" Skylar shouted to the

cheering crowd disappearing below.

Confident that Skylar and Chelsea were safely in orbit, Orion jubilantly stepped off Earth and lumbered out into space. He erupted in fortissimo song to Skylar. *"Leave roomm on yourr dannce carrd for Virgo! Cassiopeia! Andromeda! Our womenn are stellll-arrrrr!!!"*

All watched Orion and his dogs ripple the night sky as they moved, the harmonious ringing clusters in their wake tickling our ears and delighting other Constellations. Orion's voice faded in the distance, 800 light years away. Each dog arrived at its gaping empty frame, its celestial address, and took its familiar position. Orion arrived at his cosmic address and sang a twinkling, barely audible *"Goooodniiiiight, Earrrth!"*

In orbit, Skylar's Constellation Charm of Orion went silent.

He then gave Chelsea the stellar command he had heard Saturn shout to his rings: a high-pitched oscillating *"Woooo-owww-woooo-owww!"* Chelsea understood the command in spite of Skylar's funny human accent. It was *"Full Speed*!" in Star. In moments they vanished over the atmosphere to begin the adventure of a lifetime.

THE SOLSTICE SNOW BALL

The moment we saw Orion arrive home, Winter beings everywhere cheered, threw snowballs in the air, kissed their sweethearts and toasted *"Shazinga-Zasss!"* Orion was visible across the entire Northern Hemisphere and his return home meant, *"We did it!"*

"Maestro Sammy, let the Snow Ball begin!" cheered the King. In a flurry of white fur, the Samoyed Swing Orchestra launched into the *Stellar Stomp*, indicating to all that now the party would really get going.

The Castle's iridescent walls reappeared around them and Winter's Royal Family led their guests in a sumptuous banquet feast. Winter desserts are the envy of all the Seasons: rich creamy buttery colorful frosted cakes, pies, tarts, cookies, bon bons, puddings, eggnogs of every flavor, crystal candies, white chocolates, custard filled pastries sprinkled with snowy confectioner's sugar and, to top it off, the pride of Winter chefs … a colossal ice cream mountain ever re-freshing itself with new flavors! Teams of daredevil Faerie Scoop-Skiers, armed with ice cream scoops, raced downhill scooping boules like giant snowballs and catapulted them into glazed cones – some heaped ten boules high! Delectables were served all night long to keep dancers fortified. From Yuraq (Eskimo dancing) to boogie woogie to ice-hops, the fun spun the Snow Ballroom!

But it was Winter's teens whose dances rocked the castle. They had the latest rhythms and coolest moves from the other Kingdoms, especially Summer. Faeries in warmer climes reinvent music and dance like we Winds reinvent air! Some new dances were so fun and easy to pick up that they became overnight classics: the *Sled Slide,* the *Tree Line Dance* and water's favorite, *Drip Drop* (hip hop on skates, with spins so fast the ice melts!)

While the Fire Witch had banned singing, the one thing she couldn't stamp out was dancing, because Fire, as we all know, is a prolific dancer. Why, there's probably no more insanely inspired dancer than Fire, except for us Winds, that is, and Arctic men, human and Faerie. Some say they dance to keep warm, others say it's to impress their womenfolk, and they certainly did both at the Snow Ball! The mood amped up to rowdy as Faerie men of Russian heritage exuberantly burst into an explosive version of the Trepak, their legs flinging in prisiadkas (when dancers squat and kick each foot out alternately!) It's an astonishing feat of great strength and fast feet. Young Faeries of all ages joined in, showing off their athletic prowess, usually with both feet flying out from under them, tumbling in laughing heaps!

Not to be outdone, male Faeries from Greenland cut loose in drum dances they'd learned from the Inuit. These dancers were famous for their *Snowflake Pattern Dances*. The thrill was in the unexpected: as each snowflake in all of eternity is unique, so is the spontaneous dance mirroring the snowflake's shape. The lead drummer caught a snowflake and asked me to spin-chill it till it expanded a thousand times its size. Then he and his drummers beat the hexagonal rhythms (snowflakes have six arms) as their kinsmen began to dance the snowflake's 3-D form. They synchronized into three gyrating aerial circles and brought that snowflake to vibrating life! Every snowflake in the room dreamed of seeing its beautiful uniqueness celebrated next!

But that's not all, just like Inuit drum dances, Snowflake Pattern Dances were peppered with clever humor, for jokes are a key ingredient: whichever dancer evokes the most laughter from the audience is considered the winner! It was my distinct honor to bestow on Kuupik of Nunavut Winter's coveted *Hystericle Icicle* for making me laugh so hard I guffawed cracks into a castle wall!

As Swingin' Sammy's Samoyeds played into the night, the ballroom's ice-floor continually refreshed itself with smooth perfect ice, especially at the north end where the kids' theatrical performance was about to start.

Winter Solstice for Faerie children not only means sweets, presents, no school, staying up late and fancy dress balls, but it's also their big night to re-enact a favorite Norse legend. Old Winter Faeries got it from old Scandinavian minstrels. "Yule" is the tale of Sól, the Sun Goddess and Thor, the Thunder God.

For millennia, Yule had been nature's and Man's festival of Winter Solstice, the rebirth of the Sun, until it was blended into another festival of light and birth called Christmas. The more the Fire Witch tried to eradicate Yule, the deeper it took hold of everyone's imaginations. Tonight one of Yuletide's oldest traditions came roaring back to life!

Just as the Yule Pageant was about to begin, I blew a frosty breeze to calm nervous parents in the audience. The pageant, now a mega production, was originally an informal game for Faerie children to learn what Solstice means: *The moment when the Sun (sol) stands still (sistere) as it reaches its northernmost point in June or southernmost point in December from Earth's equator.*

The ballroom went dark. Lit by moonlight through the ice ceiling, the room tingled as an excited hush fell on us all, the hush of when the curtain goes up on a show!

A beam of golden light shone down onto the ice. Into the sun skated Sól, a pretty teen girl, who swirled in delight around her sun chariot. The audience went nuts. Sól and her chariot were pulled by a team of athletic children, Sól's horses. They brought sunlight to the earth, showering glitter onto the delighted audience.

But then, behind her from the underworld, a tall dark wolf puppet swooped in, operated by fast-skating strong boys – this was the hungry dark night keen to swallow the sun's light. The audience held its breath. The Wolf of Darkness chased Sól, nipped at her chariot then pounced and gobbled her up! Gobbled her chariot! Her horses! Her light! The Wolf plunged Earth into cold wintry dark.

The Wolf's minions came on next, hundreds of scary Yule Riders: creatures of the underworld and souls of the dead. Oh what costumes they wore! The Yule Riders chased and terrorized Villagers, young boys and girls with small animals, across the dark lands of Winter.

Then appeared Gnomes and Trolls, the comic relief, to whom the Villagers and the audience threw treats to avoid the mischief and curses of the darkness. The Villagers prayed for Winter's end and Spring's return, *"Sól! Bring back your light and renew the Earth!"*

And lo, Thor, a handsome young hero, appeared with two Yule-Goats pulling his chariot. The audience erupted in thunderous cheers as the Villagers waved to Thor. Thor battled the Wolf and vanquished darkness. He rescued Sól from the Wolf's belly.

She, her horses and sun chariot rose victorious to birth a new year with her immortal promise: *"Come tomorrow, the day after Winter Solstice, I will add two minutes of daylight every day till Summer Solstice, the longest day of the year!"*

The performance concluded with the cast wishing *Good Yule!* in all the languages of Earth and leading us in the final verse of the *Solstice Carol:*

> *Oh roar, Aurora Borealis!*
> *Shine your lights on Winter's palace!*
> *Bid the dark a loud 'Good Night!'*
> *Pour light in every chalice!*
> *We love for love is always in season,*
> *Always the reason,*
> *Let the Season start!*

With darkness and light duly honored, the performers were congratulated by the Royal Family and invited to a feast

CHAPTER THIRTY-SEVEN

of refreshments laid out for them. Eager to keep the children entertained all night, Winter's Master and Mistress of Games, Frisque & Frolique, announced the Deep Freeze Treasure Hunt. With hundreds of clues frozen throughout the castle, there were many paths to victory. The most fun part was exploring the castle's secret passageways, hidden rooms and roof top parapets and towers, different every year. In no time at all, a brother and sister team from Iceland found the Solstice treasure: a blue-eyed Siberian Husky puppy!

As for me, I danced into the wee hours! Oh, I made merry! The elegant but vigorous old world court dances were my favorites. I used to dance the galliard with Elizabeth I, you know! And the courante with Louis XIV! Yes, right there at Versailles. Wow, could the "Sun King" throw a party! And what a dancer!

I leapt higher than anyone else and spun our ladies to their giddy delight! Occasionally my thoughts drifted to the events of the last few days and I felt a rush of pride and joy in our achievements. I still couldn't quite believe the Fire Witch was dead. She'd been part of my life for so long, so intimately, that I wondered, *Will her Invisible Fire ever really go out? Will Earth really cool off?* Then I thought of morning, just an hour away, and practically burst with excitement.

Just before dawn I knew it was time to take my leave, though the party was still going full tilt. The festivities would conclude at midday with the Borealis Brunch when the Royal Family gives children traditional gifts of maple-candied pine cones and hats, scarves and mittens woven of Saturnalian ice. The King's faithful cook had been rationing maple syrup for centuries anticipating this day would come!

I read the pre-dawn sky and saw that my stellar friends were either on their way or already in Machu Picchu, where our secret project awaited us. I asked Queen Crystalline to safeguard the mirror for me for I travel light and knew the Peruvian heat would melt it.

The Royal Family and I then engaged in a farewell ritual not seen in a long time, *Winderlust.* One by one the King, Queen, Prince, Zhu Zhu, Gala and Lily allowed me to tenderly caress their faces, wisping their hair, ears, noses and mouths. This ritual is my most intimate expression of my love for another being and I'm happy to tell you that many humans have shared it with me and even tried to communicate with me.

Lily and I skated down the center in a few last swirls for fun. Winter Faeries blew me kisses and I blew kisses back! They threw ice confetti and cheered, *'Fair winds till we meet again!'* At the Stellar Portal, in a spontaneous whoosh I blew, *"<Hyâh 'Ooshshh-ffahh Whhújhoúhee!"* which by now you know is *"Happy Winter Solstice!"* in Wind. Out Lily and I strolled into the frigid wintry dawn.

"Fatherrrrr of the Briiiiiide? I'd be honnnored!" I gushed, completely taken by surprise.

Plans were underway for the first royal Inter-Season wedding ever. It truly was a new era as Lily, a Daughter of Autumn and Prince Cerulean of Winter were to be wed. And because my secret project was so vital, and there was Winter to launch in the Southern Hemisphere in just six months, the happy occasion was scheduled around me.

"I promise to return on the next full moon, *my soon-to-be Princcesss!"* I said, relishing the word. It was the first time Lily heard herself addressed with her soon-to-be title and it tingled her, suddenly feeling very real and daunting. "You got some practice tonight as a queen. You'll be wonderful princess!" I assured her.

"I love you, Windham. You never gave up believing in me, or Cerulean," Lily replied warmly.

"And you never gave up on me, even when the trees stopped telling me their secrets," I sighed. We breathed each other in, feeling one another's energy deeply. "Did you hear the Kingdom of Spring canceled its boycott? They're promising the return of several extinct species they hid from humans and the Fire Witch all this time!"

"Including Cerulean's beloved Polar Bear?" Lily asked.

"Especially the Polar Bear!" I replied.

It was no secret in nature that the Kingdom of Spring was Earth's DNA nursery, having memorized the pattern codes, big and small, for every Earthly being. But where Spring's *Treasure Trove of Life* was hidden was a quintessential mystery no one had ever solved. To this day it remains an elusive secret location known only to Spring Sentinels and to me. It is so secret that many conjecture it is off-planet. But all agree it does exist.

"Sing to meee, as I will to theee!" I howled to Lily as I swirled high and took off in a rip-roaring gust of joy. Below me, legions of the Blue Spruce Guard waved me off as I tickled their boughs, kicking up a fine snowy dusting.

One last Solstice tradition awaited me. As the music and merriment faded out below, another sound faded in above: the sweet snap, crackle and pop of Aurora Borealis. Yes, she's both sound and light show! Old Magnus really got in the spirit and put on such a smashing geomagnetic storm between his magnetic field and the Sun's bursts of plasma, that the night air tingled with Aurora's crackling electrical discharges.

I sailed right into her gleaming curtains of rainbow color. Oh ho! How it tickled and tingled! How can I even describe the feeling of color shimmering and dancing through me?

There's only one word for it. *<Hh'whåhh ... Peace,* in Wind.

<Wh'hoosh whøuuheh'hezj-hooph//

(See you outside!)

THE KINGDOMS OF THE SEASONS'
EPIC ADVENTURE CONTINUES IN

THE KINGDOM

OF

SPRING

TURN THE PAGE IF YOU HAVE ...

SPRING FEVER!

𝔚hen
Equinox knocks, the
Queen of Spring's song unlocks
her flowering fields and migrating flocks.
'Tis time for fun ye birds, ye fox! Winter's done
with ice and wool socks! Oh sing to the Sun in time
and space! *Run Sun, your Four Season Race! Your rays
of luminous light align and shine on the great finish line,*
———————— 𝔈arth's 𝔈quator! ————————
'Tis no greater solar sight for a Polar Knight than the tie in
the sky when day and night are equal in light! Yet dark
is the mystery in Spring's history: tales ne'er told of
deeds and seeds disloyal royal soil breeds. What
evil treason? What wicked reason? Why no
King in the Season of birth? Known to
the Stars, known to the Earth, the
answers will shock when
Equinox knocks!

- SKYLAR

SUN CHARIOTEER TO THE ROYAL COURTS
OF
WINTER, SPRING, SUMMER & AUTUMN

(SNEAK PEAK!)

G ood moods feel so good! I was euphoric flying south to Machu Picchu. The more I spread Solstice cheer, the more it energized me. Every snowcapped mountain I passed wanted to know *When's the wedding? Has Skylar met Hercules? ... Is She reeeally dead?* Several surviving tree lines invited me to stop and play our favorite Winter sport: tree snowball fights! You've seen it, where Wind bounces boughs of snow, slinging 'em loose onto passersby or neighboring trees. What humans call blizzards are actually championship tree snowball fights. And Pine Trees are the merriest, and fiercest, competitors.

Onward I flew, taking in the wintry landscape below and the snow clouds above. Of all of Winter's wonders, its palette of infinite shades of white was an endless source of artistic subtlety and genius to me. Occasionally, thin blue lines rose up like genies, slicing the whiteness in diaphanous columns of smoke from chimney fires. They'd jolt me and I'd have to remind myself that *She* was gone ... at least till Fear reinvented itself. Several times I picked up with a Southerly or Trade Wind cousin and they'd howl strains of the *Solstice Carol* like drunk sailors happily ashore after being lost at sea, confident their Season's lost spirit would now return. I didn't have the heart to tell them some things would never return.

Before I knew it, I was there – high above what had once been lush Amazon rainforest, now a struggling thirsty bowl edged by the Andes Mountains. The thinned canopy had cavernous holes and I looked and listened for my Amazonian relatives, the Trade Winds legendary for reversing direction to create the monsoon. I knew the rainforest's leaves helped trigger the start of the wet season. If they lost their vapor power, then my Wind cousins, who relied on this trigger, may be lost, too. But I pressed on, flying south into the Andes. The mountain air filled me with familiar anticipation as I found myself arriving at an old friend's abandoned estate from long, long ago: Inca Emperor Pachacuti's magnificent Machu Picchu in Peru.

sssSUUURRPPPRRRIISSSE!!!

I heard them roar up to me! Fanfares, banners, streamers, flags, bubbles, feathers, confetti, wind chimes – anything that dances in the wind was unfurled heralding my arrival. Circling the monumental site triumphantly, I viewed them all below: hundreds of humans and six Constellations, brilliantly radiant on Earth's surface in daytime. It took even my breath away, for these Constellations embodied stars far larger and brighter than Earth's Sun. There they stood midst the humans in razzle-dazzling blue-gold-green-white-red rays like beacons: Lyra the Harp, Bootes the Ploughman, Cepheus the King, Monoceros the Unicorn, Ursa Major the Great Bear and Ursa Minor the Little Bear, here for the day, gathered to perform the Picchu Protocol then back up to the Sky by nightfall.

"Winnnndhammm!! Orrrrionnnn has tolllld ussss allll! Youuuu savvvved Winnntterrr!" they rang in chiming chorus.

"And you saved me!" crackled Phrendly Phyre, whom I rescued from the poisoned volcano just yesterday. It was delicious irony that the Fire Witch had chosen to nauseate the one volcanic belly where Phrendly Phyre had been in hiding.

"¡Hola guapo!" *(Hi Handsome!)* echoed a thundering female voice over the Andes Mountains.

"¡Hola niña loca!" *(Hi Crazy Girl!)* I howled in ecstatic relief, welcoming my mischievous fiesta-loving Easterly Trade Wind cousin, Esté. "¡Me preguntaba dónde estabas!" *(I wondered where you were!)* I howled again. I sensed in Esté, a usually merry spirit, a great weight on her winds. Her part of the world was in desperate trouble and they all, unfairly, blamed her. My Trade Wind cousins were taking a beating. If the *Picchu Protocol* didn't work, nothing would. South America's Winds and last surviving slips of rainforest knew Machu Picchu's importance. They were counting on us to celebrate the Inca's Sun Festival,

Inti Raymi and Summer Solstice, *Khapaq Raymi*, and get it right.

Esté and I, Norte *(North)* as she called me, slammed into each other a warm wonderful *WHAM!* wind hug then rocketed thousands of feet up into the clouds who spun, rolled and rollicked in surprised delight. For hundreds of miles I'd seen clouds gathering here in fantastic caravans. If you're a student of clouds as we Winds are, you know what I'm talking about: no cloud is content to travel simply as an amorphous clump of white. Oh no, each dons a shape, perhaps not readily recognizable to human eyes, but it's always there. Cloud Readers get it right away. Clouds take every shape imaginable, concocted from what they see below, until the Sky is lined with vast parades of party-going titans. The party, of course, is usually a storm. But today was different, for Constellations create vast swaths of clouds when they visit (it's one of the tell-tale signs they've been here) and the party was the long forgotten ancient *Picchu Protocol.* So old was this astronomical ceremony that only the Sun, Constellations, Earth, Esté and I knew what was about to happen – and what was at stake.

Certain there were no Shroud Clouds (spies), Esté and I blew an opening for the Sun to aim its rays with pinpoint laser accuracy at 13°9'48" and …

zzzzzIIIIINNNGG! The Sun hit the gigantic Inti Watana stone, the Inca's ritual *Hitching Post of the Sun,* Machu Picchu's astronomical clock. At that same moment, shafts of sunlight shot into *Inti Mach'ay,* the sacred cave built to let sunlight in for just a few days at December's Summer Solstice. Yes, it was Summer here, for we were now well below the

Equator. Up at the North Pole they were celebrating the longest night of the year; here at Machu Picchu we were celebrating the longest day of the year! For a moment, which felt like an eternity, all went stock-still silent. Inti Watana, the solid granite monolithic curiosity, about 4' tall and 12' around, couldn't quite believe what just happened. Its old granite molecules, slow, heavy and densely packed, heard its name *sung* in Quechua, the ancient language it was carved in, the tongue of the Inca Empire – but *sung* by the *Sun!* It would know that solar accent anywhere! Could this be the re-awakening it had waited for all these centuries?

Inti Watana wondered, *Will the second ritual greeting come? Will it?*

As if on cue in reply to the stone's question, a merry salutation rang out: *"¡Haylli Khapaq Raymi!"* *(Glory be Summer Solstice!)*

The joyous Inca greeting was unearthly yet vibrant, glorious and comforting at once. It vibrated deep into Inti Watana's old granite memory. *"¡Haylli Inkakuna!"* *(Glory be the Incas!)* *"¡Haylli Tawantinsuyu!"* *(Glory be the Inca Empire!)* Inti Watana messaged back to the Sun.

The Constellations glanced at each other nervously. It was clear the Inti Watana stone thought the Incas were still in charge! I would break the news to him about that later. But his words gave us old timers pause for the Sun, the Constellations and I had known the Inca people for three centuries until their brilliant civilization fell at the hands of other humans. Now brilliant humankind was falling at its own hands. The Sun quickly saved the awkward moment, even louder than before:

"¡Haylli Khapaq Raymi!"

"Happy Summer Solstice!" rang the Constellations in reply. Oh I'll never forget the shiver of that sound – it's when I suddenly realized the humans couldn't hear a word of this cosmic dialogue.

Cepheus translated for them warmly. *"Yourrr Sunnn is sinnnging tooo youuu! Annd is wishinng youuu a Haappy Summmer Solllstice!"*

The adults looked confused, completely deaf to the growing musical crescendo. The children's young ears, however, were still tuned in to the unseen and could feel a burgeoning sound tickle their eardrums. It wasn't the adults' fault they couldn't hear it. But for a few farmers, athletes, solar physicists, artists and mystics, it hadn't occurred to most humans that their Sun might sing to them, so it wasn't something they listened for and therefore they didn't hear it. But it had been there all along … their great Sunsinger accompanying the fever of human life on Earth.

Earth's Yellow Dwarf Star's sonorous mix of low frequency oscillations, pitches and overtones rang out in a magnificent sonic bath:

SHAA-Z-Z-Z-INGA-ZASSS! ZOOS-ZOOS-ZOOS! ZINGA-ZINGGA XooNzHA-Zha-SASS!! ZuZuuZuuu=ZZZOOONN!!! ring Ring RING! sing Sing SING!

Inti Watana vibrated in recognition like when an old friend's familiar voice says hello on your phone. Though they hadn't celebrated the Sun Festival or Summer Solstice together since the 1500's, Inti Watana and our Constellar guests didn't miss a beat. Lyra, Bootes, Ursa Major and Monoceros spontaneously began to ring in contagious musical riffs led by Cepheus, the most celebrated singer of the Great 88 with his Cepheid Variables, the Cosmos' loudest stellar choir, stars ringing their hearts out. This titanic stellar hum vibrated Machu Picchu's gargantuan granite foundations, waking them from a rock solid sleep until they, too, began to hum.

The humans, whose feet now started to vibrate, began improvising on musical instruments, creating sounds as if waking forgotten ancestral voices hard wired into them. In later accounts of the *Picchu Protocol,* the children wrote how they felt a mystical, musical pull into a vast eternal energy expressing itself through them, like conduits channeling unfettered euphoria. Their melodies, harmonies and rhythms were in perfect mind-expanding sync with the Constellations. A new music was born to mankind as, for the first time in millennia, humans evolved into the next better version of themselves.

Did you know some stars sing in percussion? Yes! The wild rhythmic drumming of several human boys so completely entranced Ursa Major, the Great Bear, that with a mile-wide beaming smile she oscillated and reverberated, *"Shoooo-beeeee DooDooDoo-waaaWaaa!"* Guardian Constellation to many a jazz musician, she swung out her Big Dipper, beat it like a drum, plucked it like a double bass, twirled it then danced around it as if it were a Spring maypole! None of us had ever seen big mama bear shake her booty – at least not since the Big Bang!

"Baaa Daaa Binnng Baa Daa BooWooWOOOM!" Cubby (Ursa Major's stellar bear cub, Ursa Minor) chimed in, singing with his mother, ecstatic to break out of stiff Constellar protocol.

And not to be outshone, Lyra the Harp, whose music is known for charming rocks, strummed and plucked the harmonies it knew Peruvian rocks would resonate with most. Lyra's blue-white star Vega, the fifth brightest star in the night sky, pulsated in all directions like a cosmic disco ball.

A deep abiding joy spread, engulfing every being in the circle in warm affinity for all life. As the Constellations' glow grew, the humans' consciousness grew.

High above, Esté and I howled at each other like two rock stars vying for the mic. Then, in a moment of mathematical perfection only spoken by stars:

The stellar chant attained its UFO (Ultimate Frequency Oscillation), transportability mode, activating the second crucial part of the Protocol: Esté and I would carry the sound beyond Machu Picchu's remote realm. We took off in opposite directions. One by one they met us, our Wind cousins across the globe.

To this day, Mother Winds sing to baby breezlings lullabies about that legendary global Wind relay. Why even Windkins (teen Winds) deftly picked up the stellar chant and carried it across land and sea, transponding it to every breeze, gust and gale without losing one decimal of volume or wave length of tone.

In a matter of twenty-four minutes and twenty-four seconds, Earth's entire surface was resonating in unison. The Sun's energy, long since thwarted by a junk choked atmosphere, came in a healing form Man hadn't imagined: music carried on the Wind. Not being one to openly declare its love for Earth, for it knew most humans would repudiate such a concept, the Sun was content to hum its star song just enough to keep asteroseismologists tantalized with hints and to keep farmers' food growing. But this day the Sun radiated a harmonic banquet from the core of its being. It didn't care who believed or who didn't. It was the Sun and it knew its healing sonic vibrations were Earth's last hope.

Far beneath the Earth's crust, the Sun's music gently sank down down down, soaking into damaged hibernating forest floors, dead sea beds, scared desert dunes, scarred mountain sides, valleys and even volcanoes. The low-rumble oscillations triggered the secret restoration and nurture of beings whose lives had ended when Earth's personality changed, that is, when her climate faltered. Over the next three months until Spring's Vernal Equinox, Earth would repair underground. Daily doses of stellar song would boost damage control, transmitting the highest vibrations in the Universe to which all beings resonate in joy – or so we thought.

At twilight, we celebrated our festive lantern-lit dinner on Machu Picchu's sun-warmed stones. We'd barely raised our forks when it happened, the first horrible *JOLT!* – the jolt I'll never, ever forget.

I whipped to attention. Everyone froze. Machu Picchu, built to be earthquake proof, was trembling, the stones seemed to dance eerily in their tightly fitted construction designed to prevent collapse. The dishes on our tables rhythmically clattered;

the Constellations fluttered and flickered, trying not to giggle, for they can't resist vibrations of any kind. But this was a dark, negative vibration deep below us in the Earth, rolling to and fro like some monstrous subterranean drill. Machu Picchu sits atop two fault lines, but had been seismically quiet. This was no earthquake. And the Sun's healing chant should have calmed the Earth, not agitated it.

Then jiggle Joggle JOUNCE! A second jolt! It sent the humans screaming and scampering for cover. But there's no cover on Machu Picchu. Maternal instinct kicked in: without so much as a flash, Ursa Major supersized and enveloped us all in a vast black starry dome overhead making us invisible. This protected us from trouble above, but this menace was threatening from below.

It is common knowledge that kids have bigger imaginations than adults and this proved true among Constellations, too. Cubby, scared little bear that he was, knew his mother's effort wasn't quite right or enough. So underneath her dome, he supersized and spread himself across Machu Picchu's ruins like a giant bear rug, singing and ringing his own sweet lullaby version of the Sun's chant. One by one, everyone and everything picked up his tune, for when you're scared, singing is the best fear fighter. In particular, the warm stones he lay on vibrated so intensely it became impossible for anything or anyone to squeeze through from below.

It worked. The tremors stopped. Were they scared away? Cubby signaled us all to *Shhhh*. A deafening silence. Even I held my breath. Then an ear splitting *BOOM BLAST!!* rocked us. It shattered the air. The first sonic wave sliced Esté and me to ribbons! It pummeled quintillions of particles into Ursa Major, Bootes, Lyra, Monoceros and Cepheus in painfully loud hammering clusters. As for Cubby, he was hardest hit – the boom vibrated through the ground punching his little bear tummy hard, over and over, in horrific aftershocks. He thought he would throw up, gripping the mountain with all four starry paws with all his might. But he took it, refusing to budge.

Across from us on Wayna Picchu, the higher peak watching over Machu Picchu, we saw the incomprehensible: a smoking massive gash in the side of the mountain. Colossal boulders had been thrust from their impenetrable rock beds like jelly beans from a jar. What force could have that tonnage, that power, that aim? Was it a message? A warning?

"They'rrre loookinng forrrr it! Forrrr the Treassssurrre Trrovvve of Liiiiife! We've beennn dissscovvered, Winndhamm!" rang Ursa Major urgently.

Her words shot through me like a meteor shower. The moment Winter returned, Spring's subterranean machine had begun like clockwork. But who'd be so bothered by that as to kick a mountain in the side? Let alone do it with a bunch of Constellations standing right there? No vibration known can escape Constellar detective skills, or mine – but someone just did! … Or something.

Bootes, the Ploughman Constellation, quite at home on rugged terrain, shone the light of his bright star Arcturus onto the jagged gash in the mountain's facade, now a burning side ache. A fine black dust rimmed the open wound, but as I drew

near to sniff it, trillions of its fine particles lilted on my breezes
and dispersed every which way, vanishing before I could catch a
signature trace. It was faintly familiar but not enough for me to
confirm its essence. What was under the black dust, though, sent
a chilling shock through me. Massive holes and fissures veined
this once solid-as-a-rock rock. On instinct without thinking
I blew into the gash as far as I could go, surprised at how
impossibly deep I plunged. The deeper I flew, the hotter it grew.
Then I caught a whiff. *Oh no! NO! Not that! It can't be!* I beat a
hasty retreat – yes, I reversed! I couldn't stand the smell! That
stink! Wildly I vacuumed myself out of there, ignoring the dirt
and rocks I blew loose, holding my breath in spite of slamming
into jagged walls. It seemed the return trip had wrong turns,
razor sharp edges and points I hadn't noticed going in. At last
I burst out onto the surface gasping for fresh air. Choking and
trying to shake that noxious smell out of my essence, I zoomed
across to Machu Picchu where under Ursa Major's protective
mantle rose a din of scared, guarded whispers.

"*Cannn annnnyyonnne herrrre reeeeadd thiiiiis*
lannnnguaaaage?" rang Lyra, leaning over the Inti Watana stone.

"*Nnnot toooo clossse, Winnndhamm! Eassssy does iiiit!*
Staaay baaack! STAAAY BAACK!" cautioned Monoceros, poking
his unicorn horn into me.

"*<Hf' hwåh-hoøff// "* I blustered an apology reversing, but
kicking up more fine black dust. "*Soooorrrrry!*"

I did an abrupt one-eighty to contain myself, dying to know
what held Lyra and the rest so spellbound. I drifted up and over
to peer straight down – it was a message in very strange writing.

Those millions of black dust particles that lilted away from the mountain's gash? They were a violent silent scream that hitched a ride on my tail wind and somehow impossibly seeped through Ursa Major's stellar canopy to form itself into words on Inti Watana:

"It's old Sumerian, Cuneiform, a language from thousands of years ago," said Mimi, a clever young girl with dark skin and a heavy accent. "But its symbols don't make sense. I think it says *gib-ba ud šu-nim-ma* which roughly means block or stop Sun – no wait, heat. And Springtime … huh? That's it – I know what it says! It's *Ban Spring Fever!*"

"Who'd wannnt to bannn Sprinnng feverrr?" Lyra rang.

Careful not to be noticed, I circled slowwwly, quiiietly above to read the message another way: upside down. If this was from whom I thought it was ... I shivered, then warned myself: *Shh! Careful! Don't say a word till you're sure!* From my new position, the symbols subtly re-aligned, just for me it seemed, to read vaguely like ancient Chinese characters. There's only one Element who writes in human logograms, the one who's in every single human who's ever existed, and in every plant and animal for that matter. I fought the avalanche of memories. Sending messages had been a game for – – again I warned myself: *Shh! Stop it! You can't say it! Don't even think it – that oh-so-special name!* It had been a secret game between us when – *Cut it out! Shh! No one can ever know!* I struggled to make it out, my

ancient Chinese was rusty. Then I noticed that it, the black dust, noticed me. Of course it would, after all we'd been through. But, just to make sure, I puffed ever so gently. Yes! The dust imperceptibly tightened its lettering into Chinese characters. As best as I could decipher, it read something like:

被 捕 活 埋 需 要 氧 气 和 救 援
bèi bǔ huó mái xū yào yǎng qì hé jiù yuán

… Buried? … Alive? In the Peruvian heat I felt an evil shudder ruffle me – the worst kind of chill. There was no mistaking that vibration.

If my guess was correct, the thing about this message was its genius messenger, a puzzler bar none! Its messages always contained several layers of information, in at least two ancient languages, depending how you read it. The first one, *Ban Spring Fever,* that was easy – as long as you knew Cuneiform, or at least this scribbled version of it.

I decided to translate the ancient characters into the most common human languages, trying to crack the third level of the code: Mandarin, Spanish, Hindi, Arabic, Russian, English – aha! There it was! The translation and last clue lay in English:

Captured   Buried   Alive   Need   Oxygen   Rescue

Now if I took the first letter of each word, it spelled

C B A N O R

… just rearrange the letters and … it was beyond belief:

C A R B O N

I couldn't breathe. Could it be true? Carbonara? Held prisoner? Who on earth had that kind of power? Control Carbon, you control the planet! There could be no Spring, no regeneration of life, without her.

Who'd sabotage the Kingdom of Spring to seize control of who lives and who goes extinct?

I knew who.

Fear hadn't just reinvented itself, it had evolved …

<HaHø'å hWhee'eff >wh'hyuu-wh'hyuu//

(Ask the Season outside what it knows!)

One
Autumn night,
Dorothy Papadakos
was invited to play Night Watch
at the Cathedral of St. John the Divine,
NYC, on their giant pipe organ. Upon graduation
from the Juilliard School, she became the Cathedral's
Assistant Organist and went on to become their first woman
Cathedral Organist, a Greek
girl playing at the world's largest
Gothic cathedral! Working with Cathedral
Artist-in-Residence The Paul Winter Consort,
Dorothy's passions for improvisation & environmental
activism found a nexus improvising with humpback whales, timber
wolves, elk, owls, birds
and the Wind. As a solo performer
she is world renowned for her silent
film accompaniments. Her annual *Halloween
Horror Tour* performances pack houses across the
USA and around the world. Like Sir Windham, she is a
a world traveler, a student of languages and knows that people, like
trees, are made stronger by the storms we weather.
Dorothy loves all Seasons
but especially
loves the
Kingdom
of Winter!

www.dorothypapadakos.com

CPSIA information can be obtained
at www.ICGtesting.com
Printed in the USA
BVOW06s1816310117
474964BV00011B/100/P